HIDDEN
Gem

Ria Alice & Jessica May

All rights reserved. No part of this publication may be reproduced, stored in a retrieval system, or transmitted, in any form or by any means, without the prior permission in writing of the publisher.

The moral right of the author has been asserted.

All characters and events in this publication, other than those clearly in the public domain, are fictitious and any resemblance to real persons, living or dead, is purely coincidental.

Copyright © 2024 Ria Alice & Jessica May

ISBN: 9798339263807
Independently Published
2nd Edition

To the girls looking for their next favourite billionaire book boyfriend!

Playlist

"Kicks"- Lauren Aquilina
"I Can See You (Taylor's Version)" - Taylor Swift
"Shameless" - Camila Cabello
"Bed Chem" - Sabrina Carpenter
"Lose Control" - Teddy Swims
"Crazy In Love - Remix" - Beyonce
"Partition" - Beyonce
"Guess" - Charli xcx
"Wild Thoughts" - DJ Khaled, Rihanna, Bryson Tiller
"hate to be lame" - Lizzy McAlpine, FINNEAS
"Apologize" - Timbaland, OneRepublic
"my tears ricochet" - Taylor Swift
"Bruises" - Lewis Capaldi
"Hearts Don't Break Around Here" - Ed Sheeran

CONTENT NOTES

This story contains explicit sexual content, profanity and topics that some readers may find sensitive including death of a parent (mentioned), mention of cancer and mild violence.

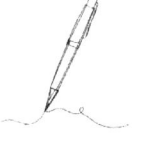

1

LILAH

The door to Timeless Treasures closed behind me and a weight lifted off my shoulders. The quaint, cluttered shop had become my sanctuary of calm in the heart of the hustle and bustle of London, a refuge from the chaos of the outside world and the sorrow that tainted my life at the moment. Rows of polished, old wooden cabinets lined with plush, purple velvet decorated the perimeter of the shop, filled with both antique and modern jewellery. I smiled at the familiar sight of Brian deep in concentration. Grey hair falling across his brow, eye-loupe in place, hunched over the new purchases whilst he checked the quality was as he expected.

"Morning Brian," I greeted cheerily. The middle-aged man straightened at my voice. He smiled but it didn't reach his eyes like it usually would. Brian was a close family friend; he was my saviour last year when my mother passed away. I took on the family home, trying to keep it afloat as it was the only home I'd ever known, but the combination of extortionate rent in Kent and the debt my brother Theo and I had inherited meant I could no longer get by on my own. Luckily for me, Theo had a flat and Brian had a shop a short tube journey away and they both welcomed me in with open arms.

It broke my heart to admit defeat and hand the keys back over to our landlord, but I knew without completely crippling myself and any future financial endeavours, I had to say goodbye to the memories she, Theo and I had created over those two decades there. We moved in when I was a toddler and now, twenty-six, it was time to shut the door and focus on myself and my career.

I hadn't had any jobs that I could really grow into before. Up until now, I mainly worked in corner shops and retail to help make ends meet at home and provide myself with a bit of pocket change to keep my sketching supplies stocked up. Especially when Mum was in the midst of her cancer battle, it fell to me to keep food on the table and a roof over our heads as Theo had already moved out and was saving for a mortgage of his own at the time. He sent me what he could to support me and visited as much as possible, so I wasn't going to let him throw away his hard-earned deposit, to dig me out of a hole.

Therefore, being at Timeless Treasures finally provided me with the opportunity to grow my interest in jewellery, expand my experience within the industry and get money together for my own deposit so I could finally get out of Theo's hair. After almost a year of what felt like constant shit and near depression, everything was starting to click back into place, and I could feel my smile appearing again.

It was safe to say, that this shop had become a home away from home, especially given that I was essentially a glorified squatter in Theo's tiny box room. The cosy vibe that emanated from the walls, the sunny disposition from Brian and the friendly, local customers that shopped here, brightened even my darkest days.

"Hello Lilah, can you meet me in my office when you're ready please?" Brian asked, his voice shaking slightly, seemingly nervous but still as warm as ever. "I was waiting for your shift to start," anxiety twisted in my stomach as I hung my coat on the hook by the door and nodded. Brian shuffled out towards his office before I had the chance to ask him what was going on.

I gave it a few minutes before walking to the back room, racking my brain for possible reasons I might be in trouble. When I entered, my eyes locked on the stranger sitting to the right of the cluttered desk where Brian was sitting in his chair, looking full of guilt. I'd never seen him like this. This fact only increased my stress levels further. The woman wore a tight pencil skirt and blazer and had an undeniable air of professionalism about her which looked out of place in the homely surroundings, causing further unease to flow through me.

"Lilah, this is Mrs Wilson," Brian introduced the blonde woman in her forties.

"Hello," I greeted the woman warily, smiling carefully in her direction. She offered me a guarded one in return and a short, firm handshake.

"Good afternoon, Miss Hart, it is a pleasure to meet you. I am a representative of Moreno Jewellery."

My heart stopped - I remembered that name. *Moreno.*

When we were children, we would spend our summer holidays on the Cornish coast, staying with my mum's friends, Carlos and Sofia Moreno and Zane, their only child. Zane and Theo were the same age, so naturally became thick as thieves, bonding over their love of outdoor adventures, sports and when they were older, computer games and girls. Even sharing a room, they were such stereotypes!

Despite only being two years older than me, I was left out and picked on at every possibility. *"You're too young to play this", "no this game isn't for girls"* and *"we don't need a third player"* was all I heard on repeat over the break. So, I was thankful that I had a bedroom all to myself which I could retreat to for some peace and quiet from the bullying from the boys. If I weren't holed up in there reading some fantasy book, I would spend my time with Sofia, learning to cook recipes from their Colombian heritage and with Mum, drawing the house and scenic coastlines.

Where Theo would be excited to have his best mate around for six weeks, I was dreading his presence as my brother pretended, I didn't exist around him and Zane only worked to isolate me further.

In the years following, the pair of them stayed firm friends, attending the same university together and spending most weekends with each other until Zane travelled back to South America. I knew he was back in

England now and that Theo had seen him regularly since his return, a year or so ago but he hadn't darkened my door since their graduation. So, what was he doing back in my life now?!

****

"I'm going to kill him. I am going to kill him!" I barged into the Gilded Cage, slinging my bag onto the mosaic floor with such force it knocked into the dark oak stool next to me, threatening to topple it over. The swanky bar was full of its usual sophisticated clientele conversing softly in the golden glow of the ambient overhead lights. The loud scrape of wood against tile earned me a few curious glances from bystanders as I threw myself down at the bar, disrupting the usually serene atmosphere but I couldn't care less at that moment. High-flying rich businessmen and women and perfectly polished celebrities typically frequented the bar, so my loud, dishevelled arrival would have definitely raised some eyebrows.

"Whoa whoa whoa Lil, please don't scare my customers!" Theo scolded facetiously. My brother had been working at the bar for the last two years and had been promoted to manager at the end of last September. It was by no means his dream job, but it paid the bills. Theo was the lead guitarist in a band, that was his real passion, but trying to make it big in the music industry and pay a mortgage without a 'normal' job didn't exactly go hand in hand. He turned towards me, his shaggy brown hair flicking at the movement. He checked his watch, clearly surprised at my early arrival at his workplace. Although I didn't fall into the category of likely patrons here, I quite often popped into the suave cocktail lounge after work. Especially given the mate's rates I received and how I got to jump the queue every time thanks to my manager bro, but it was only 3pm on a Monday…

"Who are we killing?" He pondered, as he strained my usual Aguardiente Sour into an ice-filled tumbler and placed it in front of me. I didn't thank Zane for much, but his father did have impeccable taste in alcohol which I often sneaked measures of in the later years of my teens.

"Fucking Moreno!" I griped, grabbing the glass and taking a huge swig, praying the strong liquor would wash away his overbearing existence.

"Been a long time since I've heard you complain about him, sis." An amused look spread across his face.

"He bought Timeless Treasures!" I exploded, "with zero regard for all of us working there! I can't even imagine how Brian feels right now, he's owned the place for decades."

Regrettably, I hadn't had a chance to properly talk to Brian after my meeting as he had been busy in his office for the remainder of my shift, having to repeat the same news to each of his employees. Therefore, I was yet to fully chat through all of this with him and see how he really felt about selling the company he had headed up for so long. Theo sobered.

"Shit Lilah that sucks…Unfortunately, though, that's just the big bad world of business and let's be honest, Brian wouldn't have walked away penniless. I'm sure he's sad about closing the doors and letting you all go but probably sitting on a stack if Zane had anything to do with it," he defended his best friend, much to my annoyance.

"Don't stick up for him Theo! I wouldn't be surprised if he'd tracked me down to that store. He has always had it out for me, I thought I'd seen the end of that dick!"

"Come on, you know it wasn't personal right? And surely, you're getting a redundancy packet?" My eyes rolled with exasperation as I felt myself getting more wound up. I should have known Theo would take his side, as always.

"Yes, but not much, I've not been there that long but that's not the point Theo. I couldn't care less about the money right now and more about poor Brian and my colleagues. I bet Zane coerced him in some way - that weasel!"

"Lilah, come on now, you're spiralling." Theo declared sympathetically but I was too overcome with emotion to acknowledge his words, as something else in my life was going wrong, when it all finally was going right. And at the hands of Moreno no less.

"Why am I not surprised, in the direction Zane has gone in? He makes a bit of money and starts shutting down people's livelihoods for his own gain. What a pig! In fact, what an ARSEHOLE!"

"Good to see you're still feisty, *Joya*."

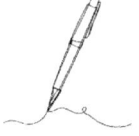

2

LILAH

I felt my blood boil at the old but familiar nickname. Rage burned through my veins, as I turned to see the face I was already expecting. There he was, Zane Moreno, but he was no longer the boy I knew from my childhood. Navy, expensive Italian suit, partnered with an outlandish silver timepiece on his wrist and ornate silver rings that decorated his strong, tanned fingers. A crisp white shirt, clung a little too tightly to his broad frame, alluding to the well-sculpted muscles that hid behind the fabric. I followed the lapel of his jacket, up to the face of the man who had brought chaos to my newly found peace.

"What's it been, a decade? Give or take? Some things never change!" He drawled in his unique dialect; a mix of Colombian heritage and London living.

"Well, some things clearly do." I snapped back, waving a hand towards his elevated aesthetic, disapprovingly. "Long gone are the surfer shorts and backward caps I see."

He scoffed, throwing his head back slightly, displacing the mane of wavy black hair, "I outgrew them," he replied matter of factly, "what are you so fired up about?" He glanced at the half-drunk sour on the bar beside me, "can someone not handle their liquor?"

The amusement flickered in his brown eyes becoming the lighter to my fuse. I stood in an attempt to intimidate him although it was futile with him still towering over me.

"How can you be so incredibly out of touch and selfish? These are real people's lives, not just data in your spreadsheet!" I spat at him. "You're pathetic, coming in here in your fancy suit and overpriced watch with that smug look about you."

A look of bewilderment crossed his annoyingly attractive face. "How many of those have you had, *Joya*? As I just said I've barely spoken to you in nearly ten years, what could I have possibly done to inspire this tantrum?"

I stood there, mouth agape for a moment, unable to comprehend the ignorance and lack of humanity exuding from the dickhead before me. I took a deep breath whilst I assessed my next move, going for the jugular or not wasting my energy on such an unfeeling robot person. After a mental count of three, I chose the latter.

I faced my brother, stock still behind the bar as if trying to blend into the background. I met his gaze and flashed him an exasperated smile, before downing my drink and slamming it onto the mahogany surface. The ice inside the glass rattled with the force, breaking the silence. I lifted my bag off the floor and walked in the direction of the door, passing the powerful figure on my left.

Just as I felt the friction between us begin to dissipate, as I distanced myself from him, a hand closed around my wrist, stopping me in my tracks.

"Delilah?" Zane questioned, visibly confused.

"Fuck off Zane." I cussed, yanking my hand from his grip. I stormed out of the bar knowing I had chosen to be the bigger person.

God, I need another drink!

3

ZANE

"Theo, please translate your sister for me?" I questioned, baffled by her outburst.

Theo handed me my usual, a double shot of Medellin Reserve rum, on the rocks, a taste of home.

"Ah buddy, you've really gone and done it this time!" He said amused, shaking his head in disbelief. I stared back at him blankly and raised my eyebrows, waiting for him to continue the explanation.

"Firstly, picture the scene. I finally have my dream bachelor pad after years of slumming it in flat shares around the city. A place to be as dirty as I want, with whoever I want, however many times a day I want." I rolled my eyes in amused disapproval. "Then I get a call from my sister, after giving up our mum's house, asking for a temporary place to stay. I get it, the past year has been tough on us both, even more so on her, I imagine, with taking on the rent and that; so, I obviously welcomed her in with open arms whilst she found a new place to live."

"Get to the point, T!" I cut in, beginning to lose my already low interest, swirling the glass in my hand.

"Okay, okay. Cutting to the chase, it's been six months now, she was *so* close to having enough for a deposit for her own place. Do you know how many chicks want to come back to yours when your sister is parading around in her underwear? It's a bit of a mood killer mate!" I flashed him a stern look of warning to get on with it, as I tried not to picture Delilah in skimpy lingerie. Despite her short fuse, it was impossible to ignore how alluring she was. Theo sighed. "And then *you* had to make her redundant."

Just like that, the image was shattered.

"The last time I checked, she didn't work for me, Theo?" I said sarcastically, whilst I wracked my brain, mentally reading through my company's staff lists - not that I had any job losses on my hands recently. Moreno Jewellery has only gone from strength to strength since migrating to London.

"Timeless Treasures ring any bells, pal?" Theo replied with a knowing grin, causing his dimples to appear.

The lightbulb clicked, our latest acquisition - of course she worked there!

"Por Dios, justo a mi." I cursed under my breath, finishing my rum in one swig. Theo replaced the drink almost immediately, with a mischievous look in his eye.

"Zaney, my old friend. We've known each other, what twenty years? And how many favours have I asked of you?"

I didn't like where this was going.

"Zero. Yet how many free drinks have I given you?" He nods in the direction of the second drink I was already tentatively sipping. "Time to pay up *mi hombre*." He rubbed his fingers and thumb together.

"And what's your price?" I asked apprehensively. Whilst capital wasn't a concern, it was the non-monetary favours that unsettled me.

"You've got plenty of stores, I'm sure there's a vacancy. Look man, she saved my arse whilst Mum wasn't well and I'll always be grateful for that. So, if you give her a job, it's a win-win for everyone involved. I'll leave you to mull it over." He winked as he walked down the bar to serve the post-work patrons arriving, leaving me to contemplate his outrageous request.

As the Gilded Cage buzzed around me with jubilance, I retired to a booth in the back for some quiet contemplation and worked through the pros and cons of hiring the redheaded vixen:

- I run a business, not a charity. If I do it for Theo, others will expect it too…but he is my best friend and has always been there.

- I certainly don't need another sales assistant…although at least she's got experience in the industry.

- People get made redundant all the time. Unfortunately, there's always collateral damage.

- She was a live wire as a teenager and she clearly still is…

Theo swaggered over to replace my drink again with a cunning smirk.

- But they've had a year of it so maybe there's something I could do… and I can't deny the intrigue I felt seeing her again today.

With the clock nearing eleven, I decided it was time to order an Uber home, as driving was no longer an option after the unplanned drinks I had mindlessly sunk.

As the city buildings blurred past, I couldn't help but replay the interaction between me and Delilah. The image of her wavy red hair cascading just below her shoulders directed my gaze to the curve of her hips. The sound of her voice ranting to Theo was oddly exciting and her defiance when she stood up to me, only enticed me further. I wanted to take in every inch of the woman I hadn't seen for so many years, but I couldn't look away from those eyes. Those piercing emerald eyes that had always caught me off guard, the reason I involuntarily stopped her from leaving. I could only pretend that I hadn't noticed the spark of electricity where my rough hand met her delicate wrist. *Dios mio*, I shouldn't be thinking like this about my best friend's little sister.

I took a deep breath and ran my hand through my hair.

As the car pulled up outside the door of my townhouse, I knew I had made my decision.

One that I thought I might live to regret.

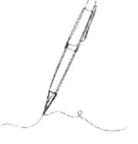

4

LILAH

Well, that was a depressing day, only four more to go before I'm jobless!

I kicked my Adidas off as I slammed the apartment door shut. The only thing on my mind was a hot bubble bath and an episode of mind-numbing reality TV - my favourite way to de-stress.

I walked towards the kitchen, following the scent of something delicious Theo had prepared, bubbling away on the hob. My anticipation was quickly replaced with disgust as I heard the voices of two men: one belonging to my brother and the other I prayed I had misheard. As I pushed through the door, my worst fears were realised.

"What the fuck is he doing here, Theo?" I gestured angrily towards the intruder, making himself at home. Before he had a chance to answer, I turned to face Zane square on and continued, "I haven't seen you in like eight years and now I get the pleasure of you ruining my day twice within the past twenty-four hours!"

A wry smile tugged at his full lips as if stifling a laugh. "That's no way to speak to your new boss, *Joya*."

"I don't know if I need to remind you, you only bought the building, not the staff." I quipped back.

"Correct, but I heard you're on the market for a new position," he retorted.

"Correct, but no thanks to you!" I mirrored in response.

"Well, let's call this an apology then." He chucked a brown envelope across the kitchen table towards me.

"If this is what I think it is, I'd rather start an OnlyFans."

"As profitable as that venture might be for you, Delilah," he smirked, "just open the goddamn letter!"

I stood frozen in disbelief at this unexpected revelation. I glanced at Theo for support, silently asking for help, but was met with only an encouraging expression. *Traitor*! I sighed and picked up the document, slowly opening the seal. Two pairs of eyes bored into me, as I scanned the job description.

"So, I would be your skivvy?" I asked incredulously.

"Personal Assistant. Turn over the page, Delilah." Zane replied impatiently. He continuously refused to call me anything but my full name and that bloody Spanish word over the years and it had always got my back up. Not even my own mother called me Delilah unless I was in trouble! Maybe that's why it irritated me so much, it was like Zane was scolding me every time we spoke.

Anxiously, I flipped it over and my eyes widened as I took in the salary that was before me. A few moments passed.

"I'll see you on Monday, *Joya!*" He winked as he stood from his seat, looking me up and down. "Oh, and by the way, the office dress code is business casual, so you might want to expand your current wardrobe...Talk to you later, T." Theo nodded in response and just like that, he was gone, leaving me dumbfounded. As I heard the front door click shut, I spun to interrogate my sibling.

"What did you do Theo?" I questioned.

"I think I got you re-employed, Lil," he replied jovially, a cheeky glint in his hazel eyes.

"As a slave for Moreno, you know I can't stand him. What am I going to do?" I said as I slumped into the chair Zane had just occupied, his cologne, an earthy yet sweet scent, clung to the air. I placed my head in my hands.

"That's a funny way of saying thank you, sis," he joked as he ruffled my hair, I groaned in response and looked up at him.

"I know I've been here longer than we both expected, but you didn't even let me try to fix this myself."

"It's not just that but this job could give you a career and get you closer to where you want to be. I know the dreams you and Mum spoke about. Plus look at this as a way for me to repay you for how much you supported Mum when I wasn't there to be man of the house," he placed a hand on my shoulder caringly. "You're not kids anymore. He's doing us both a solid and if you hate it, I give you permission to quit. But just give him a chance." Theo pleaded as he served us both dinner. I looked towards the bowl he offered me and realised I no longer had an appetite.

****

Come Monday morning, insecurity gnawed at me as I sifted through my unorganised, temporary wardrobe trying to find something 'business casual.' I wasn't going to give Zane any more ammunition to pick me apart. The sun peeked through the linen curtains - *I guess that rules out tights then!*

I sighed as I decided on a black, polyester pencil skirt that landed just below my knees and hugged my curves in a way that was both professional and flattering. I donned a green chiffon blouse and brushed my unruly ginger locks, opting for a half-up half-down style, to keep the hair out of my face. The full-length mirror, which leaned against the far wall, reflected back an image of a person I did not recognise. Anxiety twisted my stomach and I unconsciously chewed my lip, already missing the ease of my old work routine and the shop that had become my haven.

As I shuffled over to the vanity to start on my makeup, the old wooden frame, which was propped up on the dresser, caught my eye. It held a snapshot of my mother and me: simpler times, happier times. I sniffed back the threat of tears, as I applied my everyday makeup - a light coverage foundation and slick black liner on my eyes. I fastened my usual array of embellished, gold necklaces around my neck in a layered fashion, reminding myself of why I was going through with this.

I was grateful for the little room my older brother had let me call my own, but it wasn't home. There were subtle signs of my recent, hurried move like the unopened boxes of books hidden in the corner, under a pile of yet-to-be-put-away clothes or the untouched art supplies still stored within a drawer in my bed. The belongings I had taken the effort to unpack, brought comfort but looked foreign. Patterned cushions were strewn across the sofa bed, my favourite art, and various photographs of Theo, me and Mum leaned limply against the wall yet to find their permanent place. I'd give anything for her to be here to give me a well-needed pep talk right now!

I stared at my reflection in the mirror as Mum curled my hair into loose ringlets.

"You're beautiful, sweetheart!" She smiled warmly at me as I met her gaze. "This mystery boy is very lucky to be spending the evening with you tonight."

Looking down at the homemade Valentine's Day card I had received that morning, my mind raced with thoughts of who could have sent it. It didn't seem like something any of the boys in my class would have made.

I was full of apprehension at the prospect of my blind date however, if I was honest, I was glad to be out of the house this Saturday evening. Zane was visiting us in Kent for a change. Theo had turned eighteen the week prior, so his best friend had surprised him with an unexpected visit. They were finally able to go out and legally drink together - and no doubt get up to some mischief!

*I waved Mum off from outside of the restaurant after she dropped me. **Just be yourself darling**. Her words of encouragement rang through my head as I walked into the building.*

"Hi, I have a reservation under Jones for two people at 7pm please," I said nervously to the waiter, repeating the pseudonym from my card. They led me to a quiet corner of the room. We walked past lots of happy couples, enjoying a romantic evening together.

I took my seat and scanned the room as I waited for my Valentine to make his identity known. With each passing minute, my anxiety grew. Was it normal for boys to be ten minutes late? At fifteen, this was my first ever date. So, what did I know about the correct protocol?

Picking up the menu, I began to peruse the different options. What was a safe choice to eat with someone you didn't know? Garlic bread or spag bol was probably best to avoid.

*"Well, fancy seeing you here, **Joya**!" The accented male voice made me sit up straight and drop the menu to reveal my worst nightmare. Zane. My cheeks began to burn under his watch. I definitely didn't want him as an audience for this.*

"What are you doing here? Spying in the windows?" I accused, shuffling awkwardly in my seat. I looked around him hoping my date was still running late. God knows the jokes Zane would have made when he arrived. However, I spotted my brother, looking equally as amused.

"We were passing and saw you sitting all on your own, so thought we should pop in." He explained.

"Jesus, do you two not have anything better to do than follow me around?"

"We didn't want to leave you stood up on Valentine's Day especially when you've gotten all dressed up!" Zane teased, I immediately wanted the floor to open up and for one of us to fall into it.

Confusion flooded through my brain at the prospect that Zane Moreno actually cared about my feelings. "Well, that's great but if you can both go now, I'm sure he'll be here in a minute. He's probably just running late."

*"Mm yes, 'running late'," he said sarcastically with a faint smirk beginning to form, making air quote marks with his hands, "oh **chica**, no one's coming." He burst out laughing, unable to keep it in any longer. I sat there gobsmacked, unable to speak. My heart sank as I processed what he had said.*

"Zane sent you that card as a prank, sis. You should see your face!" Theo announced, as he walked up to my table and stood beside the joker, my shock clearly visible.

"What the hell is wrong with you? Do you get off on making me feel like shit?" I exclaimed as tears began to trickle down my face. "Why would I have ever found this funny?"

"Chill out Lil, it's not that big of a deal!" Theo retorted, Zane still cackling beside him. I stood up to face the villain and his ever-loyal pet.

"You are so pathetic. You're eighteen for God's sake, grow up." I insulted, my voice breaking through sobs as I prodded Zane in his chest. Finally, I remembered we were in public and noticed several tables watching the spectacle unfold. "Enjoy the rest of your night you pricks!" I said, barging my shoulder into Zane as I made my exit. Standing around the corner of the restaurant, I waited for my mum out of sight so that I wouldn't bump into the pair of them again. Now alone, I let the tears continue to fall as I

made a mental note that I would never let Zane Moreno humiliate me again.

Tearing myself out of the daydream with a shake of my head, I sprayed a few spritzes of my signature perfume - pissed off at myself for even caring about smelling good for that arsehole.

I slipped on my oldest pair of office-appropriate heels, grabbed my keys and slung the Mulberry knock-off bag that I found a dupe for on the high street last week, over my shoulder. Taking a final deep breath, I met my troubled gaze in the mirror one last time.

Get it together Lilah.

I stepped out of Farringdon tube station, ready to complete the remainder of my commute on foot. Taking in the sunshine, on an uncharacteristically warm April Monday morning, I checked the directions on my phone.

5 min walk.

A blue line on the map was all that separated me from freedom and the Moreno Jewellery offices, located in the famous jewellery district of London - Hatton Garden. With every step, I felt closer to my demise, mirrored by the sound of noughties emo music playing in my ears. *In the words of My Chemical Romance, I'm not okay!*

As I rounded the final corner, I was taken aback by the grandeur of the building before me. Beautiful red brickwork, traditional black Crittall-style windows, and an exquisite columned entranceway. For a man with such an ugly attitude, he certainly knew how to pick a gorgeous office.

Cautiously, I rang the bell to the side of the large wooden door and waited for the buzz in return to allow me in. What welcomed me was a white and grey marbled floor that made me all too aware of the click-clack that my heels made through the quiet room, as I approached the sleek reception desk.

"Name?" Queried the radiantly beautiful, blonde woman.

"Erm, hi! Li- Delilah Hart. I'm here for Zane Moreno. I'm the new PA, it's my first day, what an amazing office!" I word-vomited nervously. The bombshell didn't once look up at me as she clicked through the computer system as what felt like minutes passed.

"I love your necklace! Where's it from?" I questioned in a bid to break the awkward silence growing between us.

"Here obviously…I guess it's lucky that the PA position doesn't require product knowledge," she insulted, still looking at the screen.

I found myself longing to be back with the familiar, friendly faces at Timeless Treasures. I shifted my weight from left to right anxiously, becoming aware of every one of my insecurities: how tight my skirt was, leaving nothing to the imagination; how sore my feet already were in the heels that I had to dig out from the back of my wardrobe, which only reaffirmed my frustration as to why I had put so much effort in, in the first place!

Eventually, the receptionist passed me a branded lanyard, with EMPLOYEE emblazoned across the white card, swinging from it.

"Through that door on the right." She directed vaguely, finally meeting my eyeline. I stared back for a moment, admittedly intimidated by her radiance.

"Oh, thank you, bye!" I found my voice, took the keycard and headed for the door.

After beeping in with my electronic pass, I stood at the entrance, scanning the expanse before me. If walking into Timeless Treasures felt like home, then walking into the main office of Moreno Jewellery was like entering the lion's den. Rows and rows of dark-stained, wooden desks, paired with leather swivel chairs, lined up along the herringbone floor. Eclectic artwork and stunningly shot gemstone photography hung along the cream walls, meant to inspire the many jewellery designers into creating the next trending trinket. Behind every desk was stationed either an alternate for a Victoria Secret's runway show or a Calvin Klein underwear model. What was it with this place and the entire roster of a modelling agency being employed here?! If I hadn't felt out of place before, I certainly did now! Don't get me wrong—I knew I wasn't unattractive and had never been overly insecure, but standing there like a six among tens, it was impossible not to feel like a fish out of water.

As I entered the studio, a sea of faces peered up from their computers and design sketches, to size up the newcomer. I smiled awkwardly, quickly looking for an exit or an empty desk that might be mine to hide behind. Quiet music played through a sound system, which helped to drown out the noise of my heart thumping in my chest, as I walked past the many rows, stopping every few steps to check again for my escape route. After what felt like an eternity, I felt a light touch on my shoulder.

"Hey hun, Jacob, nice to meet ya. You look lost, d'ya want some help?" I was met by a kind face belonging to a man with wavy blonde hair and instantly my nerves began to melt away. He outstretched his hand and I met him with a firm grip, returning his greeting.

"I'm Lilah, thank you, that would be great!" Relief washed through me.

"Follow me, these other *lovely* ladies are far too busy to help!" He rolled his eyes at me, "everyone's a newbie once, I think they forget that. They just see new women as competition." He said as he placed a hand on my back, gently guiding me towards an elevator at the back of the room.

"You're the new PA, right?" Jacob asked, seeming confident in the question.

"Erm, yes. How do you know?" I queried.

"I know everything, hun!" He winked with a laugh. "Some might say I'm the office gossip, but I just like to know what's going on in my nine-to-five. Plus, the place has been buzzin' with activity since a flashy new desk was ordered and set up on the bossman's level." We reached the lift and he pressed the button labelled with an upward arrow. "If you ever need'a lunch buddy, you know where I am. Floor three by the way. Good luck up there!"

"Thanks, Jacob!" *I think I'm going to need it…* As the doors opened, I stepped inside. An overwhelming feeling of nerves filled my entire body as I watched the numbers click from one to two to three. Why did I take this bloody job? I should have told Theo, and more importantly, Zane, to stick it. I had a great CV; I could have been reemployed in minutes. Why had I willingly offered myself up as a sacrificial lamb? Whilst I was still in deep thought, the elevator pinged to announce it had reached its destination. I braced myself and took a step into the unknown as the doors opened, only to be met by a brick wall.

5

ZANE

Right, I had held out long enough and needed to leave, or I would miss my appointment. I picked up the stack of files I had set aside for my newest recruit and headed for the exit - she could meet me there if she had to. I called the elevator and checked my Cuervo y Sobrinos watch. 9.05am, five minutes late on her first day. Great first impression, Delilah! As I waited for the lift to arrive, my irritation levels rose. I knew this was a bad idea! This is what I get for doing my friend a favour. I reached for my phone, writing out a text:

> Leaving now, won't be long.
> ZM

The familiar ping of the elevator rang, as I stepped towards the entrance, still staring at my phone. A flash of red threatened to knock the items out of my arms as the scent of spiced cinnamon and citrus filled my head, dizzying my mind ever so slightly. What a way to make an entrance!

"You're late," I said bitterly as she stumbled from our collision, I pushed the documents I had recovered into Delilah's grasp, directing her backwards into the lift as she fumbled to gather them.

"Well, if your ever-so-helpful receptionist had shown me where to go instead of abandoning me, I would have been early!" She defended indignantly.

I chuckled inwardly as I thought of how Brittany could be particularly difficult with attractive new starters. "We've got an appointment to get to," I stated flatly, pushing the ground floor button. Delilah tensed her jaw whilst silence filled the elevator.

As we made our way towards the exit of the building, I smiled sweetly at Brittany at reception and watched her cheeks flush red.

"You're looking lovely as always Brittany, what an exquisite necklace!" I winked, knowing the effect the comment would have.

"Oh, thank you, Mr Moreno!" She flustered, "Have a great day with your *amazing* new PA!" Although she flashed a thousand-kilo-watt smile, the bitter undertone was evidently shot in Delilah's direction.

I heard Delilah let out an amused sigh, clearly unaffected by the dig as we stepped onto the pavement. My driver pulled the car around and stopped in front of us, I walked forward to open the door of the Maybach. As I reached for the handle, my hand was met with the soft touch of Delilah's as she grabbed for it in unison. A light ripple of electricity charged through me as I held contact for longer than necessary. Her breathing laboured slightly as I met her gaze. "After you." I offered, as I broke the tension, pulling the door open.

Delilah slid across the leather seat, her skirt riding up her thighs as she clicked the seatbelt into place. I tried not to notice her pale skin as she adjusted the length.

"Where are we headed then?" She questioned.

"I have a suit fitting near Cannon Street for an upcoming event."

"So, I get to watch you play dress up, how riveting!"

"No, you've got plenty of work to do, you can't spend the whole time ogling me," I joked. "The files you have, I need you to organise every document into date and alphabetical order."

"Yes, sir." She saluted mockingly.

****

The clock ticked over to the last hour of the day after another hectic schedule of appointments, meetings and approvals. It had been eleven months since the migration of Moreno Jewellery to London and I had only been getting busier.

My time in Colombia had been fruitful both professionally and personally. After moving to Cornwall, from my birthplace aged seven, I felt it necessary to reconnect to my roots. I did just that when I had accumulated enough money to relocate after my interest in the gemstone industry piqued. Thus proceeded many a late-night meeting with local tradesmen, over Colombian cigars and liquor, to expand my knowledge and network.

Fast forward five years, I was sitting at my desk as a member of the 'Forbes 30 under 30' list with an office in one of the most prestigious areas of London.

With the upcoming Annual Board Member's event, I should be focussed on getting our next year's strategy up to speed but all I could think about was the woman still dutifully organising files, just outside my door.

Subconsciously, I played with my lip as I reminisced on the morning. Despite our history, I couldn't deny the pride I felt as her eyes raked over my body, during the fitting, when she thought I wouldn't notice. It would appear she didn't hate *everything* about me.

A quiet knock at my door disrupted the thought as Delilah entered and strode towards me.

"All files organised in date and alphabetical order," dropping them onto my desk with a thud. Although I was aware of Delilah's reluctance to be here, I was surprised she was so willing to let it show on her first day. "What now sir, or can I be dismissed?" She said sarcastically. Heat rushed to my groin at the submissive language as it left her full, heart-shaped lips. I subtly adjusted myself as I replied in an unbothered tone.

"Trying to escape, *Joya?* Go back to your desk and I'll find you when I need you."

"Can't wait…" She replied flatly as she turned to leave. I silently mulled over various menial tasks when my empty glass caught my eye.

"Oh, Delilah!" I called, raising the vessel towards her, "I'm parched!" She returned and swiped it from my hand with a sardonic smile.

"*¡Gracias!* And you can leave the door open!" I called after her as she disappeared out of view, her voluptuous hips swaying as she left.

I rubbed my stubble with my hand letting out a sigh. To be honest, I was enjoying this power play a bit too much.

And I could get used to her calling me sir…

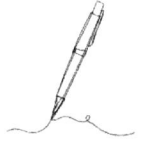

6

LILAH

"So, how was your first day with the devil man then?" The voice of my best friend Verity trilled through my device on speakerphone. I had known Verity for most of my life back in Kent and we had always been each other's go-to agony aunts for every situation. It was also a plus that she knew of the history between Zane and me.

Turning off the tap, I slipped into the bubbly paradise and took a sip from the full glass of white wine, balanced on the edge of the bath.

"Where to even begin…" I sighed dramatically. I recounted the frosty welcome, the awkward lift encounter and the journey to the tailor.

"So proceeded the next two hours of my life, watching him try on six indistinguishable navy suit jackets. It was SO boring!" I emphasised.

"Doesn't sound all that bad, at least he's easy on the eye!" She giggled. I paused for a moment as I tried not to remember the way his chiselled back rippled as he pulled on the white shirt. His olive skin peeking through as he buttoned it up. I took another sip of wine to clear my mind.

"His personality ruins it, believe me," I said in an attempt to convince not only Verity but also myself. My mind drifted to the face of the man I hated, equal parts arrogant and alluring. The sharp edge of his strong jawline accentuated by a five o'clock shadow, which conveyed his rugged masculinity. His stern expression was juxtaposed by his warm hazel eyes that seemed to look too deeply at me. My thighs clenched together at the image.

"Lil, are you still there?" Verity's voice pulled me out of my daydream.

"Erm, sorry, yes, still here. How's things with you?" As Verity ran through the events of her day, I was ashamed of the lengths I had to go to keep Zane off my mind. "Anyway, have you dusted off your sketchbooks yet? I wonder if being involved with a jewellery design company will get your creative juices flowing again?" She questioned. A long sigh escaped from my lips.

Fashion magazines covered every inch of our small dining table, intertwined with sheets of paper and pencils. Enthusiasm and laughter filled the air as Mum and I flicked through and circled our favourite items.

"Oh Lilah, look at this, isn't it extraordinary!" Mum said. "It looks like rose gold will be a big trend next season."

I watched in awe as my mum's eyes glinted with intrigue as she folded over another corner. I loved afternoons like this.

"No, I just can't face it yet." I took a deep breath as the sadness from the memory washed through me.

****

11.30 am and I'd lost count of how many mundane tasks I'd been assigned to carry out:
- Pick up dry cleaning.
- Organise the stationery cupboard.
- Make Zane a coffee (Espresso).
- Sort through junk mail.
- Make Zane another coffee (Black Americano).

I genuinely thought I was going to go mad before my lunch break. As if on cue, Zane sauntered behind my desk through his already-open office door and rested a hand on the back of my chair.

"You look rushed off your feet, Delilah!" He mused, a stern edge to his voice, pointing at my laptop screen that had gone idle. He leant across me to wiggle my mouse, his patchouli and sandalwood scent flooding my senses, causing my muscles to go rigid momentarily. "Am I not keeping you busy enough? Maybe I should extend the parameters of your role?" He stared intensely. Before I had time to process the undertone of his comment, my mind had already drifted to inappropriate scenarios.

"No, I'm quite satisfied, staring out of the window, daydreaming about not being here, thanks." I smiled sweetly in response.

"If you're craving the outside world so much, you can post my mother's birthday card, and when you get back, you can dust my desk."

"Do you want me to polish your shoes, too, while I'm at it?" I asked sarcastically, batting my eyelashes.

He smirked.

"I don't see how it's part of my job to post your personal letters. Do it yourself." I waved my hand dismissively.

"Why would I do that when I have you, *mi esclava*?" He taunted, closing some of the space between us, raising my pulse.

"You know that you can't just insult me in Spanish 'cause you think it sounds sexy!" I insisted, half to myself.

"*¡Vamos, Joya!*" He winked as he returned to his office, leaving me ruffled.

When I finished completing his slave work, his words not mine, I had a look into Zane's office to see if he was there or if I could sneak onto my lunch hour ahead of schedule. I was relieved he must have popped out for an early break himself, and with his absence, curiosity got the better of me.

I decided to have a quick nosy of the space as you can tell a lot about a person by their surroundings! I had to admit the thought of finding the voodoo dolls of his enemies - or of me - did cross my mind! I snuck into the vast room, lined with dark windows, which let a generous amount of natural light in, making my way around in a clockwise direction so as not to miss any details. Starting at the entrance, a sleek beige couch, which looked like it had never been used before, with an empty side table next to it. I continued along a bookshelf chock full of design-led books and travel journals, presumably of the many places he had visited or had on a list to whisk off to in his private jet. Finally, I faced the central point of the room. A thick, dark grain desk, which he kept impeccably minimalistic and tidy, anchored the space, with a tall leather swivel chair behind and two matching armchairs which faced it for any guests. His abandoned MacBook sat perfectly in the middle, with a simple silver coaster to the right and a family photo of him and his parents sitting around a restaurant booth, dressed to the nines. Everything had a place in this room. Although I had yet to suss out where he was hiding the nefarious objects, the whole place gave off major obsessive killer vibes. The snapshot of the Moreno's was the only touch that gave this room any heart.

I lifted the sleek frame and felt a smile form across my face at the sight of the happy trio. How two of the nicest people I'd ever met gave birth to the devil's spawn was beyond me!

"Mum! Where is Mr Ferb, have you seen him? I can't find him anywhere!" I called as I walked into the kitchen of the Moreno's house.

"No, sorry darling, but I can help you look after dinner." My mother said sympathetically whilst cutting vegetables. I headed back to the living room to continue my search to find Zane and Theo standing there with mischievous looks on their faces.

"I know one of you two took him!" I said, accusing the two ten-year-olds.

"No idea what you're talking about, Delilah," Zane responded with fake innocence. "Maybe if your room wasn't such a mess, you'd be able to find things a bit more easily."

I felt the fury bubble inside of me at his words. "So, you have been in my room then?"

"I wouldn't dream of entering that pigsty. It doesn't take a genius to know that you must lose everything in there."

"I know exactly where I left him. It's an organised mess, thank you." I thought silently in case I had misplaced him, as much as I didn't want to admit it, Zane was right. It was a regular habit of mine to lose toys amongst the piles of clothes. "So, you really don't have him then?" I asked, my bottom lip wobbling as I considered that he might really be gone for good. Looking at Theo, trying to mask my worry, I watched as he turned to Zane as if he was asking what to say telepathically.

"Oh, wait a minute, what's this behind the cushion?" I watched as Zane walked over to the sofa and revealed my beloved Furby. "How the devil did you get here, Mr Ferb?" Zane said sarcastically, dangling my poor toy by his ear. "Here, catch!"

Before I had a moment to register, Zane had launched the defenceless creature towards me. I grappled to catch him, but he fell through my fingers and landed on the floor with a hard thud. I heard a crack of plastic and sad robotic noises playing, confirming the Furby had broken beyond repair.

The toy murderers stood silent as I fought back tears. I looked up from the crime scene to see a look of guilt on Theo's face. The silence was shattered by laughter. Theo and I broke our eye contact to face Zane, who was cackling away like a Disney villain. Instinctively, Theo began to join in, mirroring his best friend and breaking my heart further.

"Come on, Theo, we've got more important things to do than hanging around with cry-baby girls." Zane declared as they rushed past me, leaving me in tears, picking up the literal pieces of my furry friend.

My eyes flicked to Zane's stupid, smiling face. This photo couldn't be more than a year old - no doubt one of the times his parents had visited him since his return to England. He looked effortlessly attractive in a casual button-up shirt, which contrasted against his perfectly bronzed skin. It's a shame I know his personality; otherwise, Zane would be quite the catch!

"Be my guest, Delilah." A raspy male voice with a hint of frustration made me jump and nearly drop the photo. Leaning against the doorframe was Zane, a scowl forming.

"Jesus, Zane, how long have you been standing there?" I asked, promptly placing the item back where I'd found it.

"Long enough to see you snooping around my office and staring mouth agape at that photo." He stated flatly in a judging tone. "I don't remember adding that to your task list for today. So, tell me, Delilah, why are you in here when I'm not?" I approached him to leave, but he blocked my exit. "Well?" He stared down at me, our height difference giving him the physical upper hand.

"I was not staring or snooping. I was merely getting to know my surroundings without your annoying presence, and it would have been a bonus to have found the doll you have of me that you must stick needles into constantly." A faint look of confusion crossed his face, "well that could be the only plausible reason for why you're such a pain in my arse all the time!" I crossed my arms defiantly in protest as he clenched his jaw angrily. Of course, I knew this wasn't any way to speak to your employer, but unfortunately for Zane Moreno, I had no respect for him as my superior.

"Let me remind you, Delilah, this is *my* office, and I'm *your* boss. Your desk is on the other side of the door." Zane bent down to my level. "I'll let you off this time, but if I find you prowling around in here again, I might not be as forgiving." He stared so intensely into my eyes that I couldn't help but break the contact. I felt heat rise on my cheeks at his dominant words and proximity.

"Noted. Now, if you'll excuse me, I'm going for lunch." I announced, releasing a breath I didn't realise I was holding as I pushed past his strong frame, placing my hands on his chest to manoeuvre around him, feeling the curve of his pec through his thin shirt material.

Thank God it was lunchtime. I had a whole hour of not being bossed around or mocked by Mr Moreno. I surveyed the break room, searching for an empty table to settle myself at. I opted for a solo table towards the back and started to weave through the seats.

"Hun!" A friendly voice called. "Lilah, over here!" I looked to my left to see Jacob gesturing for me to come over. "We've saved you a seat!" As I walked over to the round table, I saw Jacob and a curly-haired brunette occupying two of the four seats. "This is the new girl I was telling you about. Mils, meet Lils!"

I nervously approached them after the not-so-warm welcome I had received from other women in the company so far. Holding out her hand to shake mine, a comforting smile spread across her full, rouge-painted lips.

"Nice to meet you, Lilah! I'm Amelia," the stunning woman released her grip. "Jacob loves an abbreviation, as you can probably already tell!" She laughed. Immediately, a wave of relief washed over me as I returned the introduction. "Come sit down and spill the beans on being Moreno's bitch."

"We want all the gory details!" Jacob chimed in enthusiastically. I took a seat opposite the pair, placing my food in front of me.

"I've been here twenty-four hours, and I've never made so much coffee in my life. If this falls through, at least I'm qualified to work at Starbucks." The pair laughed.

"I've seen you running all over the place; he seems to be keeping you busy, at least." Jacob expressed, he looked towards Amelia and then back to me. "So, you've gotta fill us in, hun, what's the third floor like?"

"None of us ever go up there, so we're all curious!" Amelia informed, the two of them staring back at me, eagerly awaiting the juicy scoop about their - our - boss.

"Why doesn't anyone go up there?" I asked, unwrapping my bagel, slightly concerned by this new piece of information - maybe he really was hiding something!

"As friendly and polite as Zane is to us all, he's a bit intimidating." Jacob laughed, taking a bite of his sandwich.

"Plus, we don't really have any reason to. I barely have any meetings with him, and the designer's comms with him via email. Not to mention, all the conference rooms are on the second floor, so I've yet to be invited to the hallowed halls of the third level."

"Oh, right, I see. Well, it's nothing special up there! You've got a sofa, my desk and chair and the grump's office."

"Have you seen inside? I imagine he's got dart boards of all his enemy's faces!"

"What the fuck, Jacob?" Amelia mumbled through a mouthful of sushi, making eye contact with me as I tried to stifle a laugh. I was pleasantly surprised by how open Jacob was being with me. Especially considering how closely I worked with the dictator in question.

I thought back to the scolding I had received from investigating his office earlier today and how he made me feel like a naughty school kid.

"Yeah, I've been inside, there's not much of great note except it was weirdly clean and organised, a meticulous murderer comes to my mind!" The pair giggled in response as I went to continue. The memory of the family photo in pride of place on his desk appeared in my mind. A strange feeling built which prevented me from wanting to divulge that piece of information. Like it was a detail, I didn't want anyone else to know but me. Amelia and Jacob looked at me expectantly, hanging on every word. "Now I think about it; maybe he just doesn't like mess, just a boring bog-standard boss and his beige office!"

The pair of them took a breath as they realised there was no tantalising information coming from me. "Well, that's enough about work, we want to learn more about you! So, what's your story?" Amelia questioned.

For the next forty-five minutes, we exchanged basic details of our lives and their time at the company. Jacob worked in design, and Amelia in marketing. It was comforting to spend some time with the two of them after the lonely day I'd had yesterday.

I checked my watch, only ten minutes remained of the lunch hour.

"Thanks for the company, I better head off. He's a stickler for punctuality!" I declared, getting up from my seat.

As I gathered my belongings, I noticed Jacob and Amelia sharing a knowing look. "Bye, have a good afternoon!" I said, placing my bag in the crook of my arm.

"Lil, do you know Simmons bar near Smithfields? Great cheesy music and two-for-one cocktails. We go most Thursdays, here's my number if you ever fancy joining us, hun!" Jacob quickly scrawled the digits onto a piece of paper and handed it over.

"Sounds great, thanks. I'll keep that in mind. Better dash!" I grabbed the paper and popped it in my back pocket. My heart warmed at the prospect of building this new friendship.

7

ZANE

Another busy week of difficulties and decisions which caused this one (much like all the others) to vanish in the blink of an eye. Before I knew it, it was Friday, and I was back at the Gilded Cage with a comforting rum in hand. The bar was a place of polished elegance during the day, but in the evenings, it was a much more raucous affair. The air was filled with the thrum of alcohol-infused patrons battling for the bartenders' attention and the enthusiastic chatter of groups of friends deep in conversation.

"This is the last free round, okay, it's not so easy to swindle them when I'm not on shift!" Theo announced as he sauntered back to the table, precariously balancing an array of four drinks - three pints and a tumbler - on a sleek black tray. I hadn't been back in London long before Theo had scooped me up into his friendship group - an eclectic mix of three musicians who made up the remainder of Theo's band, The Velvet Echoes.

"Cheers, mate!" Callum (The Bassist) thanked Theo as he took a seat at the crowded booth. I raised my glass in gratitude. Despite his friends not being my usual crowd, I needed a way to unwind after working weeks and drinking over mindless chatter was as good a way as any.

"So, T, how's that new riff coming along?" Finn (The Drummer) asked, taking a swig of his Moretti. My mind wandered as the boys discussing their set list for an upcoming concert became background noise. I daydreamed about various spreadsheets and presentations that I needed for the week ahead; it was the curse of being CEO - never being able to switch off. Suddenly, a brazen man with a drink in hand came bellowing from the bar in our direction; I sighed heavily before I turned to confirm my hunch. It was the final member of the quartet, Sean (The Lead Singer). I could tolerate the other two, although immature, they were funny enough, but Sean aggravated me beyond words. His need to be the centre of attention in every room he walked into was the complete antithesis of my character. Although I appreciated female attention and maybe encouraged it at times, I was far too busy prioritising my business to make finding a woman for the evening my whole personality - like Sean appeared to do.

"All right, geezers?" He announced to the room as he slapped me on the back in his form of greeting, I sat up straighter in response. "I see The Suit is honouring us with his presence tonight?"

Dios mio, I wish I hadn't stayed for another drink.

"I guess we could say the same for you, Sean, what time do you call this?" Callum interrogated jovially.

"Wouldn't you like to know, Cal, a gentleman doesn't kiss and tell," he winked, sitting down in the empty seat opposite me.

"Ah, did you finally get lucky with Lilah then? Or did she tell you where to stick it for the fifteenth time?" Finn interjected. My ears pricked up at the mention of Delilah as Theo groaned in disgust.

"Can we not?" Theo whined. "I'm all for hearing the dirty details usually, but let's draw the line at my sister, for fuck's sake." Theo got up from his seat and headed for the bathroom.

"Oh mate, don't be like that, I wouldn't have made it here if I'd just fucked her! We'd be deep into round two!" Sean called after. Theo waved a dismissive hand in his direction as the door shut behind him.

I felt my grip tighten around the glass in response to the vulgar image now threatening to replace the spreadsheets. I sat quietly assessing him. A washed-out Nirvana t-shirt that desperately needed an iron drowned his lanky frame. Coupled with his greasy, mousy brown hair that had been roughly scraped back into a man bun, I failed to see what any woman would find appealing about him.

I stifled a laugh as I sipped the brown liquor, remembering the way Delilah's breathing changed when I confronted her in my office.

"Ahh, big man knows what I'm talking about!" He nudged me playfully across the table. "You know what they say about bosses and their secretaries!"

My jaw ticked as I drained the last of my drink, the familiar warmth flooding my body. I spotted Theo on his return and stood up to address the table as I decided it was my time to leave.

"Firstly, Personal Assistant, not Secretary; secondly, I have no interest in pursuing Delilah; and thirdly, I don't think hipster skater boy is her type." I shrugged my jacket on as Finn and Callum laughed in response to my dressing down.

"Well, gentlemen, time for me to head off." I declared. As I passed Sean's seat, I leaned towards his ear.

"Oh, and maybe next time you see Delilah, you can ask her what colour my underwear is?" I goaded, patting his shoulder twice in a patronising manner.

Suddenly, all thoughts of work now seemed to revolve around my PA.

8

LILAH

It was surprising how quickly I fell into the new routine. The days still dragged as Zane bossed me around relentlessly, but my lunchtimes had provided a form of solace.

Every day, I would watch the clock, counting down the minutes to 1pm when I could finally escape my prison on the top floor and relax with Jake and Amelia. I had never met two people more unlikely to be friends, but somehow it just worked. Where Jake was sunshiney and positive, Amelia was serious and pessimistic, but they both had a sense of humour and confidence in themselves that meant the opinions of others didn't matter. Think Janis and Damian from Mean Girls, but fifteen years on - *I guess that makes me Cady!*

I didn't have the opportunity to build close friendships at Timeless Treasures due to the limited staff and differing shift patterns, so I was grateful that the pair had invited me in with open arms despite their tight bond.

Making my way out of the elevator and returning to my desk, I sat down and logged back on, ready for what the afternoon had in store.

"Delilah! Come here." Zane shouted abruptly from his office. I groaned inwardly, that's my break well and truly over!

I slowly meandered into the room, ready to hear whatever mind-numbing task he had in store for me now. Three weeks in, and our relationship was as frosty as ever. Zane seemed to get a kick out of asking me to do the most basic of chores. I understand, as his PA, that it's kind of in the job description. However, I couldn't help but feel like he was taking advantage. There is only so much stationery a girl can organise - it begged the question of why he even needed to hire me for this position in the first place.

"I've written down an address for you." He handed me a Post-it note with information written on it. "There's a parcel I need you to pick up, call for a car, and you might want to hurry!" I huffed and made for the exit. "Having a bad day, *Joya*?" He asked.

"Let's get one thing straight, Zane, I'm here because I need the money, not because I enjoy running around for you all day."

"There's that feisty girl; I'd wondered where she'd been hiding these past couple of weeks behind all of the sulking!"

****

I tapped my nails on the large white box, from the swanky design atelier, I had placed on my lap, as I rode the town car back to the office. Curiosity tantalised my thoughts as I pondered on what one-of-a-kind piece could be hiding inside for Zane to wear to the Annual Board Member's event this evening - and admittedly, what he would look like in it… I might have despised the man, but any hot-blooded female with two working eyes could admit that he was gorgeous!

I dropped the heavy box on Zane's desk when I returned, causing the photo frame to rattle.

"Mission accomplished, I'm off now." I pointed at the clock, already past 5pm, thanks to the city traffic, the errand took up most of my afternoon.

"Where do you think you're going; don't you want to see the dress?" He questioned. *Dress?*

"As much as I'm a fan of that designer's work, I couldn't care less about what your trophy date is wearing this evening." I bit back, admittedly ballsier than was warranted. Zane wasn't being particularly rude, but I couldn't hide the bitchiness he seemed to bring out of me whenever I was around him.

"Don't be so hard on yourself, *Joya*." He chuckled, seeming to be in an uncharacteristically happy mood. "You have the honour of accompanying me tonight." He opened the box and slid it across the desk to me. I tried to mask the surprise on my face as he held up a silky, elegant cocktail dress. "Emerald is definitely your colour."

"It's gorgeous; I hate to think of how much it costs!" I admired stroking the soft fabric as Zane handed it to me. It's amazing how a beautiful garment could rid me of my toxic attitude. "Hang on a minute, doesn't the event start in two hours?"

"*Si*, I told you to be quick. I'll be in a car outside yours at 6.30pm. So, Delilah, don't be late." He mocked.

"Better go then!" I frantically re-boxed the dress and rushed back to my apartment, half an hour away. Trying hard not to bump into people on the tube with my awkward cargo as my frustration boiled at the short notice I'd been afforded.

I hurriedly pulled off my work clothes, chucking them on my unmade bed carelessly, and carefully took the silk dress out of its box, marvelling once again at how it felt between my fingertips. I thoughtfully stepped into the garment and revelled at the feel of it gliding up my back as I did the zip-up.

A gasp released subconsciously from my mouth when I turned to face myself in the mirror, it was hard to believe the dress wasn't measured to fit me. It moulded to my body perfectly, cinched at my waist and flowed over my hips, following the shape of my legs down to just above my ankles. The neckline was perfect! The fabric contouring my chest showed a tasteful glimpse of cleavage but was still sophisticated.

I couldn't help but smile at my reflection as I admired myself from all angles. Zane was right about it being my colour, too. My auburn hair, which I had hastily thrown into a somewhat presentable updo, glowed against the green fabric. A blush tainted my cheeks at the thought of him choosing this for me. I sucked in a deep breath to calm my mounting nerves as I started on my makeup.

In no time at all, my phone lit up with the notification of Zane's message:

Outside Delilah - Z

Hastily, I grabbed my clutch bag and headed down to the road to join Zane in his chauffeur-driven car.

"Good evening, *Joya*, you look dazzling tonight!" Zane purred as I slid into the back of the black Audi.

"You can quit the nice guy act, Zane." I rolled my eyes and tried to squash the unwelcome butterflies fluttering around in my stomach at his unexpected praise. Although I was quick to remind myself that Zane was not to be trusted and to be on the lookout for any opportunities, he had to publicly humiliate me. Why else would he have invited me tonight? I can't imagine there's many pencils to organise at a fancy party!

"It's not an act, I've got great taste!" He affirmed playfully.

"There's that self-assured man!" I said deadpan, assessing his outfit. Zane's work attire was polished, but tonight, he looked like he'd just stepped off the pages of a fashion magazine. The cream tuxedo he wore complimented him perfectly, the contrast between his sun-kissed complexion and the expensive fabric made the outfit seem tailor-made just for him - which I guess it probably was! I couldn't help but let my eyes trail over his broad frame as he played absentmindedly with his cufflinks. "So, all your other ladies were busy tonight, then?" I said in an effort to distract myself.

"No one does what they're told like you do, *Joya!*" Although I knew this was purely part of my job, the butterflies started to fly downward and red spread across my face. I looked out of the window for the remainder of the journey to mask the physical reaction my body had to him. Damn my hormones for not hating this man, the way my brain did!

All eyes fell on me and Zane as we entered the grand hall. I tried to avoid eye contact with everyone by surveying my surroundings. Ornate designs decorated the whole of the high vaulted ceilings, which loomed over the dark oak flooring. Several elaborate archways bordered the perimeter of the room, where hundreds of guests were dressed to the nines, reflecting the aristocracy of the building.

I'd never felt so like a celebrity or so uncomfortable in my life. For the first couple of hours, I followed a few steps behind Zane, drinking numerous glasses of free champagne, in an attempt to calm my nerves, as he effortlessly captivated the whole venue.

After the first round of greetings, we were approached by two men not much older than Zane. He placed his arm around my waist, almost instinctively. My skin burned beneath the silky fabric, at the touch, but I didn't pull away. "Zane, you never did introduce us to this beautiful lady?" The blonde man said, reaching for my hand and kissing it gingerly. I felt Zane's grip tighten slightly at the interaction.

"This is…" Zane began to reply.

"I'm Lilah, his Personal Assistant." I butted in, the alcohol in my system bolstering my confidence.

"I wish you were *my* Personal Assistant!" The brown-haired man leered, looking me up and down. Resulting in another pull towards Zane. I squirmed under his appreciative gaze.

"She's very good at her job, but she's unavailable." Zane defended coldly. "If you'll excuse us, there's more mingling to do." He guided us towards the refreshments, pouring me a glass of water away from the creeps.

"Thank God that's over; he was majorly undressing me with his eyes!" I laughed as I sipped from the glass, in an attempt to sober up slightly.

"It's not funny, Delilah, you'll find out soon enough how many men try to abuse their power in this industry." He shook his head in disbelief, rubbing his temples with one hand.

"Thank you for saving me, my knight in shining armour!" I mocked, placing my hand on his hard chest.

"Anytime, *princesa!*" He joked, tapping my hand kindly, still resting on his torso. We held eye contact for a moment too long before Zane continued. "With that, I think you've had enough to drink for one evening. Stick to the water for the rest of the night, *Joya.*" I playfully rolled my eyes as his usual authoritative tone returned and dropped my hand. Classic Zane, bossing me around!

He looked towards an older gentleman over my shoulder, nodding his head in their direction.

"I need to speak with my second in command; I'll be back soon, stay out of trouble, you!" He smiled kindly, leaving me on my own for the first time that evening. It was the longest either of us had gone without insulting each other; it was a refreshing yet confusing revelation. Before I'd had a moment to collect my thoughts, the two vultures swarmed.

"Lilah, darling!" The blonde greeted me. "Are you not allowed any more alcohol tonight?" He asked, nodding at the water I was holding. "Moreno doesn't know how to have any fun." He commented, replacing the glass in my hand with a flute of bubbles. As much as these men weren't the company I wanted to keep this evening, it was better than standing in the corner alone like a loser, and with this many eyes around us, I knew I was safe!

"He may seem uptight now, but he was a lot more outgoing when we were kids!"

"Oh yeah? Did you grow up together? Spill the details on Mr Strait-Laced." The brown-haired man weaselled.

"Well, there are lots of memories to choose from, but my personal favourite was when he choreographed a whole dance routine to One Love by Blue, with my brother. He used to wish he was Lee Ryan!" I divulged. The two men sniggered at the mental image I had created for them, whilst pride that my joke had landed swirled along with the alcohol in my veins.

"I thought you said you'd stay out of trouble!" Zane's gruff voice cut through the laughter as I felt his hand return to its previous spot, in a protective manner.

"Oh look, Lee Ryan's returned!"

"Give us a song mate!" The two men taunted.

I turned to see Zane clench his jaw in annoyance. "What are you two on about?"

"Lilah here has been filling us in on your childhood together." One of the men explained.

"Lucky you!" Sarcasm cut through the words. "We've got to go," he announced flatly as he once again led me away, this time out of the main room. When we were out of sight of the other partygoers, Zane turned to me, anger evident across his face.

"Delilah, do I need to remind you this is work, not a date? I am your boss, not your boyfriend, and I need you to be professional." I reared back at his words, condescension coating his reprimand. "I overlooked the obvious over drinking as you were having a good time and clearly nervous, but you've crossed the line divulging personal information about me to my peers."

"Are you serious, it was a silly story from when you were a kid, it's hardly important! You shouldn't care what those jerks think anyway! And don't flatter yourself, as if I'd have agreed to come if I thought it was a date." I argued back, slurring my words.

"I am the CEO of this company, Delilah; I need to be taken seriously, not having my Board members imagine me prancing around as a foolish child in their heads when I'm leading my next meeting." He looked at his watch and sighed heavily, "I think it's time for you to go home now, Delilah. I can finish the night on my own." Then he turned to return to the party, leaving me mortified and alone. A mix of sadness and fury rushed through my body as tears pooled in my eyes.

I hailed a cab outside the venue, giving them my address as I replayed Zane's cutting words over and over in my head. I didn't want to go home yet and stew on those feelings. I called to the cab driver in the front seat that the destination had changed.

I remembered it was Thursday and that Jake and Amelia had told me about their weekly Simmons tradition. I pulled out my phone and clicked on Jacob's contact. On the third ring, he answered.

"Oh hey, hun!"

"Are you out? I'm on my way."

****

I walked into Simmons, surprisingly lively for a Thursday night, but I guess two-for-one cocktails always draw in a crowd. I searched the busy club for Amelia and Jacob, spotting them in a booth towards the back corner. It would appear they had already stocked up on the drinks!

As I passed through the herd of partygoers dressed in casual shorts and t-shirts, I looked down at my silky gown and felt immediately out of place.

"Hey, we didn't know what you wanted, hope a Pornstar is okay?" Amelia pushed the drink across the table towards me as I sat down.

"You sounded like you needed a bev, hun." Jacob interjected, "You're looking glam this evening, where've you come from?"

I released a deep breath and took a sip of my cocktail before downing the prosecco shot. "Thanks, I did, it's been a long night. I went to that stupid work event thing with Zane." I explained, slumping over my drink. I watched Amelia shoot a curious look towards Jacob.

"You went *with* Zane? He always goes to work events solo." Amelia informed me. If I hadn't been so pissed off with the way he treated me at the end of the night, I may have felt touched by that fact. For the past couple of weeks, I'd been tiptoeing around Zane's moody demeanour and lingering glares, counting down the minutes until home time, when I could finally escape and breathe freely again. The thought that he would willingly want to spend time with me never crossed my mind. "How'd it go? I can't imagine it'd be much fun with all those stuffy, old men!" She scrunched her nose up.

"It started all right. We were actually getting on for once, and he even gave me this stupid dress to wear!" I gestured towards the expensive fabric. "But classic Zane, he couldn't keep up the good guy act all night and turned right back into his arsehole self! I'm getting another drink."

The night was still young, and I needed to forget about my boss.

9

ZANE

I had felt strangely uneasy leaving Delilah on her own whilst I went to speak with Graham, a senior member of my Board. I don't know if it was her obvious nerves, the wandering eyes of the invitees or the copious amounts of alcohol that was surging through her bloodstream, but I felt a fierce urge to protect her here tonight. Or perhaps it was just the way a boss would feel towards an employee?

I glanced back at her briefly, a knot forming in my stomach, as Graham and I headed to the mezzanine level, which overlooked the main room, providing some quiet to talk business amid the revelry.

"So, Zane, I have to say, the other Board members and I have been very impressed with the way you have transitioned the company to London from Colombia this past year, the stocks have only grown. It really is a feat that we haven't seen for a long time." Graham trilled.

"That's kind of you to say. I am very passionate about my company." I replied matter of factly.

"It shows, and we, of course, feel the same way. Money into the company is only more money back in our pockets, so what's to complain about?"

I knew there was going to be something. There was always something with him, some nit-picking point to test me. At twenty-eight, I was the youngest of my fellow entrepreneurs at Moreno Jewellery, and even though it was my company and name above the door, these old-school men constantly made it clear that they thought they could do a better job. When I moved back to London, I wanted to gather assets and experience fast, so I began to acquire successful businesses and merge them into my company. Graham was the Managing Director of one of those and had made a name for himself in this industry, therefore, I wanted someone like him as a right-hand man. He knew the UK market inside out and would be a vital support to me in our crucial first year, so I offered him a job to work alongside me on my Board.

"I'm sure you'll tell me, Graham."

"Well, my boy, we value your clever brain and company vision, but I, we, the Board, agree that we need another dazzling limited-edition product to knock our competition out of the park. You've seen Jason Sallow and his newly launched brand, Crystal Cascades." He said. Oh yes, I knew of Jason. He was some jump start TikToker who had garnered a mass of followers, making silly videos, pranking his friends and family and now thought because he had an audience that he could make some tat and it'd measure up to the quality we upheld. "You're only the new kid on the block for so long, and we need to step it up to compete and not turn stale."

I tried not to release an exasperated sigh. Why was he stating the obvious to me? Of course, I wanted to ensure the continued success of this company. And no, some inexperienced trend-hopper would not be getting the better of us!

I snuck a look out to the crowd as he continued, trying to spot a familiar redhead. Feeling my pulse quicken when I failed to find my target. Finally, I located her. I couldn't deny how beauty radiated from her this evening. I knew the dress I'd chosen would complement her, but she was breathtaking in it. Then I saw the predators circling her like she was a meal. I had to wrap this up.

"Thank you for this invaluable insight, Graham. It's much appreciated, as always. Now, I must return to the other guests. Have a lovely rest of the evening." I held out my hand to shake his in a silent agreement.

Hurriedly, I rushed back to Delilah. I was foolish to leave her alone; I had seen how they had sized her up when we spoke to them. However, as I approached, she didn't look concerned or uncomfortable, she was… laughing. They all were. What had I missed? Then the morons started bleating on about Lee Ryan, and I knew exactly what memory Delilah had fed to the wolves. I don't like being the butt of any joke, let alone from two of the most imbecilic men on the planet.

Admittedly, I may have overreacted by dismissing Delilah so harshly. I saw the hurt in her eyes when I disciplined her, and I felt a small stab in my chest as I could see the tears starting to form, which no doubt fell when I left her companionless in the hallway. Regardless, my rage had won out, and she had to learn that even though we did know each other a long, long time ago, I was a very different Zane now. I was a serious businessman, and with that, I had an image to uphold, which I worked hard to protect. Particularly as an immigrant from Latin America, I always had to prove myself three times as much as the average London-born Etonian.

I took a deep breath and grabbed two drinks from a passing waiter's tray, sinking them both in quick succession in an attempt to wash Delilah out of my thoughts. It was a fruitless exercise, all I could picture as I scanned the room now was her silk dress and how it clung to her curves in all the right places, the outline of her nipples through the expensive fabric, how tendrils of her red hair, fell in waves from her pinned up style, in such a perfect, undone way; and how no matter how many times I looked at her this evening, her emerald eyes, which were only enhanced further by the green matching fabric, mesmerised me every time.

I stood in the corner of the room, swirling another drink, mulling over my internal analysis of Delilah. Seeing the way the other men lazily dragged their eyes over her body from top to bottom, as if they had the right to, ignited a small but very apparent fire in my gut. I didn't recognise this feeling, but I knew that it made me want to pull every one of them out into the street and prevent them from ever setting eyes on her again. *Dios*, I needed to get out of here.

"Zane Moreno, as I live and breathe." I recognised the voice before I saw the speaker. "It's been too long." A hand slowly slid across the top of my back as the woman came round to face me.

Saskia Bennett, an old flame of mine. One of those people who you don't speak to for a while but fall right back into place when you reconnect. Usually, *our* reconnecting didn't involve much talking, but it had been at least three months since our last dalliance. Sleek blonde bob, dark brown eyes and pinky-sheen-coated lips. There was no denying how beautiful she was, but tonight, she looked duller in comparison to the other woman who was plaguing my thoughts.

"Saskia, it certainly has. How have you been?" I asked out of politeness. She slid closer to me.

"All the better for seeing you. I thought I'd find you lurking in a corner somewhere, looking moody and mysterious." She purred seductively.

"Am I really that predictable?" I questioned, raising an eyebrow.

"You are, but I know what I'm going to get with you. It's what keeps bringing me back again and again." Saskia flirted, wrapping her arms around my neck, facing me directly. "You know, I assume you've had all the business conversations you needed to tick off this evening. What'd you say we go and have our usual catch-up? You look stressed." She started to slide her hand down my torso towards the edge of my trousers. I stopped her from travelling further, unconsciously making the motion.

"Oh, hard to get this evening Moreno? I like a challenge."

"It's not that. Just not here. Let's head back to your hotel; we can hail a cab." I declared. A knot formed in my stomach for some strange reason. What was this indifference I felt?

Buzzzzzzzz!

The vibration from my phone snapped me out of the thought I was consumed in, and I removed myself from Saskia's grasp to answer it. The words DELILAH HART appeared across the screen as it continued to ring in my hand, making my pulse rise.

"Delilah?" I asked dubiously as she mumbled incoherently. I held the phone up to my ear, "Delilah!" I demanded this time only to be met with the muffled sound of the passing of the phone.

"Theo, thank God you've got back to us, we've been trying you for ages! Lilah's paralytic: she's slurring and barely making any sense, we're at Simmons in Farringdon, any chance you can come and get her?" A vaguely familiar second voice echoed down the line.

"This isn't Theo, it's Zane. Who is this?" I sternly asked as my mind whirred with the thought of Delilah being so inebriated.

"Oh! Uhh, it's Jake, your Lead Designer. I'm so sorry. I assumed Theo had called back; we've been trying him and not getting through!" I gripped the phone tensely. I couldn't believe Delilah was still managing to be an inconvenience to me despite not being here.

"Call him again. Have a safe night, Jacob." I concluded and put the phone down. Turning to Saskia frustratedly, "Are we leaving then?"

She smiled sensually in reply, linking my arm as we walked to the street outside. As if on cue, a black cab appeared with its light on. I hailed it down.

I'm sure Theo is just caught up at work. He must be finishing his shift soon.

"What's the destination, mate?" Questioned the driver as Saskia slipped into the back of the vehicle. I stood frozen on the pavement, a wave of concern washing over me.

But what if he's too late?

If anything happened to Delilah tonight, I couldn't forgive myself.

"The Dorchester Hotel, Park Lane," I advised. I glanced at Saskia through the door I was holding open.

"Are you getting in or what?" She asked, looking confused at why I was stalling.

"There's something I've got to do. Sorry, Saskia." I shut the door and watched the cab pull away. Thankfully, another appeared almost immediately.

"Farringdon, quick as you can," I commanded.

Pushing through the throngs of inebriated bodies, I quickly located Delilah and her friends. She was doubled over on a chair whilst Amelia seemed to be trying to get her to drink some water. Her red curls fell loosely, no longer resembling the earlier style. Jacob spotted me, and relief appeared across his face.

"Zane, I wasn't expecting you to come, but thank you so much, we still haven't heard from Theo."

"What has she drunk?" I cut to the chase as I slung her arm around my shoulder, hoisting her up.

"Honestly, we lost track. She wasn't in a good mood and kept disappearing." Amelia informed me.

"Wharrayoudoingere Zane?" Delilah said incoherently, leaning against me. Her citrus scent flooding my senses.

"Looks like I'm saving you again, *princesa*." I teased. "I'll take it from here. See you both tomorrow!" I declared to Amelia and Jacob.

"I don't need saving." She insisted as I supported her to the exit.

"I know you don't, *Joya,* but I'm here anyway," I reassured her.

As the cold night air hit us, Delilah's face turned green, and she expelled the alcohol from her body, narrowly avoiding my shoes. I heard her mumble *'sorry'* whilst still face down. In a split decision, I removed the pocket square from my jacket and offered it to Delilah to wipe her mouth. Tears streamed down her face, and I took off my blazer to drape it over her shoulders.

The taxi pulled up, and I managed to get her to stand upright.

"Come on, *Joya,* let's get you home." I ushered her into the cab and gave the driver Theo's address. For the duration of the twenty-minute car journey, Delilah lay half asleep on my lap. I instinctively played with her hair to soothe her as I texted Theo to give him a heads-up, hoping he had now finished his shift. This wasn't how I had pictured my night ending. I should have been furious at her, disgusted by her behaviour. It was clearly a mistake to invite her to the work event - there were lines we shouldn't have crossed, and yet there we were, her fiery hair cascading across my lap, her hand clutching the edge of my shirt, absentmindedly gripping tighter at every bump in the road, the warmth of her breath fanning over my thigh with each heavy breath. And as I sat there in the back of the vehicle, the rage I had felt earlier never returned.

I could have been in Saskia's bed, her familiar body intertwined with mine as it had been many times before, but the thought of meaningless sex made me feel hollow. I looked down at Delilah, so vulnerable, so beautiful in my lap, trusting me to take her home safely. I didn't want to acknowledge the dangerous feeling that spread across my chest as she snuggled closer into me.

As we pulled up at her apartment, I carefully shuffled her out of the back seat, realising she could barely stand due to the mix of alcohol and exhaustion. I bent down to carry her in a swift but careful motion.

"Wow, you're strong!" I concealed my proud smile at the first compliment she'd ever given me, "for someone with such fragile masculinity." She muttered, I couldn't help but laugh, *there's the Delilah I know.* I rang the doorbell. Within a minute, Theo swung the door open.

"Jesus! You weren't lying about how fucked up she is! Follow me." I continued to carry her towards her room. "Shit man, I feel awful. I finished work to find all those missed calls and messages and thought the worst. Thanks for going to get her, you did me a solid!"

Theo went to the kitchen to get a glass of water whilst I placed her down on her bed. I removed her shoes and put her bag on the side table, plugging her phone into the charger. As I laid the duvet over her, I stopped to take in her effortless beauty. After a moment, I turned off the light and began to pull the door to.

"I wish we didn't hate each other." She muttered sleepily, rolling over to face away from me.

Her words hit me in the stomach.

Hate? I could never hate her.

10

LILAH

"Please, can I join you guys? I love this game!" I begged, watching Zane and my brother compete on Mario Kart. I tugged on their arms, trying to break the spell the Nintendo had over them.

"For God's sake, Delilah, you're making me hit all the bananas. This is why you can't play with us." Theo barked at me.

"Well, if you let me have a go, I wouldn't have to jog you." I protested. I approached Zane. "Zane, please, please, please, can I go next? I promise I won't ask again." I gave my best Puss-in-Boots expression, making my eyes as sad and wide as possible. "Or can we do something that I can join in with instead?"

*Zane glanced over at my sibling, who was scowling back at him. "Sorry **Joya**, no girls allowed. You wouldn't get it; we aren't going to start plaiting each other's hair. You might break a nail pressing the buttons." The boys erupted into laughter. I was sick and tired of being treated less than when the two of them were united. My brother and I did everything together the rest of the year, but oh no, when Zane was here, I didn't exist! "You're cramping* *our style, go back to Mummy!" Theo patronised, not taking his eyes off the TV.*

"This is SO unfair!" I shouted. "I'm eleven, I'm NOT a baby, and you need some manners!"

My anger levels had reached their peak, and before I knew it, I grabbed the controller from Zane's hands and launched it across the room.

"Hey! Do you know how much that is?!" He looked at me bewildered, scurrying across the room to retrieve it whilst his kart went careering off the road on the screen, plunging him into last place.

"No, and I don't care. Don't be rude, and you won't be such a loser." I said, pointing at the twelfth-place position, now showing on his side of the screen.

I peeled my eyes open at the sound of my alarm. My head was pounding, and my mouth was like a desert, dry and bitter. The soft sunlight streaming through my open curtains felt like the spotlight to my shame. I groaned at the pang of nausea when I sat up as the room spun around me, a nice reminder of the copious amount of fizz I had devoured last night. I reached over to silence my alarm, squinting at the bright light from my phone. I grimaced when I saw the time - fifteen minutes to get ready for work. Great.

Slowly, parts of the previous night started to fit together like a humiliating puzzle, each piece more shameful than the last. I felt my heart drop to my stomach as I remembered how I had got back here. The memory of leaning limply against Zane's muscular frame as he supported my staggering self out of the bar and again at the memory of him hauling me out of the car like a baby. My cheeks burned at the mental image. I guess drunk Lilah decided that the humiliation at the work party wasn't enough and felt the need to take it one step further!

Wait a minute, how did I get into bed? It clicked then how Zane had tucked me in. I threw back the covers to find I was still wearing the dress, now sporting a very unattractive puke stain - *delightful Delilah!*

That's going to cost a lot to dry clean!

The anger I'd felt when he'd dismissed me still lingered but was overshadowed by embarrassment. I dreaded to think how he would lord this over me. If I still had a job that was!

Finally, I dragged myself out of bed, scrubbed yesterday's makeup off, and threw my hair into a claw clip, ready for the ungodly tube journey I was about to endure, hoping the bumpy ride didn't churn my stomach further.

Zane's office door was closed, different to usual, which relieved me as I couldn't face discussing last night yet. I wasn't rushing in there to announce my arrival, instead, I quietly slipped behind my desk. A relentless ache still throbbed through my skull, as I prayed I could get away with doing the bare minimum today. Seeing Jacob and Amelia wasn't a mistake, but the two-for-one cocktails certainly were.

I turned on my computer screen opening my emails. One from Zane, from ten minutes ago, caught my immediate attention:

delilah.hart@morenojewellery.co.uk

Morning Tasks

Morning Delilah,
Some tasks below:
- Colour code my calendar;
- Book a meeting with the Board for two weeks Friday;
- Proofread the press release attached.

Sincerely,
Zane Moreno
CEO - Moreno Jewellery

My stomach fell into my arse. He was so angry he couldn't even speak to me directly. I exhaled anxiously as the ping of the work IM alerted me.

Jacob Collins: 09:11 AM
morning sailor! are u ok? worried me as I didn't hear back from you! x

09:11AM
yes sorry, overslept and didn't have a min to reply. I've felt better but thanks for looking after me, i was a mess x

Jacob Collins: 09:12 AM
all been there babe, catch up properly at 1? x

09:13AM
perfect, save me a seat x

I sank into my chair as I began the monotonous tasks that lay ahead of me, although boring, I was glad to not be running around the city today. Zane's office door flung open, and I caught my breath, bracing myself for the ridicule. To my surprise, he stormed past, deep in conversation on his phone, disappearing into the elevator. I didn't know if I was more relieved or disappointed that he'd ignored me.

As the clock ticked closer to lunch, my stomach rumbled with hunger, and I was beginning to daydream about what I was going to devour when it hit 1pm. I had long completed the tasks Zane had emailed, and with the second wave of hangover coursing through me, I took the absence of him as an opportunity to take it easy.

The ping of the lift jolted me out of my daydream, and I quickly resumed typing nonsense on the keyboard to look busier than I was as Zane reemerged.

The sound of his heavy footsteps hitting the wooden floor filled me with dread. We couldn't avoid the topic much longer. I kept my gaze firmly locked on the laptop keys, trying to blend into the background. The sound of paper rustling as it hit my desk caused me to look up. I recognised the packaging from the bagel place around the corner as Zane placed a can of Diet Coke beside it.

"What's this?" I asked.

"Lunch," he replied flatly. I looked at him, perplexed. "Your lunch." He clarified.

"What? How?" I stuttered.

"I think you know I'm strong enough to manage two bagels and a can of Coke." The comment jogged a memory of Zane carrying me into my flat as I mentioned how strong he was - *for God's sake!* He smirked as if remembering the moment, too, and my nerves melted away at the first sign he wasn't angry. I couldn't stop my smile in response.

"Thanks!" I called after him, "Oh, and I'm going to bring the dress back ASAP, I just need to get it cleaned. For obvious reasons." I blushed sheepishly.

Zane turned back to face me, leaning against the doorway. He ran a hand through his dark, wavy hair, and I tried hard to dispel the image of running my own fingers through it.

"It was a gift, not a loan. I don't expect it back, Delilah." He said matter of factly and returned to his desk. I reached over and picked up the package, turning it over to read in black pen, *'Joya'*. I couldn't stop the flutter in my stomach.

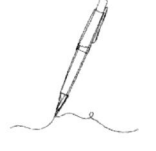

11

LILAH

It had been two weeks since I had embarrassed myself, and still, to my surprise, Zane had yet to use it against me. It would appear that the bagel he gave me was a peace offering - or he's suffering from memory loss!

I couldn't quite believe it, but working with Zane had become somewhat tolerable. He no longer scurried past with a scowl on his face when he came in in the mornings, now occasionally opting for a smile and hello, which started my day off in a much more pleasant way!

This new sunny disposition made for some complicated days in the office. Before, it was easy to ignore how attractive he was when he was the grumpiest man on the planet, but now I was finding myself confusing his newfound friendliness for something more.

This was dangerous territory. If there was one thing I'd learnt about Zane, it was never to let your guard down. I'd been burned too many times in my childhood by assuming 'this summer he would be different' and left with egg on my face when he had inevitably not changed. But on the other hand, this was the longest he'd gone without mortifying me in some way.

"*¡Felicidades Joya!* As you've been such a positive ray of sunshine this past month, I thought it was time your effort was rewarded." Zane said sarcastically as he approached my desk from his office. I braced myself for the attack. "I'm promoting you to Head Diary Manager." Okay, so far so good. He leant across with a yellow Post-it note in his hand and pressed it below my collarbone. I stilled at the contact. "That's my password, keep it secret." He winked with a full smile. The expression sent a shock between my legs, and I shifted in my seat to alleviate the building pressure.

"Lucky me, I'm honoured!" I replied sardonically as I unstuck the note, trying to play it cool.

"You should be honoured; now you get a peek into my personal affairs!" I turned it over to reveal the password. Written in black ink was the phrase 'leeryan4ever'.

"You've got to be kidding me…" I rolled my eyes and typed it into my computer.

"What can I say, *Joya?* You reminded me of a long-lost passion of mine." He tapped his knuckles on the desk and sauntered away, clearly pleased with himself.

I perused his calendar, familiarising myself and cross-checking the various appointments with my own. Not too much of interest in the personal world of Zane Moreno. An alarming number of reminders to 'call Mum' were littered across the weekdays, it was slightly amusing that he had to prompt himself to do that on such a frequent basis.

One entry that particularly caught my eye was the recurring 1pm lunch reservation at The Regal Orchid restaurant, booked into every afternoon. The only difference was his lunch buddy: Monday, Olivia; Tuesday, Haley; Wednesday, Isabelle; Thursday, Michelle; and Friday, Charlotte. It was like a real-life version of Mambo No. 5! I guess I shouldn't be surprised that the man was making the rounds. Not with his general fuck boy, billionaire aura, but I didn't appreciate the way the new information played on my mind.

As the week was coming to a close, I found myself heading to lunch at the same time as Zane.

"Regal Orchid again?" I questioned, met with a nod in response whilst he flicked through his phone, and we waited for the elevator to arrive on our floor. "So, who is it today, then? Alice? May? Or am I getting the days confused?"

Zane looked up from his device, an unusual smirk pulled at his lips. "Someone's jealous!" He accused as we stepped into the box.

"You wish!" I scoffed. The doors opened when we reached the ground floor, and I spotted Charlotte from the design team waiting eagerly by the lift. As Zane started to walk towards her, he turned back to me, amused.

"Don't worry, *Joya*. It'll be your turn soon!" He patted my shoulder in a patronising manner, leaving me shocked.

"Good afternoon, Mr Moreno." Charlotte greeted giddily. "I'm looking forward to our lunch!" At that moment, it clicked that the names in his diary were women from the company.

"Yes, it'll be good to get to know you a little better," Zane responded. I tried to hide the disgust on my face; I never thought he would risk mixing business with pleasure. The thought of Zane wining and dining the women from the office made my skin crawl. Surely, he didn't need to prey on women, he's employed, to get laid for fucks sake!

I pushed the image to the back of my mind and hoped I still had an appetite for lunch.

At 3pm, Zane returned from his fifth date of the week.

"Afternoon, Delilah, how was your lunch?" He asked, in his usual attempt to make small talk. I carried on typing, ignoring his presence. "Okay, well, mine was great, thanks!"

"I don't care about your lunch," I responded blankly.

"I'll leave you to go on with your work then." He chuckled at my attitude.

My blood boiled, watching him swagger back into his office. It would appear that he had more in common with the creeps in the industry, that he warned me about, than I first thought. Before I knew what I was doing, I had followed him into his room.

"To be honest, I think it's downright disgusting that you're using the woman in your office as your own personal dating pool. I know you're the CEO, and you're busy, but there are literally apps for everything. I'm sure you've got five minutes a day to swipe through some profiles, do it on the toilet for all I fucking care, but don't abuse your power. You said yourself how awful that is!" I turned to leave, the rage still burning through my veins. "And for your information, no, I'm not interested, so don't bother booking a slot for us."

12

ZANE

I sat silently, watching as Delilah's fury spilt out of her. I should have been annoyed at her accusations, but I stared in awe as her fiery hair fell slightly in her face, her voice quivered with emotion, and her emerald eyes blazed with intensity. I was captivated by her movements.

"Delilah, I appreciate your concern, but what happens at those lunches is none of your business, and if I wanted your opinion, I would have asked." I stated bluntly. She didn't bother turning as she cursed me under her breath and walked out.

I thought our relationship had progressed, but at that moment, I was transported right back to the day I saw her in the Gilded Cage. I'd always admired her confidence, but she always thought the worst of me, it had been that way since we were children. Granted, I did do my fair share of teasing, but we were kids, and it didn't mean anything.

"Come on, Lil, you can do better than that!" Theo shouted, chucking the ball high above her head. The sun beat down on the small cove, the serene landscape filled with our laughter and shouts, days like this were the reason I looked forward to summer. The ball sailed past Delilah, and as she scrambled for it, it landed perfectly in my hands.

"Come on, guys! Why do I always have to be in the middle?" She whined as I laughed and easily threw the ball over her head again, back to Theo.

*"You're just so good at being the piggy, **Joya**!" I ridiculed. A crease formed between her eyebrows as her face puckered in frustration and her eyes narrowed in anger. She was always the piggy in the middle, and I could tell it was getting to her, but her irritation was overshadowed by the joy myself and Theo got out of taunting her. We passed the ball back and forth to each other a half dozen more times as Delilah's face turned as red as her hair.*

"Seriously, guys?! I don't have to put up with this, you know. Just because you both get a kick out of picking on someone smaller than you!" With that, she turned and walked toward the spot where our parents had set up camp on the beach.

"I apologise for interrupting your sulk, but I have an important design meeting now, and I need you to attend to scribe." I declared, now standing over her desk. She glared up at me with defiance in her eyes. I stared back, telepathically challenging her to argue with me. As intimidating as she thought she was, her green eyes entranced rather than unnerved me.

Silently, she closed her laptop and placed a notepad and pen on top. Gathering the collected items, she stood and walked straight past me as if I were invisible and pressed the elevator button. I followed, just in time for the doors to open.

We stood in silence, only a few centimetres between us, but the space felt gigantic as we reached the second floor.

"If you could sit towards the back, six of the Board members will be joining to discuss the Valentine's limited-edition piece. Pay attention and take notes, I expect them in my inbox within an hour of the meeting concluding." I directed.

We were the first ones to arrive. I hated being late, particularly for business meetings. It told me a lot about a person and how they kept their time. If you couldn't afford me the common decency of being on schedule for a meeting, then our business relationship would fall flat pretty damn quickly. It was one of the simplest forms of respect, and not to mention, it didn't cost a penny, which was rare in this industry. Therefore, I would ensure my arrival was also at least five minutes before the scheduled kick-off. I checked my watch; the rest of the team would be here soon. I sat in the large black, leather swivel chair at the head of the long, rectangular white table. A further nine matching chairs spread around the perimeter. In the corner of the entirely glass-walled boardroom, a basic plastic chair sat off to the right-hand side. There, Delilah perched, stock-still, consumed with her despisal towards me.

I watched her deep in concentration, balancing her computer on her lap as she typed away. A line deepened between her eyebrows, just as it had when she was a child, and she chewed on her lip absentmindedly. I imagined pulling that full lip between my own teeth, thinking of a few ways to erase the frustration from her pretty face. The sound of the boardroom door opening jolted me out of my fantasy. I stood abruptly to greet my colleagues, nodding my head towards them in an unemotional greeting.

"Good afternoon, gentlemen, thank you for all making time in your busy schedules to meet with me today. After an important conversation that I had with Graham at the gala event, I thought it best that we start thinking about Valentine's product launch early!" Graham smiled proudly, like the cat who got the cream. That's the thing in business: you need to make those alongside you feel as if they hold some power or gravitas in your decisions. When, in actuality, it was always me calling the shots and steering the ship, I didn't need the likes of Graham's support with that. Of course, I knew about competitors within my industry, how out of touch would I have to be to not be aware of the inexperienced influencer pumping out generic, overpriced rubbish? "With the time ticking along to the submission date, I wanted to discuss it with you all."

"Of course, we're always happy to be involved in helping you, Zane." Graham bleated. "And always in favour of thinking in advance, you can't move Valentine's Day after all!"

I continued. "Over the past two weeks, I have been meeting individually with different members from our company to discuss their personal likes and dislikes when it comes to jewellery and what would make them more likely to purchase or put an item on their wish list." I glanced at Delilah as a vague expression crossed her face, almost like a realisation of some kind. "And in the interest of inclusion, I wanted to gather your thoughts also. So, tell me, gentleman, from your perspective, what would your wife or daughter love the most?" I enquired.

"My wife only cares as long as it's big, round and shiny. So, keep making that, and you'll forever have a customer." John, one of the other board members, *helpfully* inputted.

"Insightful John. What about you, Mark?" I asked. Mark was a senior employee at Graham's old company when I acquired it, so I offered him a seat on the Board to stay also.

"Let's be honest here; it's women we're targeting. Or should I say the husbands of these women, who are the ones actually spending all this money?" I caught Delilah stop typing and stiffen in the corner. "And what do women want? That's the age-old conspiracy. I think if we're being realistic, though, a sapphire stone in a silver setting, just like the Princess of Wales, is the perfect choice. The ladies love the royals!"

Delilah scoffed, cutting through the quiet in the room. I flicked my eyes in her direction; her expression was a bit like a deer in headlights.

"Excuse me, Assistant?" Mark whipped round to face her. "Something to say?"

"My apologies, I thought that was internal." She stuttered, "Ignore me!" She gestured with her hands to proceed.

"How preposterously rude-" Mark began.

"Delilah, you clearly have an opinion. One I'm interested in hearing, please, the floor is yours." I cut in. She shifted in her chair, causing the plastic to squeak. "Go ahead." I encouraged. I'd never seen her so nervous; it was incredibly endearing and did nothing to clear the earlier image I had of her in my head. Now I was imagining her staring up at me, on her knees, with those doe eyes. I could feel my zipper strain at the thought.

"Erm, well, you want to know what women want. Firstly, yes, we like 'shiny' things, as you so aptly put it." She pointed towards John, then turned towards her new nemesis. "Secondly, it's not just a minutely more affordable knockoff of a Duchess' engagement ring that gets us girls hot under the collar. In fact, public opinion on the royal family is only declining, particularly in the younger generations, so if you think you're going to influence us with something like 'The Royals' or 'The Kardashians' you can think again and thirdly…" with each word she exuded more and more confidence. I was spellbound. "If you bothered to do any research, you would learn pretty quickly that gold is a much higher performer than silver. Oh, and peach-toned Morganite is the gemstone of the year and is thought that to those who wear it, it brings compassion, promise and healing, making it an incredibly romantic jewel, so that might be a good place to start." She concluded.

It was deathly quiet; you could have heard a pin drop. Mark was visibly shaken, which I found hilarious to witness. But being CEO, I had to hold it together!

"Zane, aren't you going to do something about this?" He barked at me.

"Oh, definitely." I agreed, causing Delilah to blush as she awaited the discipline she was expecting from me. *Fuck!* As the red hue spread across her complexion, the previous image of Delilah begging for my cock was turning crystal clear, this was going to take a lot to shake.

"Delilah, I apologise I wasn't taking notes, as you are the scribe. Please ensure that it is all included in your record. It was incredibly helpful, thank you." I smiled warmly in her direction, which she returned timidly. At that moment, I finally saw Delilah for the confident, self-assured woman that she had always been but had now fully grown into, and I feared there was no coming back from this revelation.

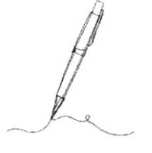

13

LILAH

What is it with the male race today and pissing me off?! I'd just started to feel calm again after the altercation with Mark. Don't get me wrong, I respect the hierarchy of a workplace, but I draw the line at blatant sexism.

The audacity of that man! To assume that all jewellery is bought by wealthy men for us poor defenceless females, it's the twenty-first century, for God's sake!

I gathered my belongings, packing my notepad and pens back into my handbag with more force than necessary, getting ready to clock out for the week. Taking one last glance at my calendar, I decided to have a look at what Monday had in store for me.

Scrolling through mine and Zane's agendas, I spotted his familiar lunch booking. I couldn't help my curiosity at who the 'lucky lass' was this time. As I double-clicked the entry, I was surprised to see Jacob's name.

Suddenly, the light bulb clicked, and I remembered what Zane told the Board Members in the meeting - these lunches weren't dates, they were work outings! God, Lilah, you've got to stop embarrassing yourself in front of your boss! Although, he definitely could have corrected me at any point during my outburst. If I wasn't mistaken, I could have sworn I saw hunger in his dark, smouldering eyes as I went on. I felt a shiver race down my spine at the memory of them locking onto mine.

My phone beeped, bringing me back to reality.

> Hurry up hun! we've got wine to drink and films to watch! xo

I couldn't wait for an evening of mindless fun at Jake's apartment without the thought of Zane entering my brain.

"Dinner is served!" Jacob appeared through the door from his hallway, precariously balancing two takeaway boxes and a bottle of wine under his arm! "Don't say I don't spoil ya, hun!"

He plopped them down on the table. Jacob's apartment was like a warm hug - every corner was full of personality, soft furnishings and bursts of colour. Ambient lighting shone throughout the space from fairy lights and candles, casting a glow. Much like the owner of the space, the apartment filled me with immediate ease. The fact we were sat cross-legged on a pile of cushions around his thrifted coffee table instead of a dining table reflected that. The image of us chowing down on greasy food, cocooned in his cosy home, was the complete opposite of the busy, stressful city life outside, which I was relieved to be away from.

"What a day!" I said, taking a hearty swig of my rosé. "I hear it's pretty full-on in the design department, how are you feeling?"

"Manic, babe. It's the same at the start of every limited-edition launch. Bossman wines and dines each of us, tells us how valued we are in the company, probes us for our best creative ideas, and then barely speaks to us for the next three months!" Jake replied, "But you know I get it, he's a busy man, I'm not expecting to be besties with the boss." He said through a mouthful of pizza.

"You are not going to believe how stupid I was today." Jake's excited eyes met mine - always eager for gossip! "I saw all these lunches in his diary and immediately jumped to the conclusion that he was fucking half the office!"

"Oh, I wish, wouldn't kick him out of bed on a cold night!" He nudged me with his elbow, nearly choking on his food. I tutted in jest.

"That's not the worst bit. I then proceeded to shout bloody murder at him in the name of feminism!" I laughed, putting my hands over my face to shield the embarrassment. "And the arsehole didn't even stop to correct me; he just let me rant on, staring into my soul!"

"Ah, that's hilarious, although I've never known him to have a girlfriend, to be fair. After the first six months of working here, I thought he *did* bat for my team." Jake joked whilst opening Netflix on his TV.

"What's Amelia up to tonight, then? Another gig?" I asked, referencing her absence from our girl's night.

"Yeah, with Josh." He said nonchalantly as he flicked through the pictures on the screen.

"Stupid question, but who's Josh?" I asked curiously.

"Ah, course, forgot you don't know their history." Jake stopped scrolling and faced me. "Josh is Mils' boyfriend. Well, he is at the moment anyway."

I raised an eyebrow.

"That was bitchy. Bad Jake. Long story short, they're more on and off than J-Lo and Ben Affleck, babe. He doesn't deserve her, in all honesty, but the girl's gotta figure that out for herself. I've told her many times, but y'know, those rose-tinted glasses and all." He shrugged, defeated.

"Yeah, I get you. Amelia's fab, I hope she realises her worth soon, or he at least steps up and treats her right!"

"Agreed hun!" He smiled kindly before pointing towards the screen with the remote in his hand, "13 going on 30?" I nodded in response and grabbed a slice, trying not to dwell on the new insight into Zane's personal life. I shouldn't care if he did or didn't have a girlfriend, but I couldn't deny the slight relief that washed over me. *How pathetic, Delilah!*

Two and a half bottles later and the next film we had put on had become background noise as Jake and I put the world to rights.

"Eugh, it really pisses me off that Danny only gives a shit about Sandy when she's completely changed everything about herself!" I declared, turning my attention back to the movie as the credits began to roll.

"I get ya; it always seems like we're having to change ourselves for the male gaze." He rolled his eyes, topping up our wine.

"One hundred per cent!" I clinked my glass to his in agreement, "so, what's going on in your love life?"

"Just dating, nothing serious. I've met a few nice guys, but no one worth settling for. What about you hun?"

"Pretty much non-existent, living with your brother is the ultimate cockblock." I laughed drunkenly. "God, maybe that's why I'm so highly strung!"

"Yeah, sounds like you need to get laid, Lils!"

"You're probably right, but that's pretty hard when the only men I speak to are either my brother, my boss or gay!" I winked, causing Jake to laugh.

"On that note, you surely can't be immune to Zane's good looks?" He questioned. He was right; I had caught myself admiring Zane's appearance when daydreaming at my desk. I could see him working from where I sat, and it was difficult not to let my eyes and mind wander. The way he played with his lip as he concentrated, the shape of his muscly frame as he leaned on my desk to talk to me, and his woody scent that would tingle my senses. "*And* you've got history!"

"Yeah, but not *that* kind of history!" I concluded, opening the next bottle.

After I returned home, I stumbled tipsily through my flat, heading as quietly as possible back to my room. I put my phone on charge, noticing the time was well past 1am when the screen lit up. After removing my makeup, I flopped onto the bed with only a long, baggy t-shirt on, my mind spinning slightly from the alcohol. Moments of the day swirled alongside, but every thought led me back to the image of Zane and how he stared at me across the conference table. I could have sworn I saw a fire burning behind his gaze, causing heat to pool between my legs.

I reached for my bedside drawer, my hand finding the small silver bullet tucked away. *Jacob was right; I do need to ease this tension.*

Laying back on the pillows, I closed my eyes; my thoughts clouded with the image of close encounters and fleeting looks, which only fuelled the anticipation further. I switched on the vibrator, allowing my mind to wander and give in to temptation. I pressed it against myself, causing my breath to hitch. I imagined Zane, his hot breath against my neck and his toned body firmly against mine as I moved the toy in deliberate circles on my clit.

The pleasure built, my other hand making its way up my body, lifting my top and landing on my breast. I pictured his rough hands on my skin and his mouth tugging on my nipple as I moved in time with the motions of the device.

"Joya." I imagined hearing his husky voice whisper in my ear, causing a groan to escape from me. My hips bucked as I lost myself in the fantasy. The higher the tension rose, the more I wished Zane was here to give me release.

As I pushed myself closer to the edge, my breath came in rapid gasps with the vision of him kissing his way down my stomach to the heat between my thighs. The buzzing of the vibrator, paired with the intense daydream, caused the building pressure to come crashing down over me in waves. My back arched off the mattress, and I clamped my free hand over my mouth to muffle my moan. I turned off the bullet and let it fall onto the bed next to me. My legs tingled from the intensity of my orgasm, and I lay there for a minute, allowing the sensation to consume me.

After a blissful moment, the clarity began to seep in.

Oh fuck, I just masturbated over my BOSS!

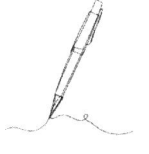

14

LILAH

"So, how was your weekend?" I asked Amelia as we waited for the coffee machine to heat up. Nothing started my working week off better than a piping hot flat white. It worked wonders to wash away the weekend. I placed two cups on the side, ready for the sweet nectar.

"I went to this little underground indie gig, I found them on Insta a few weeks back and managed to snag a ticket for me and my boyfriend. How about you?" Amelia responded. She was always looking for new and upcoming artists and loved discovering acts before they made it big, which she featured on her music blog. I watched the cups fill with coffee from the automatic machine.

"Cool, I saw your post actually, they looked great! So did you and your boyf. Josh, right? Jake mentioned him Friday night!"

Amelia smirked.

"Dread to think what he said about him; Jake isn't exactly Josh's biggest fan!" She said, shaking her head amusedly.

"Ah no, he was nothing but complimentary." I lied, hoping she wouldn't see right through me.

"You don't have to protect my feelings, Lilah. I know Josh isn't everyone's cup of tea, but I hope you get to meet him soon so you can judge that for yourself." I smiled supportively in response. "Anyway, you never told me what *you* got up to!"

"Ha, sorry for leaving you in suspense! Not a lot, really, trying to save as much as poss so I can finally leave Theo's!"

"Oh yeah, how's that going?" Amelia questioned whilst frothing the milk.

"I'm finally able to put some money into savings now that I've cleared the remaining debt my mum left behind, so that's something at least. Hopefully, by the end of the year, I'll have enough for a deposit as I really don't want to rent if I can help it." I explained as Amelia handed me my drink.

"That's good news, if you ever want company on any viewings, let me know. I'd better go for my first meeting, nonstop at the moment! Have a great one." She waved casually as she headed out of the staff kitchen.

Settling down at my desk for the day, I peeked into Zane's office and let out a relieved sigh at the sight of the empty room. I must admit, after the events of Friday evening, I was feeling quite anxious to see Zane's face in real life!

I opened his calendar to see when I could expect him and saw an all-morning meeting with his accountant. A wave of calm washed over me at the realisation that I had a couple of hours to myself. With that, I put on my favourite playlist, on Spotify, through the speakers upstairs and settled into my to-do list.

While singing along to my most played song by the Paper Sunsets, the elevator pinged. I glanced at the opening doors. They revealed Zane in his usual office attire, a grey suit, white shirt and a dark patterned tie, holding two white bags of what appeared to be takeaway food - poor Jake doesn't look like he's getting the five-star treatment like the others. The serenity I had been previously experiencing had been destroyed. The sight of him sent shivers through me.

For fucks sake, why do I have to have such a physical reaction to him?

I turned back quickly to my computer and fumbled to find the Spotify tab.

"Sorry, I'll turn this off. Two secs!" I babbled, not looking at him.

"Oh, it's fine, I like it, leave it on!" He returned, strolling past my desk. "And I like the singing too." He winked at me with a laugh and walked into his office. The action intensified the shivers into electric shocks.

Jesus, he heard that…

Zane poked his head around his office doorway.

"Delilah, I need a word with you, can you come in here in five?" I nodded timidly in response as he shut the door. I considered all the reasons I could be getting summoned, none of them particularly positive after I bit his head off, but annoyingly, his assertive tone sent me right back to my Friday night delusion.

I knocked on the door sheepishly, ready to accept my fate. I entered the room to see the takeaway boxes, still closed, set up on his desk, with two paper plates and wooden cutlery laid out. Hopefully, this would be quick, given Jake was due to arrive any minute, and I didn't particularly want an audience for my scolding. The smells emanating from the mysterious boxes made my mouth water and began to conjure up oddly familiar memories.

"I took on board what you said on Friday…" Zane began.

"Firstly, I would like to apologise for my outburst. It was completely unprofessional…" I cut in.

"Uh-uh! Let me finish." He held up a finger to silence me, and I instinctively obeyed. "As I said, I listened to what you had to say, and I know you were against going out for lunch with me. So, I brought lunch to you." He gestured towards the boxes in front of him. I stood for a moment dumbfounded.

"I thought you were due to have lunch with Jacob today?" I recalled the appointment I had seen on his calendar.

"I was, but I rescheduled. I had more important matters to attend to. Please, sit." I did as I was told and settled into the black leather chair to face him, trying to hide the unusual buzz I felt at the word 'important'.

Zane began to open the boxes, and I immediately recognised the contents. I surveyed the feast of Colombian delicacies, and my stomach growled in anticipation. The rich food sprawled out on Zane's pristine desk was quite the juxtaposition.

"Is that *Bandeja Paisa*?" I asked, he nodded in response, "Oh, I haven't had that since your mum made it when we were kids. It was always my favourite!"

"I know, it's mine too. I've been trying to find the best authentic food since being back in London, and this tops them all. Couldn't forget *empanadas* either!" He loosened the knot of his tie and pulled it from his neck, laying it on the desk. I watched his long, tanned fingers undo the top two buttons of his shirt. Suddenly, I was hungry for more than just the food.

"You can start, *Joya*! You're basically drooling!" He said with a laugh as I realised the length of time I had been lost in my thoughts.

"Thank you." I began scooping the rice and meat onto my plate as innocently as possible. "In all honesty, though, I am sorry for what I said to you. I know now that I was wrong, and you're not working your way around here." I smiled apologetically.

"Wow, Delilah Hart apologised to me. I never thought I'd see the day!" Zane smirked, grabbing an *empanada* as I rolled my eyes. "But y'know, I suppose I could if I wanted to." He joked. Zane wasn't generally arrogant, but he wasn't blind to the effect he had on women. He took a bite of the pastry, and I tried not to focus on his tongue when he licked his lips, distracting myself with the taste of my childhood. I couldn't stop noticing the smallest details of him.

Note to self: do not fantasise about your boss.

"Don't get used to it, Moreno. It's not often I'm wrong. Anyway, what's the occasion for this lunch?"

"We've been working together now for nearly three months, and I realised we've barely spoken about anything other than work. Thought this would be a good way to catch up. So, tell me, what's happened over the last eight years?"

"Well, that's quite a long time to recite. But you know, nothing too noteworthy other than losing my mum, my childhood home and my job, so I wouldn't call it a particularly positive decade, but it can only get better, right?" The earlier smirk disappeared from his face, replaced with a look of empathy. I wasn't used to seeing this level of emotion from him, which made me feel a surprisingly conflicted mix of unease and comfort.

"I was truly sorry to hear about Esmeralda, Delilah. I know I'm probably the last person you'd want to talk to about it, but I knew her for many years growing up, and I always thought fondly of her. I know my family came to the funeral; I'm sorry I didn't make the effort to join them."

I smiled sadly at the memory of my mum's funeral. Even a year on, the pain was still very much there and I missed her every day. I too regularly found myself, in the months since her passing, reminiscing back to those days on the Cornwall coast with her. As I was often left out of Zane and Theo's activities for being 'a boring girl', I spent most of the time with mine and Zane's mum, drawing the views and growing my love of art. A passion that sadly seemed to die with her.

"I also wanted to tell you that I didn't know you worked at Timeless Treasures. I'm not saying it would have changed my decision to buy the business had I known, it was a great addition to the roster, but I wanted you to know, it wasn't personal."

This admission stunned me slightly. Although I knew how ridiculous it would have been if he had really hunted down my location to inflict some pain into my life, hearing him confirm that he hadn't been out to get me was comforting.

"Thanks, I appreciate that. I'm okay, really. Anyway, I wanna hear about your crazy successes, it's a lot more interesting than my life." I changed the subject, closing the door on those memories for the day. It was oddly charming seeing this side of Zane, for the majority of my life, I had seen him as cruel and dismissive towards me, so to discover he had a heart was a nice surprise!

15

ZANE

The look of sadness on Delilah's face caused my chest to tighten and I felt the urge to shield her from her pain. I reminisced for a moment over the first day Delilah started working for me. Truth be told, even though I hired her to help Theo, I always enjoyed teasing her as a child and thought it would bring some interest to my day. Watching her run around after me, just like she used to when Theo and I would make our games 'boys only'. However, as we'd gotten to know each other again, she'd begun to bring out a different side of me. I'm not sure how to explain it but I no longer wanted to push her away, I wanted to keep her close.

"I loved Cornwall but craved to know more about my heritage. You won't find too many Latin Americans strolling around there. So, I decided to pack my bags and head back to the homeland. I learnt so much about this industry and it all took off from there.

Ironically, I then began to miss England, so I decided it was time to expand the business and come back to my second home, and you know the rest from there!"

"So, there was no lady to keep you in Colombia then?" She questioned. I spotted the intrigue in her eager eyes as she waited for my reply. I took a bite of my food to prolong the suspense.

"No one special enough to settle for. I'm too busy fucking all my staff members remember?" I watched as her cheeks glowed red with embarrassment. A cocky grin spread across my face, as I invoked the reaction. "Why, are you interested, *Joya?*" I flirted. A second wave of pride hit me as her face turned even redder. It turned me on to toy with her like this.

"Pfft, yeah right." She clearly bluffed, her body language telling me a different story.

"While we're on the topic, any boyfriends I should know about who might be jealous of you obeying all my demands?" I teased. She played nervously with her hair, her mind clearly elsewhere. With each twirl of red, I imagined sweeping the food off the desk, bending her over it, wrapping her hair around my fist and pulling her head back as I fucked her hard. It seemed we were both living out the same scenario, catching sight of her nipples poking through her thin shirt. My cock hardened at the thought of her moaning my name.

"No, I'm not interested right now." She said, in an attempt to compose herself.

"You must be batting them off, *Joya!*" I purred, enjoying the effects of my words.

"Anyway *boss*, is there anything work-related you wanted to talk to me about? Or will I be visiting HR after this lunch?" She quipped. Although she was joking, the mention of my position brought me back to reality and I realised I was playing with fire. I'd never crossed that line with an employee, and I'd made an internal promise to myself that I wouldn't risk that now. Let alone with one who was also my best friend's little sister!

"No need Miss Hart. Where do you see your career heading? Any interest in joining the Designers or Strategy? You seemed to have a lot of knowledge of trends in the meeting." I diverted the conversations back to a safer land.

"Yes, I could see myself heading in the direction of design, but I don't have any of the qualifications so it might just be a pipedream in reality." She said, looking downcast as she picked at her food.

"Well, let me treat you like a Designer then. Tell me what *you* think we should base the new launch on. I'm interested in hearing your perspective." I encouraged.

"Oh, you're not getting that information from me, that easily." I looked at her surprised. "I'm your PA, *not* your Designer. Promote me or my lips are sealed." She shrugged her shoulders cheekily.

"Fair point. I'm sorry, no one could fill your position if I agreed to that currently." I declared, giving her a knowing look. "But let's see what the future holds."

A moment of silence passed as we finished our meals. I glanced at the clock, my 2pm meeting was fast approaching.

"There was one more thing I wanted to mention." Delilah's beautiful eyes met mine with an enthusiastic look. "I have an important meeting in Paris on Thursday, it will be an overnight trip, and I wanted to know if you could join me?"

"What do you need me for? I'm sure you can find someone in France to make you a coffee?" She sassed.

"Yes, Delilah but you impressed me last week. We are meeting with the successful entrepreneur, François DuBois to discuss a potential collaboration and it might be of interest to you?"

"I'm sure I could make myself available." She giggled.

"Great. I'll send you the travel details if you could please find a hotel for us two and a good spot for dinner. There will be three of us for the reservation."

"Yes sir. Looking forward to it!" She smiled. I was happy that she agreed to join, however I feared this would be a turning point in our relationship.

****

I piled the last few items of clothing into my suitcase. Only nine hours until I would be collecting Delilah and heading to Kings Cross St Pancras station.

After completing a mental checklist, I concluded that I had packed everything required for the trip and zipped up the case, placing it by the door.

I walked across the wood floor of my bedroom, to the ensuite bathroom and switched on the light. The warm glow reflected off of the black subway tiles, which matched the dark shower. I turned the dial on to allow the water to get to heat, as I undressed. I was about to step into the shower when my phone buzzed. I lifted the device off the granite vanity to see Delilah's name.

> What time can I be expecting you in the morning, Mr Moreno?

Blood rushed to my dick at the title. *Dios mio, Delilah, the things you do to me.* I started to type a reply when my erection caught my eye. If there was ever an inappropriate time to respond to an employee, it was now.

I groaned, placing the phone down and stepped into the warm running water to clear my head. As the stream ran over my body, I could only imagine what it would be like if she were to join me here. How her long, damp, red hair would cling to her chest; how the droplets would run over her breasts; and how her curves would feel under my rough hands as I pressed her up against the cold tiles. My cock throbbed harder as I imagined pulling one of her erect nipples into my mouth.

I braced myself against the wall, closed my eyes and clenched my jaw as I fought the urge to indulge further. My efforts were fruitless as even with them shut, all I could picture was Delilah on her knees, the water racing over her perfect body as she looked up, taking my full length in her mouth like a good girl.

I let out a curse under my breath, enough was enough. The thought alone was getting me close. I couldn't spend the next twenty-four hours with this painting in my brain.

Goddamn it!

I finally caved and fisted my cock. It was already dripping pre-cum and swollen as I worked towards my much-needed release. Shamefully, I pictured what Delilah would look like with her mouth around me as she moaned greedily with each thrust, the feeling of entangling my fingers through her wet hair and the image of her eager, emerald eyes begging up at me finally tipped me over the edge.

As the rush of dopamine spread through my body, I changed the dial to cold to wash away my sins. I promised myself I wouldn't cross this line again. I needed to exercise some self-control; I couldn't allow myself to get caught in this web.

I typed a quick reply after getting dressed and got into bed. This was going to be a long trip.

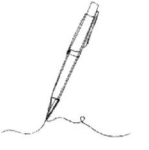

16

LILAH

I was a bundle of nerves as I anticipated the car pulling up outside, I waited on the pavement with my suitcase by my side. I couldn't tell if I was more excited to be going to Paris or to be going to Paris with Zane.

After the lunch we had on Monday, my feelings were more complicated than ever. In the past three months, I had gone from hating the man to mentally fucking him and obsessing over every little interaction.

I'd be lying if I said the thought of twenty-four hours alone with Zane wasn't thrilling me slightly. Although I had assured myself to bury any explicit thoughts of my boss deep in the mind vault.

The familiar black town car rounded the corner and stopped in front of me. Zane appeared from the back driver's side and put my bags in the trunk.

"Morning *Joya*, good to see you're early for once." He smirked and reached up to close the boot. His white

BOSS shirt rode up as he raised his arm, revealing a portion of his sculpted lower abdomen. I bit my lip unconsciously.

"For Paris, I'd always be on time. But for you, I'm a bit less eager." I tapped him sarcastically on the shoulder, noticing how firm his body felt beneath the thin material. Heat burned in my palm from the touch. I quickly got into the back seat and composed myself.

Zane slid in next to me. His woody scent filled the vehicle.

"What's the plan then?" I asked.

"We'll head to the hotel when we arrive, feel free to order some room service as we won't be heading to the offices until 4pm to meet Mark. He's been there for the past day or so, liaising with the head of the other company. Then we'll get some dinner and head back for the night." He explained. Ugh, I had forgotten Mark would be joining us…

"How are you feeling about the meeting?"

"Fine, I've been prepping for this for weeks now. I have an answer ready for any question, so bring it on." Zane assured. Normally I would be put off by this level of cockiness but coming from Zane, it came out as confidence instead of arrogance.

"I've never been to Paris before!" I gushed. "I may have abused the company card slightly; I upgraded my room to get a view of the Eiffel Tower."

"I don't blame you, it's beautiful at night. Enjoy yourself, *Joya*." He responded warmly.

The remainder of the journey was filled with polite conversation and comfortable silences at times, which I was relieved about after the immense stress I felt throughout our lunch on Monday. I swore he could see right into my mind, picking at the images that were less than professional.

Arriving in Paris was everything I had imagined. Beautiful architecture, Juliet balconies adorned with flowers and boulangeries on every corner. It was like stepping into a postcard.

As we pulled up to the front of the Shangri La Hotel, in our transfer, the building was quintessentially Parisian. A smile swept across Zane's face.

"Not just a pretty face, hey, told you I booked a bougie one." I joked.

"You're right, it's beautiful." He said, staring at me so intensely I had to look away. We entered the lobby, and I was blown away by its grandeur. Patterned, marble floors covered the entirety of the space, with gold accents and vintage furniture as far as the eye could see. An enormous stairwell curved at the end of the building, under which the reception desk was situated, ready to greet us.

"Two rooms, under Delilah Hart, ready to check in please," I announced to the woman with a smile. I stood eagerly as she searched through the system for our bookings.

"Ms Hart, you only have one room under your name. The premier suite. Here are your keycards. Breakfast is served between seven and ten. We hope you enjoy your stay."

"One room?" Zane queried.

"There must be some sort of mistake, I booked two rooms for two people. Please check again?" I begged, panicking slightly.

"I can assure you there is no mistake. The booking was one room, two people." She confirmed.

"Can I book a second room then please; I'll take anything you have?" I flustered, Zane, laughing beside me.

"By all means Delilah, stick it on my card." He goaded.

"I'm afraid we are fully booked for tonight. If there's anything else I can do to help, please let me know." The receptionist turned back to her computer, ending the conversation.

I looked at Zane, stressed. "I can stay elsewhere, it's not a problem."

"Ah don't worry *Joya*; I won't fire you for your inability to book a hotel room. We can top and tail like we did as kids." He joked ruffling my hair. I sighed accepting my fate, as if this trip wasn't going to be hard enough.

I tapped the keycard on the door of the suite and was taken aback by its beauty. This room was bigger than the whole of Theo's apartment. I walked through the large entranceway until I reached the balcony. Unlocking the door, I stepped out onto the huge stone terrace. Holding my breath as I looked out at the view beyond. The Eiffel Tower was there in all its glory, crowned with a bright blue, cloudless sky.

Circling back into the suite, I entered the bedroom to find Zane lying across the bed, with his arm folded behind his head, causing his bicep to bulge, reading the room service menu. His unkempt black hair fell effortlessly, with one prominent curl lingering on his forehead.

If the Eiffel Tower was extraordinary, then Zane was breathtaking.

"You're looking very comfortable; guess I'll be on the floor then!" I dug.

"Look at this bed, *Joya*. There's easily room for the two of us. Don't be shy, I won't bite." He laughed, as he tapped the space next to him.

I gulped, sitting down on the unoccupied side, as I resigned myself to the fact I would be sharing a bed with Zane Moreno tonight. "What do you want to order?" He asked, passing me the menu.

Our room service arrived, which Zane brought out to the balcony. I thought I had died and gone to heaven. Here I was, sitting in the heart of Paris, having just finished a Croque Monsieur, whilst staring at the Eiffel Tower. Not to mention, with my hot billionaire boss for company - who I noticed was glancing at me more than the famous landmark.

"Where is this office we're heading to then?" I asked, to break the silence.

"Rue de la Paix. The jewellery district of Paris. Essentially Hatton Garden but in France."

"Why does everything sound better in French?"

"*Je suis d'accord, bijou!*" He spoke fluently, leaving me stunned. The accent evoked a physical response, causing my nipples to tighten and my mouth to fall open.

"I agree, *Joya*." He repeated slowly to translate believing my frozen expression was due to misunderstanding.

"What does *Joya* even mean? You've been calling me that for years!" I questioned, regaining my composure.

"I'm surprised you've never looked it up!"

"I considered it, but I assumed it was an insult to be honest and preferred blissful ignorance. But now I'm curious."

Zane leant across the table, resting on both of his elbows. He stared into my soul with his chocolate-brown eyes.

"It translates to jewel," he said matter of factly.

"And why jewel?" I replied, leaning instinctively towards him, meeting his gaze, leaving mere inches between us. The electricity emanating from him was palpable.

"Well, Delilah, if you must know, when I first met you, your eyes reminded me of emeralds, the stone of my homeland. I've never been able to deny how beautiful I found them, so I gave you the nickname and you never asked, so I just continued it." He explained. The surprise sentiment of the name caused my whole body to flush with heat. I would have never imagined the name he had been calling me all these years had been a compliment. Zane flicked his eyes from mine to my lips. It looked like he was going to kiss me. I *wanted* him to kiss me. All it would have taken was a small movement forward and his mouth would have been on mine. I'd never be able to come back from that.

"You should have told me sooner," I whispered.

He was close enough that I could feel his warm breath ghosting over my lips, causing fire to burn hotter within me. Zane moved slightly in my direction. Quickly, I leaned back, out of the danger zone, and crossed my arms to kill the tension, even though it almost pained me to do so as I focussed on the ache thundering between my legs. I needed to remember this was a work trip. I was his employee, and he was my boss. This was not a romantic holiday.

Zane mirrored me, sitting back in his chair, crossing his ankle over his knee, allowing his arm to drape over his groin. "I should get in the shower." I declared and walked back into our room, gasping for air.

17

LILAH

The meeting room was much like any conference space. We could have been in London, Paris or another nondescript office building. All I could focus on was Zane as he conducted the meeting. There were six of us in here, and every person seemed to be captivated by his words.

Back in his CEO attire, a dark navy suit and matching tie, Zane looked edible. How could one man look so sensational in both his casual and work clothes? I needed to get a hold of myself.

I tried to take notes as he ran through each point of his presentation meticulously, but I was the image of a schoolgirl, doodling her crush's name in love hearts, as I scribbled incoherently.

Zane finished his section and handed the conversation over to Mark to run through numbers.

Sitting back into the chair opposite, he cast a smile that was only meant for me, knocking me further off course.

I tried to avoid his eye line as I noted down Mark's speech, but I could feel the weight of his gaze for the duration of the meeting. Finally, Zane concluded the final points and Mark, the other staff members, and I excused ourselves to allow Zane and François some privacy to discuss the finer details of the deal.

Mark approached me with a smug look in his eye.

"So, I see Moreno has brought the eye candy with him. Lucky us. Let's hope you're on your best behaviour this time!" I squirmed as he leered at me. This wasn't the reaction I had anticipated from Mark, after our heated discussion in the design meeting, but somehow this slimy attitude was even worse than I could have imagined.

"I'm purely here to do my job and go home. I'm not here for your entertainment." I stated.

"Shame, we could have some fun together." Mark shrugged. I rolled my eyes in disgust and went to find a quiet corner to complete the minutes. I shouldn't have expected anything different from a man who clearly had no respect for women.

A quarter of an hour later I was back in Zane's company as we arrived at the fancy French restaurant for dinner. Unfortunately, with Mark in tow.

"I think today calls for a toast. Whatever the outcome, thank you both for accompanying me and let's hope we get the result we came for." Zane raised his flute of champagne, clinking it with ours. I looked opposite me, making eye contact with him and smiled encouragingly. Mark sat to his left, although conventionally attractive, he was Zane's opposite. Blonde hair, blue-eyed pretty boy with a sleazebag attitude. Next to Zane, any level of charm paled in comparison.

As we tucked into our meals, Zane's phone rang. "Excuse me, I need to take this." He announced, disappearing to a quiet part of the room, leaving Mark and me in an awkward silence. I picked at my spaghetti, trying to avoid any reason to speak to him. Just as Mark had mustered up the courage to talk, Zane returned from behind me, placing his hands on my shoulders. I looked up at him, thankful for the interjection but overwhelmed by his closeness. His scent was dizzying.

"Well team, it would appear the celebrations need to continue. Mr Dubois has agreed to sign with us. The deal is on!" Zane spoke elatedly.

After he settled the food bill, we all piled into a cab to a well-renowned underground bar and headed to the VIP area to find a booth to occupy. When we reached the table, a bucket of ice and champagne waited as well as three glasses and a tray of tequila shots.

We were all overdressed for the laidback venue. Zane removed his tie and jacket, folding it over the back of the seat, in an attempt to fit in more with the revellers. As if that man could ever avoid standing out - he was out of this world! I took off my blazer to reveal my black, tight pencil dress underneath. We took the shots to celebrate, and the music filled my veins as I turned to Zane excitedly.

"Come and dance with me?" I asked, pulling at his rugged hand. The champagne filled me with a new sense of confidence, so much so that I barely even remembered that Mark was sitting next to him. He beamed back at me, running his free hand through his shaggy hair.

"I don't dance *Joya,* but don't let me stop you." He released my grip.

"Suit yourself!" I shrugged and headed to a gap in front of him. I let the music consume me, swaying my hips to the beat and swishing my hair around. I glanced towards the men sitting opposite me, only caring about one particular set of brown eyes as they raked over my body appreciatively, following every twist and turn. My movements became more deliberate, more sensual. I could see the way his lips parted and his eyes darkened. My skin burned at the trail they were leaving; I couldn't help but smile as I locked eyes with him.

I spun around again to notice Zane's seat was now empty and felt a pang of disappointment as I glanced around for him. I turned my body back towards the crowd, getting swept back up in the revelry. A pair of hands slid over my hips, as I felt hopeful that Zane had joined me. Facing my partner, I was disgusted to see Mark's smarmy face looking down at me with a shit-eating grin. I stepped forward abruptly to release his grip.

"Moreno has finally gone off somewhere and left us alone." He slurred, "I've seen the way you've been looking at me tonight and your flirty jibes." He reached forward for me again.

"You are seriously mistaken Mark; I have not been giving those vibes to you."

"Don't play hard to get darlin', you've already got me where you want me. Come here." He grabbed my wrist and pulled me towards him.

Before I even knew what had happened, I'd slapped him across his stupid face. Mark shouted out in pain.

"What the fuck is going on?" Zane barked from behind us.

18

ZANE

I was stunned by the situation before me.

When I left, Delilah was still a vision. She knew exactly what she was doing to me, giving me those eyes and moving in that way. I needed a break to stop myself from doing something I would surely regret. I didn't expect to find her distressed in the hands of Mark. They both stared back at me, refusing to answer my question.

"Don't make me repeat it," I demanded.

"You need to get control of your employee, the disrespect she repeatedly shows me is totally unacceptable." Mark bleated, like a weasel. I looked between the two of them, rage boiling my blood. I needed to get myself and Delilah out of this situation.

"We're going Delilah, grab your jacket. I'll speak to you soon, Mark." I declared as I followed behind Delilah to the exit. She was silent for the ride back to the hotel, which I mirrored, as the anger consumed my thoughts, after what I had witnessed. She seemed to be handling herself okay, but I dread to think what could have happened if I hadn't returned when I did.

Entering our shared room, I left Delilah alone in the bedroom, whilst I changed into a t-shirt and joggers in the living area. I returned as she was rifling through her belongings, muttering a frustrated *shit* under her breath.

"What's wrong?" I questioned, chucking my shirt and trousers into the top of my holdall beside the bed.

"I haven't packed any bloody pyjamas. I guess I'm sleeping in this dress!" She gestured to the totally inappropriate sleep attire she was currently wearing. She began to brush her hair aimlessly whilst I contemplated the options.

After a quiet minute, I sighed and pulled my grey t-shirt over my head, tossing it on the floor next to her. "Take this."

She glanced down at it before her eyes met mine. They travelled down my bare torso longingly, the image even better in reality than what I had fantasised about only twenty-four hours earlier. I could feel my chest heaving as she surveyed me. "What are you doing?" She asked.

"Well, it's that or a collared shirt, so take your pick. You needed something to wear, now you've got something." I clarified.

She timidly reached for the item and thanked me, before scurrying to the bathroom. With a sigh, I climbed into the king-sized bed. Settling myself into the pillows, whilst I bored a hole into the ceiling, anticipating her return. I replayed the evening's events. I wanted to wrap my hands around Mark's neck for laying a finger on Delilah. *I can't wait to wipe that smug sneer off his face.*

The bathroom door creaked to reveal Delilah, my t-shirt loosely draping over her curves, long enough to just cover her arse. She looked so beautiful and so goddamn, *mine.*

Cautiously, she climbed in beside me. The silence was deafening between us. In unison, we turned on our sides to face each other. I felt my heart rate quicken at the closeness of her. It was impossible to imagine she could be even more radiant but somehow with her makeup removed, in the dim golden glow of the bedside lamp, she achieved just that.

"Delilah, I-"

"I'm sorry-" we spoke at the same time.

"You have absolutely nothing to apologise for." I implored, staring deeply into her captivating green eyes.

"I thought you were angry with me." She confessed, averting my gaze.

I sat up on my forearm, her eyes flicked to my tensed bicep. "Why would I be? Mark has no right to take advantage of you, even though you look incredible tonight." I assured; the last sentence was out of my mouth before I could catch it. She blushed in return, her doe eyes now blinking up at me like I'd hung the moon. *Fuck she's got to stop looking at me like that!*

"Well, thank you for saving me."

"You were handling it, *Joya*, you could always stand up for yourself." I rolled onto my back, my head resting on my arm, looking in her direction.

"I just feel like an idiot. He said I was looking at him all night," she paused, taking a shaky breath, "but it wasn't him I was looking at."

I didn't reply. The tension was tangible. I was walking on thin ice, mere inches away from shattering our professional relationship and destroying the boundaries I had set for myself. I couldn't face her any longer and leaned over to turn off the lamp, enveloping us in darkness.

"Goodnight, Delilah," I concluded. I took a deep breath to compose myself.

"Goodnight, Zane," Delilah replied next to me. Exhaling shakily, giving herself away to the same inner turmoil she was experiencing. I closed my eyes, willing myself to sleep but the image of Delilah dancing, grinding her hips and that fucking look she gave me, sent me to insanity.

"Fuck it!"

I spun back to a waiting Delilah and crashed my mouth against hers, surrendering to my impulses, and holding her face in my hands. She matched my pace with equal fervour. Desperately, I lost myself in her as I bit her lip. She let out a soft moan of my name which threatened to push me completely over the edge.

I needed her. Every inch. I searched her body with my hands, yearning to discover every part, as she did the same to me, tangling her hands in my hair, keeping my mouth glued to hers. She pushed herself closer to me and I felt the curve of her breast against my bare chest. I groaned into her mouth and moved my hand under her shirt to palm her soft peak. She whimpered as I pinched her nipple in between my fingers. Her leg slipped over mine and she began to grind against my upper thigh, moving her hips in slow deliberate circles. I could feel the heat of her as her breaths became more ragged, it was intoxicating.

"This is crazy!" She panted with arousal. The three words were like a cold bucket of water bringing me back to Earth. She was right, this *was* crazy. I was on a work trip with my Personal Assistant…my best friend's little sister! This had gone too far. I pulled back immediately, trying not to notice Delilah's swollen lips and glazed-over eyes, as well as my throbbing erection. I turned over not wanting to see the rejection on her face.

"I'm sorry Delilah. Goodnight."

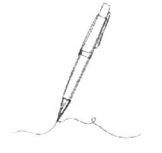

19

LILAH/ZANE

LILAH

Bright, morning sunlight streamed through the chiffon curtain onto my pillow rousing me slightly. I chose to snooze a bit longer, squeezing my eyes tightly shut to avoid the glow. I could feel the warmth of him wrapped around me and for a moment I let myself snuggle closer, the steady rise and fall of his chest comforting me in my hazy state. I gave into the sensation as our breathing synced and a content smile formed across my lips.

The buzz of my phone vibrating on the bedside table awoke me from my slumber. Opening my eyes, the surroundings came into focus, and I realised I hadn't dreamt last night.

I looked down to see Zane's toned muscular arm, draped across my waist. The sight of it caused a mix of emotions to swirl through my body.

Ten hours ago, I imagined waking up in his embrace, sleepy-eyed and cosy after our night together, but as the morning shone through, my feelings had taken a one-eighty. That familiar feeling of rage bubbled through my veins, as the humiliation set in. Classic Zane, any excuse to mortify me. I felt so stupid as I glanced upon his angelic-looking face whilst he still slept blissfully. *What a dick!*

I rose abruptly, throwing him off me carelessly.

"Delilah?" Zane rasped sleepily, his voice cracking slightly in an annoyingly sexy way. Without giving him a second look, I stomped towards the bathroom and slammed the door, hearing a tired groan come from the bed.

Good morning, arsehole.

I took a moment to gather my thoughts in front of the mirror, realising I was still wearing his fucking t-shirt!

"Ugh!" I scoffed at the image, as I pulled the grey fabric off my body, the smell of him filled my senses, as it passed over my head. I whipped around to the shower behind me. I had to wash him off of me.

As the steam enveloped the room, I lathered up the bubbles across my skin as last night replayed through my mind. The thought of the hunger on his face as he gave in to temptation; the feel of his strong grip as it explored my figure desperately; and the conflicted look in his eyes as he brutally rejected me.

I wrapped the towel around my body, which only just skimmed the tops of my thighs. I cursed inwardly, remembering I'd left my bag and today's clothes in the bedroom where Zane would be waiting. I had to return to the crime scene.

Carefully, I edged open the door. Zane was sitting on the end of the bed, leaning forward on his parted knees. He had pulled on a pair of black jeans but was yet to cover the hard ridges of his bronzed chest. He appeared to be deep in thought but looked up, through his unruly curls, at the sound of creaking wood.

His eyes seemed to darken at the sight of me, barely covered, metres away. Zane's mouth parted, as if about to speak, causing me to freeze in motion at the thought of what he might say. After a moment, he looked away to a vacant corner of the suite, hardening his jaw.

Silently, I passed him to my bag and began gathering my outfit for the day: a white linen sundress and tan sandals. Turning back to the bathroom, a flash of Zane's bare back was all I saw as he skipped ahead of me. *I guess I'm changing out here then!*

Hurriedly, I threw on my clean outfit, chucking his grey top I had used as a nightie, onto his side of the bed. The door clicked and Zane emerged, wet hair from his apparent shower and now fully clothed. I noticed the white BOSS shirt he was wearing. Surely it couldn't be the same one he had travelled here in. He wouldn't have given me his only clean alternative last night…He's a billionaire, who am I kidding? He's probably got twenty of the same top! As if he'd ever do anything that selfless.

Zane's voice broke the awkward silence. "I called the driver; the car will be here in the next ten."

Usually, he would ask me to do that. I realised how desperate he must have been to get out of this situation, away from me. I really wished I'd booked separate carriages home now!

As expected, for the remainder of our journey, you could cut the tension with a knife. It's amazing how long a two-and-a-half-hour train ride could feel with the embarrassment of kissing your boss and being rebuffed hanging over you. We only spoke again as we approached the exit of St Pancras station.

"My car is waiting around the corner."

"I'll get one of these." I cut in gesturing to the queue of London taxis lining the road outside, pre-empting the dismissal from him. I opened the back passenger door of one of the cabs and began lifting my suitcase.

"Delilah, I-" Zane started, I turned to look at him, our eyes locking for a second, "I'll see you Monday." he continued, releasing my gaze. I let out a breath I didn't realise I was holding.

ZANE

My chest tightened as I watched the black cab drive around the corner. I could have made her mine. I could have buried myself in her and never looked back. The way she begged me with those emerald eyes, I knew she wanted me as badly as I craved her.

The only thing that held me back was the last remaining tatters of my self-control. I'm her boss, and fraternising with my staff would be breaking every moral code I'd always upheld, but more importantly, she was my best friend's little sister. We'd spent so many summers together; I knew deep down how protective

Theo was of her. He would never want her to be with a man like me - someone who had no time for a relationship and a man whose business would always come first, so taking her would be reckless.

    I'd had a taste and that was enough. Time to shut the door and move on. However, I feared having an inch would only make me want to go the mile.

****

"Come in!" Mark ordered as I knocked on the door of his office. He was located in the same building as Graham. They had kept the site in Mayfair when our companies merged so I agreed they could be based here rather than move to my Hatton Garden headquarters. I walked in and made sure to shut the door behind me.

    "Ah, Zane. What a pleasant surprise. I had been expecting us to chat after Paris, but you needn't drag yourself across the city to visit me especially. I wasn't that cut up about what happened." He greeted me cheerily, standing up from his desk and offering his hand to shake.

    "Yes, well I thought this conversation would be better had face to face. Do you have five minutes?" I asked flatly, keeping my hands firmly in my pocket. Mark retracted his offer and wiped his palm awkwardly against his trouser leg.

    "Of course, take a seat. I assume this is in regard to Delilah's lack of professionalism that evening?" Mark said as he sat back down, gesturing to the seat in front of him, although I remained standing. "I'm sure you're sorry to see her go, but a necessary action given the circumstances." An irritatingly smug look spread across his face that I couldn't wait to wipe off.

"Oh, Delilah hasn't been dismissed." Surprise flickered in his eyes as I continued. "I'm here to talk about *your* lack of professionalism." Mark's initial shock turned to horror as he processed my words.

"I'm not sure what you're referring to…we were all having a few drinks and a good time in the bar! It was Delilah who-" He babbled.

"You're right everyone *was* having a good time until I returned from the bathroom to find you inappropriately touching my Personal Assistant." I interrupted him as images of Mark and Delilah replayed in my head and jealousy coursed through my veins.

"Zane! Come on! Did you not see how she was looking at me?" The fact he was trying to justify his disgusting behaviour caused bile to burn at the back of my throat, I clenched my jaw, knowing I had to choose my next words carefully.

"I think Delilah's reaction would prove otherwise Mark." I bit back.

"She was embarrassed in front of her boss. She was into it until you showed up." He pointed at me.

"I dread to think what would have happened if I *hadn't* shown up. It's obvious you don't have any kind of understanding regarding consent." I hammered my fist on the desk between us, rage getting the better of me as I imagined the possible outcomes had I been minutes later. Mark waved his hands in confusion.

"She was wearing that tight dress and dancing like a slut, she was practically begging for i-" Before he could finish, I rounded the desk, clearing the space between us. I grabbed the collar of his shirt, pulled him to his feet and shoved him against the wall.

"I suggest you don't finish that sentence." I spat at him. "You're a pathetic man if you thought her clothes or dancing were any kind of invitation. If you ever so much as breathe in her direction again, it'll be the last thing you'll do." For the first time since bringing up Delilah, I saw a glimpse of fear in his eyes.

"Okay okay, I get it! You want her all to yourself. I don't like sharing my playthings either." Without thinking, I slammed my fist into his face, a fresh wave of fury sweeping over me. A pathetic cry left Mark's mouth as a loud crunch filled the air.

"Did I fucking stutter? Don't go near her again Mark. Now get out of my sight and don't come back." I released my grip causing him to crumble to the floor, clutching his broken cheekbone in agony.

"What the fuck, Zane?!" Mark shouted, a satisfying bruise blooming across one side of his face. "You're fucking crazy!" He began to scramble back to his feet.

"I told you. Get the fuck out." My voice was low and even, I could hardly believe it was coming from me. Mark must have noted the venom too and without another word weakly scurried towards the door leaving his personal belongings behind.

I slumped into his chair, running a hand through my dishevelled hair.

God, what have I done? I wasn't a violent person, especially at work but Delilah caused me to lose control in a way I never had before.

20

ZANE

After my run-in with Mark, I had to push personal matters to the side and get back to business. I spent the remainder of my morning at Graham's studio with other senior members of my board for an urgent discussion on an important matter. It turned out that Jason Sallow appeared to be imitating Moreno Jewellery designs that were yet to hit the market.

We had been noticing over the past few months, similar silhouettes and motifs being used in their products in line with a number of our unreleased pieces. We had put it down to following trends and coincidences however after a TikTok live that Jason did yesterday teasing an upcoming release, we could no longer deny the blatant forgery.

Thus proceeded a four-hour meeting to discuss the protection of our intellectual property, how he could have gotten his hands on internal documents and the likelihood of this happening again. My company used the best cyber security team, so on one hand, I was at ease, but I had to admit that I was nervous about the possibility of our limited-edition being at risk. Especially when we hadn't determined the root cause of the leak, though it was only a matter of time until that came to light!

Now back in my town car alone, I was relieved to be returning to the confines of my own office. I needed some peace to reduce the explosive feelings that had been coursing through me after Mark's foolish comments, and the confirmation that someone in my business was not to be trusted.

As assured as I was knowing there was a team delving into this further, I couldn't deny the apprehension I felt at seeing Delilah for the first time since our uncomfortable goodbye on Friday. I carried the longing look she gave me in bed in my mind all weekend. No matter how much Medellin Reserve I drank, the image of Delilah's breathtaking face, flushed red with arousal, never left my mind. *Mierda, I need to kick this habit!*

The world was against me. As the lift doors parted, there she was in that fucking pencil skirt, which clung to her perfect arse. Jacob's eyes widened at the sight of me.

"Oh Mr Moreno, sorry we weren't expecting you back. I can go and eat downstairs now!" He blathered, beginning to gather up the food they'd laid out on Delilah's desk.

"No Jake, sit down. This is my lunch hour and my desk, there's no rule that only Zane and I can be up here!" Delilah defended as Jake sheepishly looked between the two of us.

"Stay Jacob," I confirmed, pacing to my office but choosing to leave the door open. I didn't give Delilah a second look, but the radiance of her beauty was burned into my memory.

"Eek, that was a bit frosty!" I heard Jake giggle.

"That's Zane, he's always grumpy. Welcome to my life." Delilah complained, I was ashamed to admit it bruised my ego to hear that. I tried to drown their voices out, busying myself with the emails I'd neglected all morning, but I kept being drawn back to her.

"So anyway, show me this Dan guy then. I can't believe you've only been talking since Saturday and you're already meeting up tonight. He must be sooo fit!" Jacob excitedly said through a mouthful of food. My ears pricked up and my body involuntarily tensed at the sound of this anonymous man. As if there wasn't already enough adrenaline running through my body.

"Yeah, he's pretty hot, here," Delilah responded, met with a gasp from Jacob. A mix of curiosity and jealousy enveloped me.

"Fuckkkkk girl, I'm surprised you're not already there! I'd be calling in sick!" Jacob joked.

"Haha, I need the money but bang on 5pm, I'm out of here and going straight to his." I heard the pair dissolve into laughter as Jacob cheered her on. Red mist clouded my vision as fury set in. I couldn't hear any more of this. I got up and shut the door to them, harder than necessary, hearing Jacob quietly release an 'ooo' at my reaction.

I spent the afternoon hoarded in my office, trying not to imagine Delilah's evening with another man. A quiet knock on the door cleared the thought momentarily. Delilah's head popped around the door frame, stunning me. My mind went blank.

"If that's everything, I'm going to be off then." She stated matter of factly. I looked down at my Cartier watch, noticing it was only 4.30pm. It's one thing for her to brazenly brag about her upcoming conquest, right outside my door but to try and leave thirty minutes early, is blatant disrespect.

"Trying to sneak out early, Delilah?" I queried, with a raised eyebrow.

"I'm telling you I'm going, there's nothing sneaky about it." She replied stubbornly, crossing her arms in front of her.

"And I'm telling you, you finish at 5. Sit back down and wait." I ordered. She went to argue, met only with a hard stare from me which silenced her. With an irritated huff, she skulked back to her desk.

Twenty-five minutes later, she returned full of indignation.

"I'm leaving *now,* I'm sure you won't miss me for five minutes." She declared.

"Actually Delilah, we need to have a word. Come in and shut the door." I pointed to the chair opposite but ever defiant, she remained standing by its side, refusing to follow my order.

"Yes?"

"I do have something you could do."

"Stop it, Zane, I know what you're doing. I'm not

stupid, I know you heard me and Jake earlier. You're an arsehole but I never took you for the jealous type."

"I think you've forgotten your place, Delilah." I said, making my way round to the front of the desk to face her. She stood up straighter in an attempt to match my stature, but I still towered over.

"You had your chance, and you let me go. Now you can't face the idea of me with another man." I took a deep breath as I placed my hands down on the desk, either side of her hips, my knuckles whitened as I gripped the edge of the oak. Delilah glanced down at my hands and then back up to my mouth as I licked my lips. A cocktail of anger and longing burned in her eyes.

"Admit it." She challenged with a shaky breath and with that, the last thread of my self-control snapped. I kissed her hard, claiming her mouth. My left hand snaked around the nape of her neck, fisting her red locks between my fingers. Delilah returned my intensity as our tongues fought for dominance and she moaned into my mouth.

"Get on the desk," I demanded, breaking contact momentarily.

"You can't tell me what to do." Delilah dared as her hands searched my torso.

"I think you'll find that's exactly what I can do between the hours of 9 and 5." I goaded, groping her full breast with my free hand.

"Sorry to disappoint, it's 5.05, looks like I'm off the clock." She panted breathlessly against my lips, as she fumbled with my buckle. I let out a groan in response, moving my hands to her shapely hips, easily lifting her onto the desk and positioning myself between her parted thighs, never breaking the kiss.

"Whilst you're dripping all over my desk, you'll do exactly what I tell you." Her cheeks blushed a delicious red and her breath became shallow highlighting her building arousal. "Take off your top, Delilah."

I watched her as she hastily unbuttoned the blouse, obeying my orders for once. Each second that passed was torture as I longed to discover every inch of her. My patience ran out and I ripped it open, popping off the remaining buttons. Delilah's breath hitched at the motion. I allowed myself to bask in her beauty. She wore a white lacy bra that cupped her swollen breasts, which were threatening to spill over. Her rosy nipples teased from behind the material. I reached around her back and unclasped the garment with ease, throwing it idly onto the floor along with her discarded blouse.

"Espléndida." I breathed out as my mouth found the erect bud of her nipple, sucking eagerly. My zipper strained against my pulsating cock begging for release as she leaned onto her hands, arching her back. I trailed hot open-mouthed kisses down her body towards the apex of her legs. I knelt, pushing her tight skirt up around her slim waist. I draped her thighs over my shoulders, pulling her panties to one side to reveal her glistening pussy. I groaned at the sight and imagined how good it would feel sliding my cock into her.

"Please." She begged. A smug smirk curved across my lips at the sound of her longing.

"Wait, didn't you have somewhere else to be?" I pulled back slightly as I purred. She whimpered in response, wrapping her legs tightly around my neck, and pulling me back closer.

"That's what I thought." I kissed along the inside of her sensitive thigh, my mouth meeting her as I dragged my tongue over it. Delilah shivered in response, trying to conceal her moans.

"Everyone will have left, you can scream as loud as you need to, *princesa*!" Her hands found their way into my hair, pulling me tighter against her core. I sucked her clit furiously and slid two fingers inside her, stroking her most sensitive spot. She threw her head back in pleasure.

"Zane," she gasped, "I'm gonna co-" I quickened my pace as she caught on her words, circling the bundle of nerves, lapping up her juices eagerly as she exploded on my tongue. She bucked her hips as I slowly licked her through the waves of her orgasm. I pulled my fingers out of her slowly, wet with her climax, and sucked them into my mouth, revelling in the taste of her. I stood to gaze upon her. She was a vision. The mess of tangled auburn waves and euphoria across her face only increased the level of my own pent-up arousal further. I had to have her. Now.

"Fuck me, Zane!" She demanded staring at me with hooded eyes, her face still flushed from her climax.

"I don't have a-" I started.

"I'm on the pill. I need you inside me, Zane!"

I laughed devilishly as I finally released my raging erection from its prison, pre-cum already dripping over the pulsing head. I saw Delilah's eyes widen at the sight of its length as she quickly scrambled to untie my tie and open my shirt. I looked at her thong, which had repositioned, blocking my entrance to her. Effortlessly, I tore the thin scrap of material off her body, dropping it out of the way.

I teased the head of my cock against her wet folds as she mewled needily. Her emerald eyes implored me to fill her up completely.

"Would you have begged your date to fuck your pretty little cunt tonight, Delilah?" She cried out in frustration, pushing her hips against mine, looking for any kind of friction.

"Please?" She whined. "Stop teasing me!"

"You look so pretty begging for my cock." I taunted, pinching her nipple. "Never forget, you're mine, *mi Joya*." I slammed into her as she screamed out in pleasure. I paused for a moment whilst she twisted her hips, adjusting to my size.

"You're so big!" She panted. I held tightly onto the curve of her hips, beginning to build a steady rhythm as she dripped all over my throbbing dick. "And you feel so good!" My pride soared as I thrust deeper into her wetness.

"You're taking my cock like such a good fucking girl." I praised. She wrapped her arms around my neck as I thrust into her hard, quickening my pace with each movement.

"*Fuck*, you feel even better than I imagined, *mi Joya*." I desperately buried deeper into her warmth as she lifted her hips to grant me greater access. Feeling my own orgasm building, I reached down to draw circles with my thumb over her clit. "Come on baby, I need you to come for me!" I whispered in her ear, her citrus scent flooding my senses, bringing me closer to the edge. After three sharp brutal thrusts, I felt her pussy clench as she came around me for a second time, matching my own release. I came deep inside her, collapsing against her chest. I removed my hands from her body and placed them down on the desk to support myself. Basking in her beauty again, planting a soft kiss on her swollen lips as I caught my breath.

Oh, mi Joya, what have you done to me?

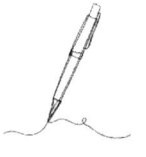

21

LILAH

I revelled in the aftermath of the best orgasm of my life, as Zane tenderly placed a kiss on my shoulder, pulling out of me. I took a moment to compose myself, letting out a breath as a content smile played on my lips. He began to re-button his now creased white shirt, as he smugly smirked in my direction, whilst my heartbeat slowly returned to normal.

"Well, that's the first time you have willingly done as you're told, *Joya!*" He winked, booping me on the nose. Rolling my eyes, I sat up on the palms of my hands.

"If that's all then, I better be off on my date!" I joked, jumping down off the desk. My legs felt like jelly from the intensity of my climax. I steadied myself, pulling my skirt back over my legs and smoothing it down. Zane paused in response, making eye contact with me, as he buckled his belt. "A girl's got needs, I haven't had a good fuck in ages!"

Zane straightened at my comment and closed the distance between us. He grabbed my wrist, pulling me against his strong body and grabbed a handful of my arse tightly. "Oh yeah? That's not what you were saying when you were coming all over my cock, Delilah." Just like that, my breath quickened again, and I could feel the arousal begin to wet my thighs further. Any witty remark I could have said died on my tongue as flashbacks to the way Zane fucked me to submission played in my mind, resulting in a pathetic whimper escaping. He tucked a lock of my red hair behind my ear and traced my lip with the pad of his thumb.

"Where'd you want to go for dinner, *Joya*?" He asked, I could feel his breath inches from my mouth, as butterflies danced in my stomach.

"I can't-" I responded as he buttoned my lip with his thumb.

"Uh-huh, I know you're not busy, you cancelled your date." He interrupted, knowing he had me all to himself, as he caressed my chin.

I took a moment to think over the proposal. Was it reckless to pursue this with Zane? Was I going to end up hurt in the process? It's not like he's been particularly nice to me in the past, why would this change now?

Who was I kidding? Of course, I was going for dinner with him!

"Hmm, let's go to that Colombian place?" I played down my excitement as he stared sweetly at me. His usually perfectly styled curls now unruly from my fingers raking through it desperately.

"Are you sure? We can go anywhere you want to in the city?" He questioned, as he passed me my bra and blouse. "You'll probably want to put these back on!"

I laughed, only just realising I was still topless after being so enamoured with the man in front of me. A hint of self-consciousness threatened to take over, however it disappeared at the way he was gazing at my body. Pulling my arms back through the blouse I began to cover my modesty, as I remembered the final couple of buttons had been destroyed in the chaos. Tucking in the front of the shirt to hide the destruction, a coy smile tugged at my lips at the memory.

"I'm sure. It was great and I've got eight years to make up for!" I insisted, and he smiled in response. "Have you seen my thong?" I searched around the office for the discarded material.

"I'm not sure it's of much use to you now I'm afraid," Zane replied smugly, holding up the flimsy underwear that was now ripped down the seam. "I'll hold onto it for you." I watched him with a dry mouth as he tucked the white fabric into his trouser pocket for safekeeping. "Ready when you are, *Joya*!" He smacked me on my backside, shooting electricity through me.

We walked the short distance from the office to the small, family-run restaurant, opting for a table at the back. Everything about this place screamed cosiness from the photos on the wall of various generations and Colombian scenery; to the mismatched furniture and dim, warm lighting emanating from the various wall lamps.

"*Hola,* Mr Moreno, so good to see you again!" An older gentleman greeted us with a strong accent.

"Please José, how many times, call me Zane!" He insisted as the tanned man patted him on the shoulder.

"And who is this lovely lady?" He gestured to me with an inviting smile. Zane replied in Spanish resulting in the two men sharing a laugh. I cast a look at Zane, raising my eyebrows in question as to what the joke was that I'd been left out of. He responded with a wink which coupled with the thick, Colombian accent made me swoon. The pair continued to converse in their native language, whilst Zane ordered for us.

"Lovely to meet you, Delilah. I'll have your food with you both shortly!" José smiled kindly and headed towards the double doors of the kitchen.

"You know, it's rude to insult someone when they don't understand what you're saying." I kicked him lightly under the table.

"Who said it was an insult, *mi Joya?*" Zane smirked, causing palpitations in my chest. It wasn't lost on me that my nickname had evolved. I noticed it had slipped out in the office.

My jewel. Mine.

Zane repeating it here, proved to me it was intentional and not just in the heat of the moment. I tried not to let my mind wander at what that might mean.

"I'll give you the benefit of the doubt this time, Zane."

Before we knew it, steaming hot plates of delicious food were paraded to our table. I began tucking in immediately, hungrier than I realised. God, how I loved this food!

As the meal progressed, we made comfortable conversation, whilst satiating our appetites.

"That was amazing! Thank you for showing me this place." I exclaimed gleefully, with a full belly.

"You're welcome, I knew you'd love it!" Zane replied, placing his cutlery onto the empty plate in front of him. I wiped the corners of my mouth with my napkin before folding it on the table. I tried to pluck up the courage to divulge the burning question whirling around my head.

"Zane?" I asked warily.

"Hmm?" He looked up at me, his deep chocolate eyes overwhelming me and making me feel incredibly nervous.

"Can I ask you a question?" He nodded in response, leaning in to listen intently, giving me his undivided attention which only increased my anxiety levels tenfold. His chest was exposed slightly at the open buttons and missing tie causing my thoughts to haze. "What happened in Paris?" I blurted out coming back to reality.

His eyes momentarily flicked away from mine, as if taken aback by the question. He swallowed, thinking about his answer.

"I was full of conflict that evening. What happened with you and Mark. My friendship with your brother. And I'm your boss, Delilah! I had drawn so many boundaries for myself, that I knew if we crossed, I could never come back from, so I pushed you away that evening to protect those lines and I'm sorry." He paused whilst his words washed over me in stunned silence. "But the idea of you being with someone else, made me realise I need you all to myself." I felt heat burn across my cheeks at his admission. "Maybe it was selfish, but I couldn't let you walk away from me today," he confessed.

"I couldn't deny it anymore either and I'm glad you stopped me from going." I matched before touching on a sensitive subject. "Did you see Mark today when you went to the Mayfair office?" I asked sheepishly, taking a nervous sip of my drink. Zane released a sigh as he absent-mindedly played with the silver rings on his right hand,

"I did." He stated bluntly, averting my gaze.

"I'm guessing from the look on your face, he didn't apologise or take ownership of his actions?" I stated. Zane stared at me directly now, a stern look on his face as if replaying the events in Paris or today perhaps, in his mind.

"No, he did not." He responded, equally as monosyllabic as before.

"So when will I next have the pleasure of seeing him again?" I asked, nervous to hear the answer. Zane wasn't an aggressive person from memory but how he was talking now, I wouldn't be surprised to find Mark's obituary in the paper tomorrow.

"You will never have to see him again, Delilah." He said, reaching for my hand. "And I can't imagine he will be taking advantage of another woman ever again."

I held his gaze for a moment as he traced circles on the back of my hand with his thumb as if I could watch the earlier events if I looked deep enough into his dark eyes. Considering Zane was sitting here and not being escorted out by armed police right now, led me to believe Mark was alive and breathing but I was certain that pretty boy face of his had been wounded if Zane's swollen knuckles were anything to go by.

A strange feeling of warmth filled me. I didn't condone violence but gross fucking men who couldn't understand the word 'no' deserved a little reminder now and again. The tenderness in Zane's eyes returned as he must have rid himself of Mark's memory.

"I've had a great evening." He announced softly.

"Me too, but let's definitely not tell Theo about tonight. Or anyone at work for that matter!" I laughed awkwardly.

"So, you don't want to do this again?" He asked sarcastically, continuing to drag his thumb over my knuckles.

"I didn't say that, but let's keep it under wraps for now."

"I'm glad we're on the same page, *mi Joya*." He squeezed my hand in agreement. "I'll pay the bill and let's head out." Kissing my hand as he stood to speak to José. I could see his arm muscles protruding through his white shirt as he paid for our meal - he looked heavenly! We began the short walk back towards the office, which was in the same direction as my tube station to get home.

"I'll drive you back," Zane offered as we approached his black sports car, which was parked outside the office.

"Oh, you're fine, it's a really quick tube ride!"

"You're not wearing any underwear, Delilah, get in the car!" There was no arguing with that logic! He opened the passenger door as he ordered me inside.

He started the engine and pulled out of the parking space. After ten minutes of driving down the surprisingly quiet, city roads, his hand rested on my upper thigh. Heat burned where his skin touched mine and I was instantly turned on again at the thought of his rough hand being so close to the bare moistness between my legs. I squeezed them together to relieve the tension. Zane noticed from the corner of his eye and smirked. His hand crept further under my skirt and my breath quivered.

"Are you okay, *mi Joya*?" He teased, playing innocent. I shot him a look that was both glaring and imploring as I parted my thighs slightly in a silent plea for him to touch me. He laughed gruffly at the effect he was having on me. "You're so needy!" He growled, not taking his eyes off the road.

His fingers continued their journey until they reached my sensitive, swollen bud. I released a moan at the contact, leaning my head back against the leather seat.

"*Fuck*, you're soaking." He groaned, beginning to play lazily with my clit as I circled my hips in time with his movements. "You've thought about this before haven't you Delilah?" He purred, and I nodded along in a half-daze. "I bet you've touched that pretty pussy thinking about me finger fucking you until you scream my name." He quickened his movements, and I whimpered. Thank fuck this man drove an automatic! "Answer me, *mi Joya.*" All I could concentrate on was the building pressure in my lower stomach, thoughts were becoming incoherent as I reached up to grab the sides of the headrest.

"Zane, please. I'm gonna come!" He glanced over at me, finally making eye contact but to my disappointment, his fingers stopped.

"I asked you a question, Delilah. Answer me." He held my orgasm hostage. My thoughts scrambled as I tried to remember the question, so caught up in my pleasure and frustration, to take it on board.

"I said, you've played with this wet little cunt thinking about me, haven't you?" I nodded desperately. "Use your words, Delilah."

"Yes!" My answer spilled out in a sob. "Please let me come!" I begged desperately as I looked at him to find he was annoyingly composed. Why did he look so good when I was on the edge of shattering completely? *"*Zane, plea-" Before I could finish my appeal his fingers quickened to a punishing rhythm, and heat pooled between my thighs.

"Tut tut Delilah, you're making a mess all over my expensive leather seat." He scolded with a sinful grin. "You'll have to make it up to me somehow." I nodded enthusiastically at the request.

"Whatever you want." I agreed, panting.

"Good girl. Show me how pretty you are when you come for me." He ordered, gripping the steering wheel so tightly that his knuckles whitened on his right hand. With his permission, I released the tension. Wave upon wave of pleasure ripped through me as I shuddered through the climax, crying out in ecstasy. Zane moved his hand to my thigh stroking reassuring circles against my skin then back to rest over the gear shifter.

"That's my girl." He praised. I sat limply in the passenger seat, my head lolling to the side to stare wistfully at Zane as I caught him already gazing at me, pupils dilated with arousal.

"How are you so good at that?" I whispered with admiration which was met with a smirk.

I reached out towards him as he caught my hand in motion, bringing it to his lips to plant a soft kiss. He placed my hand back on my leg which I immediately relocated to his groin. I felt his engorged erection through his suit trousers and wanted to give him the release he had just provided me.

"Don't worry about it, Delilah," Zane said softly. I looked at him with confusion, did he not want me to return the favour? Feeling a bit self-conscious, I tried for his buckle. He reached down to place his hand on mine to stop it with a knowing smile. "As much as I want your hand wrapped around my throbbing cock, maybe not outside your brother's apartment door, *mi Joya*." He nodded out the window towards my building, realisation hitting me that the journey was over.

"I wish you could come up." I pouted, not caring about how pathetic I sounded.

"Goodnight, Delilah." He said softly, leaning over to kiss me gently on the mouth.

I stumbled out of the car giddily, making my way to the front door. I looked back in the direction of Zane's car to see he was still parked outside watching me walk away. I opened the door, turning back to give him one last look and a small wave goodbye as I stepped inside and shut the door to the outside world.

I entered the apartment, to find Theo was still awake, beaming in the kitchen. He was the last person I wanted to see right now!

"Hey Lils, late night, guessing the date went well then?" He nudged me with his elbow. "Will there be a second?"

"Erm, yeah, we'll see. I'm going to bed!" I scurried off in the direction of my room, hearing Theo laughing behind me. "Just remember to use protection, I'm not ready to be an uncle!" God, if only he knew who he was joking about!

Climbing into bed, I reminisced on the unexpected events of today. I started Monday hating Zane Moreno and ended it begging him to make me come for a third time today.

Self-doubt clouded my elation now that the post-orgasm bliss had dissipated and I was no longer in Zane's presence.

What if he decided to push me away again?

What if I'm not worth breaking his own rules for?

As I scrolled aimlessly through my social media to try and distract my thoughts, my phone buzzed in my hand. The flicker of Zane's name sent a shiver through my body, where previously it was anger and irritation, it was now replaced with anxious excitement.

> Sweet dreams, mi Joya. I'll be thinking of you. Z

My heart filled with warmth at the sentiment of the message and I was going to bed resembling a teenager, giggling and kicking my feet.

I wondered what Tuesday would have in store!

22

ZANE

No matter what I did, I couldn't remove Delilah from my thoughts. The feel of her smooth skin, the sound of my name on her lips and the way her body begged for mine. I knew she would be trouble for me, but she was my kryptonite.

I had never allowed myself to break one of my rules before but the prize I received for breaking this one, was well worth the self-contempt. However, I had to remember why I had set them in the first place. I was the CEO of a prosperous business and the future of that success rested on my moral compass. I couldn't allow anyone to discover my weak spot, which as of recently, was Delilah. My competitors could destroy me if I was distracted and took my eye off the ball and I had worked too damn hard to let that happen.

I knew I couldn't eliminate Delilah from my life completely, but I had to be clever about how we proceeded. She suggested keeping us a secret and as much as I wanted to declare it to every person that laid eyes on her, that she was *mine*, she was right. There was too much risk to have our connection out in the open. Not to mention the ramifications it would have on my friendship with Theo if he ever were to find out.

I pulled up outside the office, in the same parking spot I occupied every weekday and smoothed my hair in the rear-view mirror. Today would be like any other Tuesday. Despite the fact, I fucked my Personal Assistant on my desk a mere fifteen hours ago. At the thought alone, I felt my cock begin to harden. I opened the car door so the cool breeze could douse the burning arousal in my veins.

I leaned across to the passenger seat, picked up my briefcase and began the short walk to the office. As I walked along the stone pavement, passing black railings, I began to read through emails I had received overnight on my phone. Glancing up from my device, as I reached the gateway to the building, I became transfixed on the figure coming into view, walking along the street towards me.

Red tousled hair, blowing in the breeze threatened the clarity of my mind. I wanted to grab her and take her, right here, not giving a fuck who was around. I stood frozen in place, no doubt emulating a fucking nodding dog, as she grew closer in proximity. Her curves were accentuated by that infuriatingly tight black skirt. Did she know that it drove me insane?

"Good morning, Mr Moreno. Beautiful day isn't it." Delilah innocently made small talk, patting me delicately on the shoulder as she turned into the entrance. My skin seared at the touch.

I was dumbfounded.

She was heavenly.

I picked my jaw off the floor and followed hastily behind her.

I shook my head to clear my thoughts. *I must regain some composure here.* Brittany's greeting was like white noise as I passed reception. I threw her a quick smile, eyes still fixed in the direction of Delilah heading through the main office.

Finally, I caught up with her as the steel grey doors began to close on the elevator, Delilah already inside, smiling coyly at me.

"In a rush this morning?" She teased at my obvious sprint to make the lift before the doors shut trapping me outside. Away from her.

"I've got a busy day ahead of me. Every second counts. It's good to see you've arrived on time for once." I retorted, staring straight ahead, avoiding her gaze at all costs. I would lose myself entirely if I looked into those emerald eyes.

"I want to make sure my boss has the best impression of me. I wouldn't want to receive disciplinary action." She stated. I clenched my fists to keep myself from shattering the final chain of self-control I had left. "Although, on second thought, maybe that wouldn't be so bad." She giggled sensually.

Dios mio. I risked a glance in her direction and found her green eyes, round and hopeful. Snap went that chain. Before I knew it, I was pushing her curvy frame up against the cool steel with the weight of me, wrapping my hand around her jaw, pulling her face towards me and claiming her mouth in a kiss so intense that it erased any idea that we were *just colleagues.*

Her hands wound their way into my hair desperately, and her teeth nipped my bottom lip as I grabbed her breast over her shirt in the precious moments we had before the doors opened, and we succumbed to the actuality of our day. She released a whimper as I tightened my grip on her and deepened the kiss. Fuck I didn't want this to stop.

"Floor three" came booming through the speakers of the car, a harsh wake-up call from our frenzy. I stepped back, releasing her from my grasp and adjusting my shirt, which had become untucked during our tryst. If I wanted any kind of integrity to remain, we couldn't get caught making out like teenagers. Delilah remained panting against the wall, a smirk forming across her flushed face.

"Good morning, by the way, *mi Joya.*" I smiled, leaving our bubble and entering our reality.

After emailing Delilah her list of tasks, I decided, like a fucking coward, to stay holed up in my office with the door firmly shut for the remainder of the day. I couldn't allow myself to cave into these desires again. Not here.

When 5pm came around, after what felt like a lifetime, I risked heading for the exit. To my relief, I found Delilah's desk empty and left to head home.

As if fate was laughing at me, I had plans with Theo this evening at the Gilded Cage. His friendly, clumsy face beamed at me across the room as he sat in a quiet booth, a round of drinks already set up on the table.

"Zaney baby, happy Tuesday, brother. How was your day? Anything exciting happening in *Casa Moreno* then?" He excitedly asked, taking a sip of his beer as I slid into the leather cushioned seat. Flashbacks to his sister leaning back on my desk, legs spread sprang to mind.

"Nothing worth reporting to you, Theo, no." I took a swig of my Colombian rum, steadying myself. I wasn't a nervous person naturally, in fact, I'd most definitely been referred to as arrogant at times in my life, but sitting opposite my best friend, knowing the events of yesterday, I'd have had to be dead to not feel some sort of remorse. "What's new for you?" I asked.

"Big plans, big plans. We have our first headline gig coming up in a couple of weeks. You've gotta come, man. You're my number one cheerleader." He winked, causing me to roll my eyes.

"Wouldn't miss it for the world," I assured.

"I've been meaning to ask, how's Lils been getting on? Did you give her a pay rise of somethin', she was walking around like a bloody Cheshire cat this morning."

Shit.

"Erm, no, she must just really be enjoying the role. Who wouldn't enjoy buying me coffee every day?" I replied in jest. Theo looked at me, cogs whirring as he rattled through a list of thoughts.

"Well, she hated it on the weekend. I thought she was going to quit after your Paris trip, dude. I don't know what happened, but she was fuming!"

"Honestly, I couldn't think why," I replied nonchalantly.

Shit.

"Hmm, odd." Theo took another careful drink of his lager, eyeing me suspiciously. "Ah! How did I forget? She had her date last night and definitely enjoyed herself. She was a mess when she came through the door. Good for her, I guess!" He laughed, and I felt every muscle in my body go rigid. "For a moment there, I thought it was you giving her the favours. How fucking gross! But I know I can trust you, bro!" His laugh evolved into hysteria as he nudged me across the table, causing a pang of guilt to reverberate through me.

"You know our relationship is tenuous at best." I watched him as he shook his head aimlessly. "So, tell me about this gig then?"

Anything to change the subject. I was right; this path I was headed down with Delilah was dangerous territory, and it was going to throw everything in my life into disarray.

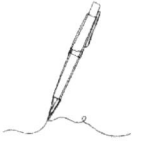

23

LILAH

I sighed as I got to my desk and found Zane's office door shut again. It would seem he's resorted to hiding from me since our extracurricular activity two nights ago.

His hot and cold attitude was giving me whiplash! One minute, he's passionately pushing me up against the mirror in the elevator, and the next, he's shutting me out - literally!

I'd decided to give him until lunchtime, but if his only form of communication was via email again, I'd be giving him a piece of my mind! As if on cue, my inbox received a new email from Zane. Today's to-do list. So, it would appear he'd chosen cowardice for the second time. Maybe I was naive to think that sex would change anything between us, there were years of teasing and taunting in our past; presumably, a man like Zane isn't foreign to meaningless hookups. Although, I'd hoped that Monday might have meant more to him.

Three and a half hours later and, Zane was still hiding in his office. Time's up, buddy! I opened the IM chat and began typing frustratedly:

> 12:38 PM
> Are you going to grace me with your presence today?

> Zane Moreno: 12:39 PM
> Sorry, very busy.

No busier than last week when he made any excuse to talk to me!

> Zane Moreno: 12:40 PM
> But you look very pretty today.

My irritation spiked as I watched the three dots appear and disappear again. My patience had snapped, and I found myself barging into his office to confront him head-on.

"If you've got something more to say, you can say it to my face," I shouted at the stunned man behind the desk. Zane stared back, speechless, and sat bolt upright in his black leather chair, wearing his usual business attire. He was irritatingly drop-dead gorgeous. "Oh, so now you have nothing to say again. I'm fed up with this, Zane, I'm not being strung along for whenever you can be bothered to give me attention. What do you actually want?"

"We're at work, Delilah." He stated coldly, but I could see the fire blaze in his coffee eyes.

"That's not an answer. *What do you want?*" I demanded.

He rose from his seat, leaning forward onto clenched fists on the desk. His eyes darkened further as they bored into mine.

"You."

I scoffed in response to his declaration.

"I want you, *mi Joya*. I hate myself for being such a coward, but I can't control myself around you. You cloud every one of my thoughts, and we agreed to keep this quiet at work, but goddamn, I want you every minute of the fucking day."

I felt my anger dissipate at the confession and heat burned through every vein in my body. In a split second, I closed the short distance between myself and the desk and grabbed him by his tie, pulling his mouth to mine. Instantaneously, I felt his restraint vanish as he gave in to his primal urges and grabbed the back of my head, holding me to him. Our tongues collided as we deepened the kiss. Zane pulled away and began to move around the desk to meet me.

"Don't move," I commanded as I walked around the table, meeting Zane's confused stare. "Sit back down." He tentatively lowered himself back into his seat, his eyes scanning my body hungrily. "You don't need to worry about losing control. Let me be in control for a change." I dropped to my knees and parted his legs, so I was face to face with the bulge in his trousers. His chest heaved as I unbuckled his leather belt and released his raging erection from its confines. My eyes widened at his full length and heat pooled between my thighs at the memory of him filling me up. I licked a long stripe up the underside of his dick.

"Fuck, Delilah." Zane breathed as he gripped the arms of his chair, as I took him into my mouth and down my throat. I paused for a moment to adjust to his size before settling into a steady rhythm as I swirled my tongue around his head, my arousal burning through me. He stifled a moan as one of his hands knotted my hair into a ponytail, the other gripping onto his headrest.

"God, *mi Joya*, your mouth feels so fucking good!" He moaned, and I hummed around him proudly, sucking harder as I looked up to find his face twisting in pleasure. He began to thrust his hips along as I bobbed up and down his length, his hand tightening around my head, keeping me at the mercy of him.

I revelled in this power. The knowledge that I was the one to give him pleasure. He was the boss, but at this moment, I was in charge. Pressure continued to build as I resisted the urge to touch myself. The room filled with hushed, ragged breaths and the slick, wet sounds of my mouth working him towards an orgasm.

"Such a good girl, taking every inch of me so well." He whispered through gritted teeth. I couldn't take it anymore. I reached down under my dress, my fingers finding my pulsing clit. My breath hitched around his cock as I began to play with myself in line with his movements as he ruthlessly fucked my mouth, drool leaking down my chin.

"Are you enjoying choking on my dick, Delilah?" He asked, holding my gaze.

"Mmhmm," my movements quickened against my wet pussy bringing me closer to release. In one swift motion, he had me bent over his desk, holding my arms behind my back with one hand, as I heard the other one undo and remove his tie.

"While you're in my office, the only one who's going to make you come is me." He growled as I felt him bind my wrists together, the bite of the material sending waves of pleasure through me. I whined in both frustration and anticipation as he removed my underwear. My legs quivered as I felt the air breeze against my sensitive sex.

"Such a pretty pussy." He complimented me as he pushed a finger inside of me, curling it to hit my most sensitive spot. I cried out.

"Shh, Delilah, or I'll have to stop." He warned, positioning himself at my entrance. "Are you going to be a good girl while I fuck that tight little cunt of yours?" He whispered in my ear, the heat of his breath sending goosebumps over my whole body.

"Yes, sir," I vowed as he slammed into me. Blinding pleasure ripped through me at the force. Mercilessly, he continued to ravage me; it took every ounce of willpower not to scream his name and risk exposing us to the entire office.

"That's it, sweetheart, don't make a sound." He instructed. I closed my eyes tightly and gritted my teeth as he held onto my hips, deepening his thrusts. A sharp smack against my arse caused a yelp to escape my lips, the silver rings on his fingers branding my skin deliciously. His right hand snaked around my face to cover my mouth.

"Now-now, Delilah, I know you don't want me to stop." My eyes rolled back in pleasure as he nipped at my neck. "Does this prove how much I want you, *mi Joya?*"

"Mmhmm," I muffled through his fingers in agreement. I arched my back to allow him greater access, wishing desperately that I could touch his skin. My vision hazed as Zane drove the fingers of his left hand deeper into my flesh, pumping his cock faster into me. My muscles began to constrict with my impending orgasm.

"That's it, baby, come all over this cock for me." My body convulsed at his words as I gave in to the overwhelming sensation. With it, any lingering doubts about his feelings towards me were washed away as I felt him release inside me. A string of Spanish curse words spilling from his mouth.

I slumped onto the wooden desk, as Zane pulled out of me and untied my hands, kissing his way up my back towards my mouth.

"Don't ever question how I feel about you, Delilah." He implored as I kissed him back.

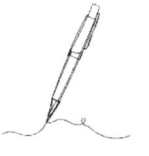

24

LILAH

9pm on the dot, and Zane was texting me that he was outside. After our moment of passion in the office earlier, I was looking forward to our first official date this evening. Zane was yet to divulge the details, and butterflies were swarming in my stomach.

I opted for a little black dress that pinched in at my waist and fell over the curve of my hips in the most flattering way, pairing it with chunky black heels and my signature gold jewellery. My hair fell in perfect ringlets down my back, with my fringe framing my face, which I had accentuated with more makeup than usual to make sure I looked and felt my best. Although this was not the first time Zane and I would be alone together, tonight felt like a turning point in our relationship, which heightened my nerves like crazy.

I rushed down the hallway to leave but was met with Theo, cross-armed, leaning against the door frame.

"Hey, Lil!" He greeted, "Big date?" A shit-eating grin spread across his face.

"Yep." I answered, emphasising the P, "If you could get out of my way, please?" I gestured towards the door he was blocking, trying not to make eye contact with him in case he could somehow read my mind.

"Aw, my little sis is all grown up!" He went to ruffle my hair, and I dodged out of the way to avoid him messing up the style. "Don't do anything I wouldn't do with Danny boy." I groaned in reply as he stepped to the side, allowing me to run for the exit.

"Bye, Theo!" I said, scurrying out and closing the door behind me. As I reached the road, I glanced back up at our second-floor apartment and spotted Theo peering out of the curtain, hoping for a peek at 'Tinder Dan' after the only information I had offered up to him previously was his name and that we met on the dating app. I flipped him off sarcastically as I began to walk.

Thank God Zane had the good sense to park down the road! He knew how nosy my brother could be…

My heart fluttered as I spotted Zane in a full black suit, missing a tie which exposed part of his sculpted chest, leaning against the shining town car. Words died on my tongue at the sight of him, and a cocky smirk spread across his full lips.

"Good evening, Delilah." He said as I realised, I was staring at him gobsmacked. He leant off his car towards me, placing a soft kiss on my cheek, the unusual tender greeting caused my heart to skip a beat.

"Good evening, Zane." I found my voice, returning the hello. He walked ahead of me to open the back passenger door as I began to slide into the seat.

"You look absolutely beautiful tonight, *mi Joya*." I blushed as he shut the door behind me. I greeted the regular driver, who had often ferried me around during work hours. My eyes followed Zane as he crossed the front of the vehicle to take his place next to me behind the driver's seat.

"You don't scrub up too bad yourself," I replied. With Zane back in the vehicle, the driver closed the partition to afford us some privacy. "Where are we headed tonight then?"

"All in good time, Delilah." He responded, picking my hand up and pecking the back of it. If he kept up with these romantic touches, my heart might have stopped completely! As the car began to move, it simultaneously ignited my excitement. Music came through the speakers, and I recognised it immediatcly.

"Is this Paper Sunsets?" I questioned.

"It is. You inspired me." Zane shot a wink in my direction. My chest warmed at the thought of him discovering music through me.

"You have to stop looking at me like that, or we are going to have a repeat of Monday evening," I warned, as desire burned deep inside me. He chuckled to himself and turned his attention out of the window, placing his hand dangerously high on my thigh again. We sat in comfortable silence as anticipation of what the night had in store filled my thoughts.

Entering an underground car park, we were driven up to an elevator on the far side of the building. The two of us walked into the lift, and Zane pressed the 'R' button on the panel inside. The lift rose out of the basement level to reveal a spectacular view of St Paul's Cathedral, with an incredible sunset painted across the sky through the glass wall. I caught my breath at the sight as Zane reached for my hand, squeezing it slightly.

"This is breathtaking," I exclaimed.

"It is." He replied, never taking his eyes off me. I felt the crimson heat spread across my cheeks at the obvious compliment, holding his hand back tightly as we rode past the remaining levels.

The elevator doors opened to an expansive rooftop with festoon lighting draped across the width of the terrace. A friendly maître d' greeted us as we stepped into the scene.

"Good evening, Mr Moreno. Your table is ready; please follow me." She welcomed us. We followed dutifully behind, passing several tropical plants and many empty seats. I hoped that wasn't a bad sign!

"Just here. I'll be back in a moment to take your orders." She headed off, leaving Zane and me at the most central two-seater table, which was adorned with lit candles. I took the seat that Zane had pulled out for me.

"Oh wow, Zane." I breathed in admiration. "This is the most beautiful place I've ever been!"

"You deserve it, *mi Joya*." He assured as the waitress returned with two tumblers of familiar-looking liquor and two menus. I took a sip of the amber nectar, feeling the warmth of the alcohol run down my throat.

"Hmm, I recognise this! Is this what you and Theo used to steal from your dad's liquor cabinet?"

"Correct. And I know you used to steal it from us, too, so I guess you like it!" He winked, causing me to laugh. "Medellin Reserve, it's the only spirit I drink these days. Reminds me of home."

We perused the menus whilst we decided on our respective meals. I watched Zane's expression as he scanned the paper and played with his lip in concentration. How can it be that such a minimal movement can look so sexy?

"So, you've been here before then?" I asked, taking a sip of my drink, referencing the familiarity between him and the staff and how they knew his name and drink of choice without asking.

"Many times." I felt my heart sink slightly as I considered that this might not mean as much to him as it does to me. "With family, Delilah." He assured me, reaching across the table to hold my hand. I looked away from his gaze, feeling slightly embarrassed that he could sense my obvious jealousy.

"Were you always the only people here, or is it just not busy on Wednesday nights?" I joked, gesturing to the ghost town around us.

"I wanted to be alone with you. Rest assured; they were all compensated greatly for giving up their reservations this evening." Giddiness flowed through me at the idea of Zane going out of his way to personally ensure the rooftop was free for us tonight. Although money didn't necessarily impress me, it was a very romantic gesture. We placed our orders with the waitress before I took a long sip of the brown liquor.

They returned again with two plates of steak frites, medium rare and a large bottle of red wine. Zane thanked her, and she disappeared again, leaving us alone to eat together whilst admiring the three-sixty view of the London skyline.

Zane began to pour me a glass. "This is a Colombian Rioja. I discovered it when I was living back there. I know what you're thinking: Colombia isn't known for its wine but trust me on this." I took the glass and swilled a sip in my mouth, savouring the fruity taste as I pretended to know anything about wine.

"Hmm, good choice. What a hidden gem." I complimented, taking a bite of my tender steak. I was shocked by how it melted in my mouth, groaning involuntarily. Zane's eyes flicked to mine. "Be careful, Delilah, or I'll be sending the staff home early." His eyes darkened as his Adam's apple bobbed with a deep swallow. Goosebumps covered my body at the loaded statement.

Coyly, I cut another piece of steak and began to chew it, avoiding Zane's eye contact, refusing to rise to the challenge.

"As much as I would revel in the pleasure of round two, this is the fanciest restaurant I've ever eaten at, and I'm not letting my steak get cold!" I rebuffed in jest. Zane was unable to stifle a laugh at my response.

"My apologies!" He held up his hands in surrender, "who am I to come between a girl and her food?" He replied, tucking into his own meal.

"So, Theo's gig on Saturday, that's pretty exciting. Their first headline show and at Koko no less!" I said animatedly.

"Yes, he mentioned it. I'll be there." He confirmed. I tried to hide my smile at the thought of a Saturday evening in his presence.

"Great! I felt like a teenager sneaking out this evening." I confessed.

"I don't feel good about lying to him, Delilah, but we'll tell him when the time is right." I couldn't deny that the only part of that sentence I could concentrate on was how he felt about us.

"I wouldn't worry about Theo. He thinks you're Tinder Dan! Our secret's safe for now." I laughed, with the alcohol buzzing through me.

"That's good. Although if Dan did come anywhere near you, I'd have to kill him. *Tú eres mía, mi Joya.*" Zane purred without a hint of humour. My thighs rubbed together to dull the ache caused by his caveman attitude. Usually, that would be a turn-off for me however, matched with Zane's unbridled confidence, I'd never seen anything hotter.

I tried to hide my disappointment at the evening drawing to a close whilst Zane settled the bill and tipped the staff. We re-entered the lift silently, hand in hand, with a palpable tension between us. One quick glance and all bets would be off.

Zane released my hand abruptly. "Take off your underwear and give them to me now, Delilah." I took a minute to register what he had instructed. "Don't make me repeat myself."

I unfroze and quickly struggled with my underwear, shimmying them down my legs. I hurriedly passed the lacy garment to Zane, who remained stoic as he tucked them into his trousers. I felt my heartbeat intensify as we made our way back into the car.

"You've been driving me crazy all night, Delilah," Zane growled as the engine roared, and we began our journey home. I felt my thighs slick with moistness. Zane repositioned into the space in front of me and parted my legs. He groaned in appreciation at the sight of my pussy wet and ready for him.

"Who does this needy cunt belong to?" He asked, his face so close I could feel his warm breath fanning over my most private area. My breath hitched as he kissed the sensitive inside of my leg.

"You," I confessed breathlessly as he placed another kiss on the other thigh. His chest growled with delight at the confirmation.

"Don't ever forget it."

Before I had time to absorb his words, his tongue began to devour me. He tongued my clit, licking and sucking like my pleasure was all that mattered to him, focused but not rushing. The warm orange light from the passing streetlamps caused shadows to form across his handsome, chiselled face as he stared up at me. My hands wound into his curly hair, pulling his face tighter towards my core.

I moaned his name as he slipped two fingers easily inside, stroking my walls in time with his tongue. The cold sensation from his silver rings sent shivers as he groaned against me, causing my legs to begin to shake with my fast-approaching release.

He expertly worked me towards my orgasm, tracing lazy circles with his tongue as he continued to pump his fingers inside me.

"Don't stop!" I commanded breathlessly as the pressure built, my back arched, and my thighs tightened around his head. A scream ripped through me as Zane continued to lap at my swollen pussy, guiding me through the hardest climax of my life. I pushed his head away when the sensation got too much. A light sheen of sweat misted my skin, and my legs finally stopped trembling as I lay slumped against the leather seat, my pleasure satiated. I hoped that the partition was soundproof!

I looked down, with heavy eyelids, at the God before me, still on his knees, as he smiled back. He wiped my juices from the corners of his mouth with his forefinger and thumb before sitting back on the seat beside me. I instinctively lay my head on his shoulder, closing my eyes to stay in the moment. I felt him wrap his arms around me.

"I hope that was good for you, *mi Joya.*" He placed a kiss on my forehead.

"*Fuck*, I don't know how it could be any better than that!" I declared in adoration as I tried to steady my still-ragged breaths. His chest rumbled beneath me with a chuckle.

"High praise indeed, sweetheart." He said, intertwining his fingers in mine. I rode the remainder of the journey, cocooned against his strong frame as I revelled in the afterglow of our date, very aware that I'd lost yet another pair of underwear to Zane Moreno.

At this rate, I'd be out by the end of the month.

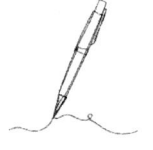

25

LILAH

It had been three days since my escapade with Zane in his town car. I blushed at the memory of his head between my legs and the intensity of the orgasm he inflicted on my body.

How could the man who caused me so much anger and infuriation for so many years, be the same person to give me so much ecstasy and euphoria?

I pondered the thought for a moment as I brushed my red hair aimlessly at my makeshift dressing table: a handheld mirror precariously balanced on top of a pile of books on my chest of drawers. I was fighting an internal battle between what I wanted and what was right. When I was with Zane, like at the dinner on Wednesday night, it felt as if it was only us two in the world. His radiant smile caused butterflies to soar within me, and his tender touch struck a fire inside. But at work, there were still remnants of the Zane of my past, who drove me to insanity. I know we had agreed to keep things low-key in the office, and he is *still* my boss, but I thought he might have adopted a slightly friendlier attitude towards me.

That was the juxtaposition of Zane Moreno: cold, direct businessman by day; warm, passionate sex-God by night, and I was merciless to them both!

A shrill ring of my doorbell brought me back to Earth and away from the image of Zane's rippling abs.

The front door opened to reveal Amelia standing there, bottle of bubbly and duffel bag in hand. I greeted her and led her through to my room, where we began to get ready for the gig.

"Thanks again for agreeing to come, I think you'll really like Theo's band!" I said, unscrewing the Prosecco and pouring it into two glasses, handing Amelia hers, who was sitting cross-legged on my bed.

"Thanks for the invite, you know I'm always on the hunt for new artists to listen to and write about. Plus, to be at someone's first headline gig is pretty special. Is Jacob coming?" Amelia responded, taking a big sip of her drink.

"Unfortunately, not, I think he's got a date, so that's exciting! I don't really know anyone else going. Apart from, heads up, Zane might be popping along." I informed. Amelia narrowed her eyes in confusion.

"Why is our boss going?" I felt a cold sweat appear on the back of my neck.

"He's Theo's best friend," I replied, matter of factly, her expression softening.

"Of course! I forgot you all knew each other before. Well, that'll be weird to spend my Saturday evening with Moreno, but hey-ho. I'm going to go and get dressed, be right back!"

I let out a sigh of relief as Amelia headed to the bathroom to get changed.

"Yeah. Weird." I responded absentmindedly. Tonight was going to be a test for us. How do we act around other people? And not just any old people: my brother and co-worker, his best friend and employee! I chugged some of my bubbles to wash down the anxiety.

Amelia returned, looking sensational! She wore a tight, ruched black dress, which showed off her insanely long legs. A leather jacket hung off her shoulders, which matched her biker boots. A mix of both silver and gold jewellery was layered around her neck and wrists, which looked exquisite against her dark skin, and finally, her shoulder-length curly hair had been styled into a half-up-half-down look, loose tendrils framing her angled face. She looked the epitome of a cool music girl!

"You look great!" I exclaimed.

"Thanks, so do you! I love the merch." She replied, referencing the white Velvet Echoes band tee I was wearing, which I had tied at the front and matched with a black denim skirt. Slipping on a pair of off-white Adidas trainers, I checked the time on my phone.

"We should probably head off!" Amelia nodded in return as we gathered our things, and I took one final look at myself in the mirror. Anxiety flooded at both seeing Zane and knowing we had to keep any signs of whatever it was we were doing completely secret.

As we stepped out of the cab, I saw a long queue of people trailing out of the music venue, a buzz of chatter and excitement in the air. Great sign!

The perks of being the little sister of the headliner meant Amelia and I could slip right past the forming horde and straight into the venue, retrieving an 'AAA' lanyard each from the box office desk.

The first support was already on stage, belting out a rock indie song I didn't know and warming up the gathering crowd as we headed backstage to see the boys before their slot.

I could hear them before I opened their dressing room door. It's incredible how much noise four grown men could make!

"Is there a headline band in here?" I questioned, throwing the door open to three almost thirty-year-old topless men wearing near-on matching jeans and Converse - I scanned the room to see their singer was absent. "Couldn't have put a shirt on, bro? I have company!" I joked, giving my brother a high-five. "This is Amelia, my friend from work I told you about."

Amelia and Theo looked at each other. I watched as her eyes flicked over his bare chest and back to his face. Theo looked equally stunned as he took Amelia in.

"Erm, hi I'm Theo, it's lovely to meet you." He wiped his hand against his trouser leg before holding it out for Amelia to return the shake. I think that was the first time Theo hadn't made a joke or taken the mick out of someone in the whole twenty-eight years of his life!

"Hi, I'm Amelia. I'm looking forward to hearing you guys play." She smiled timidly.

"I think I told you; Amelia writes a music blog..."

"So, play well tonight, and I might feature you!" Amelia butted in.

"Oh wow, that would be amazing, cheers! I'll make sure I put on my best show for you, Mils!" He flirted in response - there's the normal Theo!

"How are you all feeling?" I asked, turning towards the rest of the band.

"Oh, you know me, sis, easy breezy!" Theo rebuffed; I rolled my eyes in response.

"What a liar! He's been shitting himself all day!" Callum interjected. "Honestly, Lilah, don't listen to a word he's saying, he's just showing off in front of your new friend!" Theo nudged him in the rib.

"Shut up, man!" Theo bit back, looking slightly embarrassed. I liked seeing this side of my brother, for all the jokes he dished out, it was nice to see him in the firing line for once!

Amelia and I headed to the long plastic table at the back of the room, covered in drinks and snacks that the band must have requested on their rider. Opting for a can of light beer, I popped it open whilst looking around the room. Just the band, a couple of random guys I didn't know and Amelia. I tried to ignore the slight pang of disappointment I felt at not seeing the Latin American lothario.

At that minute, the door swung open, my anticipation rose and was swiftly dispersed at the sight of Sean, their slimy lead singer. I'm surprised I didn't sense the bravado coming through the door first.

"Nice to see the groupies are already here!" He said smugly, winking at Amelia and me. She tutted and rolled her eyes heavily at his comment. "Although, I don't know this one!" He said inquisitively in her direction, closing the space between us.

"And you won't know me!" Amelia responded, waving him off. I spotted Theo glancing over, watching the exchange from the other side of the room as he pulled a shirt over his head.

"Ever the gentleman, Sean," I said sarcastically.

"I know you love it!" He said seedily, snaking his gross arm around my shoulder, making me feel sick to my stomach just like I always did in his presence.

"Ugh, you wish!" I attempted to shrug him off of me to no avail. "Okay, get off now, Sean." He just laughed and squeezed me tighter. I shot a look over at Theo, hoping he was witnessing the unwanted attention I was getting so he could intervene, but he was now back in deep conversation with the other members of the band.

"She said get off." My body froze at the familiar Colombian voice. Standing beside us in the doorway was Zane, in all his breathtaking glory, dressed in a black linen shirt and dark jeans.

"Fun's over, boys. The Suit's here!" Sean mocked as he removed his arm from me; however, I sensed the unease in his voice. You'd think a simple no would be enough to deter Sean, but unfortunately, it seemed he only responded to male demands.

Diverting my gaze to Zane's direction to thank him, I realised he had already walked away and was standing, saying hello to Theo and the rest of the band. I tried to squash the sadness I felt that he didn't directly acknowledge me. However, I needed to remember our agreement. He's here for Theo - not for me.

"Five minutes 'till you're on!" A scrawny guy from the venue popped his head in to inform the band. Nervous conversation filled the room as they prepared to take the stage. Joining the main group, I stood next to Zane but didn't dare to look at him.

"Break a leg!" I wished, giving Theo a fist bump for luck. "See you out there."

Shuffling through the bustling crowd, Amelia, Zane, and I found a place towards the front to watch the set. Amelia and Zane made small talk as we waited for them to start.

"I bet we aren't who you expected to spend your Saturday night with!" Amelia joked.

"I've had worse company." Zane smiled politely in response.

"Although, I guess you two spend quite a lot of time one one-on-one most days, so not too dissimilar!" Amelia pondered. It seemed I had lost all ability to make conversation as I tried to avoid eye contact with Zane, praying that the start of the music would save me.

"I suppose we are quite well acquainted." He replied, a smirk tugging at his lips that only I would recognise. At that moment, the lights went out as the band entered the stage. Thank God, as it covered the crimson now painting my cheeks.

For the entirety of the hour-long set, I was hyper-aware of how close Zane was to me and how we had still barely said two words to each other. Heat burned where Zane's body was against mine due to how packed the crowd was. No matter how much I danced or tried to shuffle away, I couldn't avoid contact. I opted for pure ignorance and threw myself into singing the lyrics back to Theo and his friends as they claimed the stage, forcing myself to forget the man less than a centimetre away.

26

ZANE

Although it wasn't my usual scene to see Theo enjoying himself so much on stage, with the crowd loving every minute, it was tough not to feel pride for my best friend.

I ordered a round of drinks for the band and the entourage to celebrate their successful evening. As I returned to the table they were occupying at the side of the stage, I took up a seat at the opposite end to Delilah, determined not to blow our cover.

"So, were we good enough for a feature?" Theo pried jokily in Amelia's direction.

"You'll have to log on to find out; I don't give spoilers." She quipped. I took a sip of my drink as I watched the pair converse.

"I guess you'll have to give me the details then." Theo flirted shamelessly; I turned away as I didn't need to watch my friend in the pursuit of a one-night stand.

My phone vibrated in my jeans pocket, causing me to stop drinking my pint. As the screen lit up, I saw Delilah's name. I glanced across the table at her with scepticism, but she was deep in conversation with Finn from the band.

> Guess what colour underwear
> I'm wearing xx

My eyes widened, and my zipper strained at the provocative text. I quickly typed a reply.

> This isn't an appropriate way to text your boss, Delilah.

I shot a look towards her as she received my message and smirked whilst sending her response.

> Guess what colour underwear
> I'm wearing - SIR xx

Por Dios, this girl is going to be the death of me. I clenched my jaw before replying.

> If you keep talking like that you won't have underwear on for much longer.

Delilah giggled at my most recent text.

"Ooo, Lils, who's got you smiling like that? My bet's on Tinder Dan!" Theo nudged Delilah as she quickly hid her phone.

"Wouldn't you like to know!" She snapped back.

"I'm surprised you didn't invite him to show off your mega cool brother!" He teased.

"Who's to say I didn't." Delilah shrugged, finishing her drink. Even though I was pretty certain that the infamous Tinder Dan would not be making an appearance this evening, I couldn't deny the anger I felt at the idea of her speaking to another man - albeit imaginary!

I watched as Delilah tucked her phone into the back pocket of her denim skirt and stood up from her seat. She walked past the back of me without giving a second glance and headed for the backstage corridor. Although I could sense this was a challenge, I was powerless to ignore it. I slowly sipped my drink, surveying the table to time my escape. After the longest minute of my life, I couldn't take it any longer.

I traced Delilah's steps down the clinical-looking corridor. Several grey doors lined the walkway. My instincts told me she had gone back to the green room, so I headed there in the hopes I was correct.

I cracked the door of the room slightly, doing a quick scan for the red-headed vixen however, the room appeared empty. Frustrated, I began to pull the door closed when a sweet voice broke the silence.

"Took you long enough, sir." Delilah purred. I pushed it open fully to find her sitting with a beer in hand on the leather couch that was hidden slightly behind the door. Every time I saw her, I forgot how beautiful she was. Her auburn hair dishevelled from the concert, and those green eyes, round and begging, pupils dilated with arousal, stunned me for a moment in the doorway. "Well, are you joining?"

I dutifully took a seat beside her as she handed me a can of beer from the rider.

"Are you going to divulge me then?" I questioned, my cock throbbing at her closeness.

"Whatever do you mean?" Delilah flirted innocently.

"What colour is your underwear, *mi Joya?*" I questioned directly. Delilah put down her drink and leaned across to close the space between us as she whispered in my ear.

"Why don't you find out for yourself?" Her citrus scent swirled through my senses, intoxicating me further. I placed my drink beside hers and pulled her onto my lap with ease, causing her skirt to rid up and her legs to spread as she straddled me.

Whilst I reached under her denim material to pull down her panties, Delilah's breath became shallow, and goosebumps appeared on her skin as she anticipated my touch. Where I was expecting to feel lace, I was surprised to be met with bare skin.

"Well, *mi Joya*, you bad girl." I breathed into her neck as I started to rub her clit with my thumb. She moaned, beginning to rock her hips against my erection.

Delilah reached down to unzip my trousers and free my cock, already hard and ready for her. I lifted her and lowered her onto it, causing us to groan in unison at the sensation.

Immediately, she began to ride me desperately, greedily chasing her orgasm. I moved my hands to her hips to guide her rhythm as she dug her nails into my shoulders, trying to keep herself from screaming. I'd never seen anything so beautiful; her red hair fell in disordered curls, her perfect face flushed and contorted in pleasure.

"Look at you, Delilah, riding my cock like a filthy little slut." Her pace quickened further at my dirty words. "You couldn't stay away from me for even one night, could you, *mi Joya*?"

"You couldn't either." She gasped breathlessly. I spanked her as I watched her full, perky tits bouncing under her shirt. Delilah moaned my name in response. It was at that moment that I noticed the top she was wearing and that the full band's faces were displayed. I caught a look at Theo's goofy face printed on the fabric and swiftly pulled the top over Delilah's head to rid the image of my friend and expose her bare breasts. I sucked her right nipple into my mouth and swirled my tongue around the sensitive bud, Delilah hissed at the feeling, gliding her hand up my neck to tug at my hair. I thrust my groin in time with hers, deepening our pleasure.

"Fucking hell!" She whispered, trying to keep quiet as her orgasm approached. Her body convulsed as her pussy clamped tighter around my dick, biting her lip in an attempt to conceal her scream as she came around me. I continued to grind into her as she slumped onto my chest from the power of her climax.

The sound of footsteps in the corridor caused us to freeze at who the approaching person could be. I met Delilah's shocked eyes and placed a finger over her lips to silence her as the steps got closer. I released a breath as the anonymous passerby continued beyond our room.

"That was close!" She sighed, giggling.

"It's not over yet, *princesa*," I informed, as I scooped her legs around my torso and lifted her, before carrying her across the room and pushing her back against the door. Delilah wrapped her arms tightly around my neck, holding onto me as I increased my thrusts. "No one's going to interrupt me wrecking your sweet little pussy now," I growled into her ear, she bit my shoulder as her legs constricted around my waist, and my cock hit the sensitive spot deep inside her. I picked up speed, thrusting into her punishingly. Her second orgasm crashed over her in full force as she mumbled incoherently, I didn't slow my rhythm as she rode the wave of her pleasure. I felt her quiver in my arms at the promise of a third.

"Zane, I can't take it!" She exclaimed, trying her best to stay quiet as her brain malfunctioned.

"You can do it, angel." I praised, her muffled gasps echoed my rhythm, I could tell we were both on the brink. Her pussy rippled around me, causing my own orgasm to tear through me with such force my vision hazed. "Come with me, *mi Joya*," I instructed as my name fell from her lips in a moan she couldn't hold back. I clamped my hand over her mouth, but it was futile, our bodies moved together, an electric current of ecstasy connecting us in the most primal way as the pleasure consumed us until she was limp in my arms. Placing a soft kiss on her lips, I pulled out and began to lower her legs to the floor.

"Zane, I honestly don't think I can walk right now!" She laughed deliriously, staring up at me with adoration in her eyes. I chuckled in response, placing her down on the sofa. I reached for her t-shirt, strewn on the floor to the side of the seat.

"Next time, please don't wear a top with your brother's face on it. It does nothing for my guilty conscience." I winked, passing it back to her.

"Noted!" She laughed, pulling the top back over her head and smoothing her red hair down.

God, she looked incredible freshly fucked!

"Are we going to talk about your lack of underwear?" I raised my eyebrows in question.

"Unfortunately, they seem to keep going missing!" She said, giving me a pointed look, "and my boss pays me pennies, so I can't afford to keep replacing them."

"I'm sure there are other perks to the job?" I said, leaning down to hold her chin.

"I guess you could say that." She smiled as I placed a hard kiss on her mouth. "We better get back." I helped her to stand and watched her leave before me so as not to arouse suspicion. Delilah glanced back at me as she opened the door. Her green eyes round and full of longing.

"Go." I laughed, giving a wink as she scurried off back to the group.

As I waited for the distance to increase between us, before I returned, I retrieved my now warm lager and took a hearty swig.
I was playing with fire, but I goddamn loved being burned.

27

LILAH

The next month blurred past in a confusing concoction of romantic dates, mind-blowing sex and being almost completely ignored at work.

Outside the office, Zane would treat me to lavish outings, book entire cinemas out to screen my favourite films whilst engorging ourselves on sugary snacks, idyllic helicopter rides with dreamy views of the London skyline and more extravagant rooftop dinners with the finest cuisine. Every date ended with sex that somehow seemed to get better every time however, the conversation about telling people about us only seemed to be getting further away.

"God, Lilah, the things you get up to while I'm stuck in Kent. Sounds like a film!" Verity exclaimed. I watched her blue eyes widen through my phone screen, which was propped up against old cookbooks stacked on the dining room table, as she tried to process the mind fuck scenario I just explained. Theo had a shift tonight, so I was safe to sprawl out and talk about my boss wherever I pleased.

"Tell me about it, V!" I sighed, sipping my Sauvignon. I saw the way Verity's face lit up as I divulged the ongoings of my current life, but I was struggling to match her excitement. Things were colder than ever when it came to work. Zane's door may as well have been welded shut with how often he came to speak to me. Gone were the flirtatious comments, lingering touches and double entendre, replaced by strict professionalism. I was lucky if I got a 'Morning *Joya*' before he scurried off and communicated solely through email. I knew it was in the interest of keeping things under wraps, but I couldn't help the doubt that was clouding my mind.

"I see you're drawing again?" Verity said tentatively, twiddling her blonde hair, nodding through the screen towards the pencil I was clutching, breaking me out of my thoughts.

"Lilah darling, I've had some ideas for the next collection." My mother excitedly told me. Her jet-black hair fell in front of her face as she began to sketch out a new design in a brown leather sketchbook. She pushed a tendril behind her ear and continued to draw the various clusters of jewels that were spilling out of her head and onto the page.

I loved watching her draw. Her enthusiasm and passion were infectious, and I couldn't help getting swept away in these daydreams with her. It felt like every month, she had another idea for a jewellery collection, but she'd never tried to sell her ideas anywhere. We would plan and fantasise about the day she would become a famous designer, but so far, it was still just a pipedream. But I believed in her.

"What do you think, Lilah? Would you wear this?" I was thirteen. There was no way I would be able to afford the masterpieces my mum dreamed of creating, but if I ever won the lottery, I'd buy them all three times over, that was for sure. She had such talent, at least in my eyes.

I looked at the design. A trilogy ring. Two pear-shaped emeralds anchored a circular brown jewel, set onto a gold band with intricate swirl details.

"Of course, it's amazing, Mum!" She beamed a wide, toothy grin in my direction as she continued to refine the artwork. She was so beautiful. My mother had olive skin and dark locks, which completely juxtaposed my pale and auburn looks, but the one thing I did inherit from her was her bright green eyes.

Her eyes looked like they were mined straight out of a rock to the point that my grandma named her after them as they were so unique - Esmeralda.

She began to sketch out another design in her notebook, this time for a necklace. Every one of her designs revolved around a cluster of emeralds, which represented me and her and a cognac diamond, which reflected Theo's hazel eyes. Our tribe. It had always been us three against the world since my dad left when I was still a toddler.

Her jewellery was so personal and so thoughtful, and I couldn't wait for the day that the world knew how good she was.

I looked down at the notepad in front of me. The old, familiar leather-bound book that I shared with my mum.

"Yeah, I guess I felt inspired," I pondered. It had been well over a year since the idea of digging out the old sketchpad filled me with dread, but something had changed in the last month, and I found myself itching to create again. A coy smile formed on Verity's angelic face as it appeared she was holding back from saying something.

"Oh, spit it out, V!" I exclaimed, knowing that it wouldn't take much for Verity to divulge her thoughts, especially when she'd had had a few alcoholic bevs! Verity took a sip of the drink she had poured for herself for our virtual wine night.

"Well, I know he's still being a bit of an arsehole, but he clearly makes you happy, or you're delirious from all the orgasms!" I nearly spat out my wine.

"Verity!"

"What? I'm jealous!" We burst into laughter.

"Anything new with you, V?" I asked.

"You know, the usual, countless rejections from casting directors, too many auditions to count, and a general lack of self-belief that I'll ever become an actress, but other than that, peachy!"

"Oh, Verity, you'll get your big break one day, I just have a feeling about it!" I assured her. I had been friends with Verity since primary school, and from the moment I met her, she had dreamed of being a famous movie star! She went to a performing arts university and signed with an agent straight from her final showcase, but a few years on, she was yet to book anything particularly exciting. "I miss you so much!"

"I miss you too; I promise I'll come and visit soon. Just taking all the shifts I can at the mo." Verity sighed.

"Sucks being an adult and having to make money doesn't it." I held my glass up in long-distance cheers as Verity mimicked the motion.

"Well, at least your boss is fit! And you have some great company perks. If you catch my drift!" She winked on the screen.

"Haha, yes, I get your point!" I laughed.

"I have to deal with gross Pete making sleazy comments to me all day at my cubicle." Verity made a fake gagging motion. Pete was one of the other salesmen at the office job she worked at in between the advertising jobs she booked, and he had the BIGGEST crush on her. But rather than ask her out or be a normal human being, he was just creepy and slimy and made crude comments to her around the clock.

"Oh babe, I can imagine. You need to kick that dude in the balls one of these days. Or failing that, report to HR!"

"So true. Although I do have another audition next week for a book adaptation. Supposedly a very sought-after role, so keep your fingers crossed for me, and maybe I won't be here much longer!" She mimicked her words with her hands.

"Oh, how exciting, that sounds amazing. You've got this, V! Knock 'em dead." I encouraged.

The two of us continued to chat the night away, losing track of the time. When I crawled into bed, I felt a weight had lifted off my shoulders; it's amazing what a couple of hours of therapy with your best friend can do.

28

ZANE/LILAH

ZANE

The Moreno Jewellery Board Summer Ball. Next to Christmas, it was the biggest event on our company's calendar. Considering it was only Directors, Board Members and their plus ones in attendance, it ran up the bill of a full company party. I was looking forward to the second London one as much as I looked forward to doing my tax returns. However, with Delilah by my side, albeit under alternative public pretences, I felt like I could conquer anything.

    Previously, I had always attended these events solo, enjoying the freedom to turn up and leave as I wished without the need to agree it with a date. However, being here with Delilah somehow made the work obligation feel more bearable. As we ascended the grand stairs outside of the old building, I glanced over at her. She looked out of this world in a sapphire blue satin dress that draped over her curvy frame perfectly. Behind her wavy red hair, she looked somewhat downcast and had been uncharacteristically quiet in the car here. I reached to squeeze her hand to comfort her but caught myself before making contact as I remembered we weren't alone. Instead, I placed my hand on the small of her back, just like I had on our first work outing together. I felt her tense under my touch.

"Are you ok, Delilah?" I asked, concerned about her reaction.

"Why wouldn't I be?" she responded, looking at me with a smile that didn't reach her eyes.

"I'm glad you're here with me," I assured her quietly as we walked through the entrance. Delilah hummed flatly in agreement. Before I had the chance to pry further, I began to spot members of the Board. With that, it was showtime!

Whilst Delilah headed to get some drinks, John caught eyes with me and gestured to join him.

"Good evening, John, are you enjoying yourself?" I asked, with no regard for the answer. John was another original member of my board upon my return. He was great at his job but was always living in the past and rarely wanted to venture out into new avenues.

"Another wonderful party, Zane! But that's not why I wanted to talk to you. I wanted to raise my concern about not seeing any designs for the Valentine's launch yet. As you know, time is a-ticking!" John said, sarcastically tapping his watch.

"I can assure you, it is at the top of my priority list, and I'm receiving designs to review daily. However, the tech company looking into the root of the potential leak hasn't completed their audit, and I want to ensure the security of our systems before sharing the chosen design for launch." I explained.

"Oh, for goodness sake, Zane." John exploded, forgetting his place. "You can't hold it ransom at the unconfirmed threat of it being stolen. Just share the design so we can put this all to bed and think about the next collection!"

"Are you questioning my judgement, John?" I narrowed my eyes.

"Of course not, I would never dream of it. But I must admit, I want to see something soon, or I'll be concerned you have nothing at all!"

"Enjoy the complimentary drinks, John. I'm sure we'll speak soon." I turned, not giving him a chance to answer.

"Definitely." I heard him call in response from behind me. I knew John was set in his ways, but for him to undermine me in this manner was surprising even for him. I tensed my jaw as I walked towards the bar, needing to wash away the bitter taste in my mouth and the anxiety of the impending deadline. When I reached the mahogany bar, I scanned the room for Delilah, knowing that just having her close would ease my mind slightly.

I was about to order myself a rum when I felt a hand snake around my waist. I turned to see Delilah, but I was met by a pair of distinctively less mesmerising eyes.

"Hey, stranger," Saskia purred. I pulled myself out of her grip, offering her a friendly smile.

"Good evening, Saskia."

LILAH

I picked up the two drinks I had ordered for me and Zane and headed back into the crowd to locate him. I must have walked in a full circle as I found myself back at the opposite end of the bar and still had not discovered him.

Typical Zane to leave me alone at a work event!

The sound of shrill female laughter caught my attention, and to my surprise, I found Zane and a threateningly beautiful blonde woman in the midst of a conversation, only a few metres from where I had just been standing.

I watched in disbelief as the woman shamelessly flirted with Zane, twirling hair and giggling obnoxiously. To his credit, he didn't appear to be returning the enthusiasm.

I approached the couple and forced Zane's drink between them on the bar.

"Medellin Reserve," I stated as I locked eyes with him, he resembled a deer caught in headlights but nodded in thanks.

"Who's this Zane? Got a girlfriend I should be worried about?" The blonde looked me up and down, judging my appearance. It took all of my willpower not to roll my eyes at her bitchiness.

"No, she's just my PA." I froze in disbelief.

How dare he.

I could feel Zane's eyes trained on me, waiting for my reaction, but I didn't dare look at him as rage consumed me.

"I'm just here to deliver his drink," I said through gritted teeth, throwing a fake smile in the woman's direction and turning to walk away. I felt Zane's hand wrap around my wrist, stopping me in my tracks.

"Delilah?" Zane queried.

"I've got work to do." I ripped my hand away and beelined to the door. I needed to get out of here.

As I retrieved my jacket from the concierge, I heard footsteps rapidly approaching.

"Delilah! Wait!" Zane called after me. I ignored him and continued out of the building, fighting back tears. I couldn't cry here; it wouldn't take much to put two and two together if anyone saw a concerned boss running after his sobbing PA. But then again, that's all I was to him, apparently.

***Just** his PA!*

The sentence rang through me on repeat. Now, I didn't expect him to announce he was sleeping with me, but to reduce me to a mere employee was insulting. He couldn't even muster the word 'friend' - or my fucking name!

The footsteps dissipated the further I got away from the party. A mix of both relief that he had given up the chase and disappointment that he'd let me go that easily flooded my body. I marched towards the nearest tube station, which was around a ten-minute trek away. I held my jacket over my head to shelter from the summer rain, knowing the cab fare would be astronomical from here and hoped the walk would help to clear my head regardless.

"Delilah!" I heard from the road. "Get in the car." I turned to see Zane in his black sports car, crawling along beside me.

"Get back to the party, Zane, you've got lots of people to entertain!" I rejected. "My shift's ended, I can go home. You didn't need to come out here to remind me this isn't a date this time!" I hadn't expected this work event to end in tears like the last one, but I guess history repeated itself.

"Please, Delilah, you'll get soaked. Just get in, and let's talk." He called again. His car took up the whole road along with the rows of parked vehicles, preventing any traffic from passing. Whilst I contemplated my next move, multiple cars began to queue behind him, honking their horns and shouting abuse at the 'knobhead' obstructing their route. "I'll block this road all night if I have to, Delilah." He said above the beeping, holding his hands up off the wheel to prove he wasn't joking. Not wanting to cause a pile-up or make the news because of a road rage incident, I reluctantly got into the vehicle.

I stubbornly turned to face away from him. Silence filled the car as I watched the raindrops slide down the window.

"Delilah, let me explain. Nothing was going on between Saskia and me. You've got nothing to worry about." He said in an attempt to reassure me. I scoffed at the idiocy of this man's brain as if he thought that's what I was upset about!

"*Mi Joya,*" Zane started.

"Don't fucking call me that!" I exclaimed, snapping round to face him. "I'm not your anything; I'm *just* a PA, remember?" I shouted, emphasising the words.

"Oh, Delilah, I didn't mean anything bad by that. You know, at work, that's all you *can* be to me."

"Well, maybe that is all I *will* be to you then."

"You don't honestly mean that," Zane stated, his voice breaking slightly and his grip tightening on the steering wheel.

"I'm getting pretty sick and tired of being made to feel like a million dollars on weekends and evenings, but between the hours of nine and five, like I don't fucking exist to you!"

"We discussed this; we agreed to keep it private."

"Yes, we did, but it's been nearly two months, Zane and we've barely moved forward. What am I to you? Your skivvy in the day and fuck buddy at night?" I raised my voice in frustration.

"You can't possibly think you don't mean anything to me?" Zane matched my tone. "I'm risking so much for you!" I couldn't believe what I was hearing.

"You've got to be kidding me; you're not risking anything, Zane, let's be real. If anyone found out, they'd high-five you for bedding your assistant and say get in there, son, while I'm branded the hussy trying to get ahead in my career with under-the-table favours! And anyway, you don't have to worry about that as you act like I'm invisible. If I mean that much to you, how come we've never even spent the night together? I've never even been to your place, for fuck's sake." I exploded, anger coming off me in waves as I turned back towards the window to watch the streetlights blur past.

We sat in awkward silence for the remainder of the journey back to mine. *I guess he doesn't care then!*

He stopped the car on an unfamiliar road and got out, walking round to my door, and opening it for me.

"This isn't my address, Zane?"

"I'm well aware Delilah. It's mine." He offered me his hand to help me out of the car, which I tentatively took. He led me through the gate and up the pathway as we reached the black heavy door of his townhouse. He turned to face me.

"I've never felt this way about someone before, especially with the added complexity of our professional relationship and Theo, so forgive me for the stupidity of my actions." He confessed, "But believe me, *mi Joya*, you mean so much to me." He cupped my face and pulled me in as he crashed his mouth against mine. His words washed over me, replacing the anger in my veins with a foreign but equally as strong emotion. The earlier threat of tears welled in my eyes at his revelation, as he unlocked his door and guided us inside. Our kiss was passionate but not as frantic as usual, there was a tenderness to Zane's touches, and his hands caressed my jaw as his tongue explored my mouth. Before, I was curious about the inside of Zane Moreno's house but right now I couldn't care less as he lifted me into his arms and carried me upstairs, our kiss never breaking. My surroundings became unimportant background noise to my real focus.

Zane lowered me onto the edge of his bed, keeping his eyes on me as he began to unbutton his shirt. I sat wide-eyed, taking in the man in front of me as he dropped his shirt onto his dark wooden flooring, revealing his chiselled torso. I lazily dragged my eyes over his frame as he appeared to be revelling in the unlimited time we had.

"Stand up, Delilah," Zane commanded, still wearing his suit trousers, unbuckling his belt. I swallowed deeply and stood up. I started to shuffle my blue dress over my head when Zane's hands replaced mine. He took his time rolling the fabric up inch by inch to reveal my lacy thong and bare chest. A hungry smirk tugged at his lips at the sight of me, causing the wetness between my thighs to increase. He turned our bodies towards a full-length mirror propped up on the far side of his room.

"Look at you *mi Joya,* so beautiful." His breath ghosted over my neck. I stared at the woman in the mirror whom I barely recognised, lips swollen from our kiss, hair damp and wild around my face from the rain and pupils dilated with arousal. I watched in fascination as Zane reached around, tracing the contours of my body, he paused to feel my breasts and pinch my hardened nipples, sending a shock through me. My eyes locked on his face as he stared. I'd never seen anyone look at me the way he did. He made me feel like a Goddess.

"We look good together," I whispered breathlessly. Zane chuckled devilishly in agreement, kissing the nape of my neck. His right hand moved between my thighs; my breathing quickened as he started to rub my wet clit.

"You are perfect, Delilah and all mine." He growled the second half of the sentence and I whimpered in response, my body leaning limply against him. He continued to stroke my most sensitive area, increasing the rhythm as I began to feel my arousal dripping down my leg. "You're so wet for me, *mi Joya.*" He praised, slipping two fingers inside me with ease, replacing the pressure on my clit with his thumb.

Zane wrapped his free arm around my waist to keep me stable as my body began to shiver at the signs of my first orgasm.

"See how pretty you look when you come for me, sweetheart." He instructed. Normally I would feel self-conscious and couldn't think of anything worse than seeing myself come undone but in Zane's grip and at the receiving end of his praise, I stared at my reflection as I fell apart in his hands. "Good girl."

He swept me into his arms and guided me down onto his soft, white bedding. His sandalwood scent emanated from the covers flooding my senses. He dropped his trousers and boxers to his ankles, stepping out of them, to free his erection. My jaw slacked as I took a moment to take in the God in front of me. The dim light emanating from the lamp cast shadows across his perfectly sculpted abs, broad chest and strong, tanned legs. My mouth watered at the sight of his full length and a plundering ache hammered between my legs at the anticipation of him being buried deep inside me. Although this was far from our first time, being in his home and seeing him completely naked, brought back an excitement just like that first day in his office.

"Lie down Delilah." He smirked, I dutifully lowered myself back onto the mound of pillows at the head of the bed and glanced down my body to watch Zane as he began to plant soft kisses up my leg. When he reached my begging pussy, I felt my heart rate quicken as he parted my thighs, draping my legs over his shoulders to gain better access.

"God I can't get enough of this sweet cunt of yours," he groaned, flattening his tongue and licking a line through my folds. I moaned at the contact. "That's right angel, no need to be quiet here." I succumbed to my arousal, throwing my head back in ecstasy against the plush pillows as Zane ravaged me. Quickly bringing me towards my second orgasm. It crashed over me, leaving my body limp and boneless.

"You're incredible!" I breathed in awe, barely having time to register before he slid his hard cock inside of me. I moaned at the feeling. Unlike our previous frantic escapades, Zane took his time, grinding into me with long, slow movements, drawing out every second of pleasure. I screamed his name like a prayer as he brought us closer to the finish line.

"Fuck!" I cried as he drove deeper into me and sucked a sensitive spot on my neck. "Right there, plea-" My pleas died on my tongue as my third orgasm wrecked my body with such a force that left me breathless, every nerve alight as the pleasure built to an almost unbearable peak. My eyes squeezed shut and my muscles tensed as I was overcome by waves of raw, pulsating ecstasy. Zane fucked me through my orgasm, groaning in my ear as he came. I opened my eyes to find him staring at me before he placed a delicate kiss on my lips.

"You will be the death of me, Delilah Hart."

We climbed into the covers and Zane took me into his arms. I lay in his embrace feeling safe and content as we both caught our breaths before our urges took over again - this was going to be a long and very enjoyable night!

I blinked a couple of times as the morning light came streaming in. Glancing at the space in the bed beside me, I noticed it was now unoccupied, causing my stomach to drop at Zane's absence.

As I fully awoke and sat up against the expansive wooden headrest, I began to make out the clatter of pots and pans coming from downstairs, followed by the delicious scent of food being made which had travelled through the house and up the stairs. My worry immediately was replaced with hunger after the all-night sex marathon. Zane and I revelled in the unlimited time our first private night together gave us, unencumbered by the threat of someone finding us. Stopping only to rehydrate before getting straight back to business and exploring every inch of each other's bodies until we eventually crashed out in the early hours.

Now that my anxieties had subsided, I began to take in the room around me. A place that was heaven to me last night but that I didn't take a moment to register when I first entered it.

Raw wooden panelling accented the room which was complemented by cream-painted walls. Abstract, monochromatic art was hung above the bed, framed by two lights which hung from the ceiling on either side. Zane didn't have much in the way of personal belongings like photographs or sentimental trinkets, yet his personality still managed to shine through in his well-organised but immaculately decorated bedroom.

The door opened to Zane, wearing only a pair of black Calvin Klein boxers, holding a tray with two plates of steaming food and glasses of fruit juice.

"Good morning, *mi Joya*. I hope you're hungry!" He announced, as he approached, passing me a bowl of homemade shakshuka with sourdough bread on the side. I quickly began to eat, realising just how ravenous I was.

"This is delicious!" I complimented, as I continued to shovel in the lightly spiced tomato sauce with a piece of bread.

"Not just a pretty face." He joked, grinning, winking at me, causing a jolt to surge through my body at his drop-dead handsome smile. "I've been thinking, I want to show you, my homeland. I want to take you to Colombia." He declared, a hint of apprehension in his voice, that I would reject him.

"Oh, wow Zane, I would love to but-"

"It's all arranged, we're going tonight. Don't worry, I've cleared it with your boss." He smirked, cutting in, leaning across the bed to kiss me.

"What would the office think or Theo for that matter, if we gallivanted off to South America together at a moment's notice, they'd surely suspect something was up?" I said breaking the kiss, bringing us back down to Earth. We weren't like a normal couple who could publicly go off on international vacays. He cupped my face in his hands.

"To them, it's a work trip back to the heart of Moreno Jewellery. But to us, it's a moment to be in paradise together. Just me and you." I couldn't help but smile widely at his words as he released me from his tender grip and settled beside me on the bed.

My heart swelled at the romantic gesture, no one had ever done something like that for me before and it showed how much he did truly seem to care. I was ecstatic to see the place Zane felt so strongly about as well as to continue this well-needed alone time. If it was anything like the past twelve hours, I was in for a treat.

29

ZANE

Delilah sat opposite me staring out of the window of my private jet as we flew over the Atlantic Ocean. I often retreated home when work became overwhelming and having Delilah by my side brought even more comfort.

Last night I broke every rule I had ever set for myself professionally: don't fornicate with a staff member, don't invite them to spend the night and definitely don't take them on a holiday! However, what I'd been learning about Delilah, is that she makes me want to smash those boundaries with a sledgehammer and she makes every minute of the chaos worth it.

Spending the night with her felt different than our usual dalliances. I found myself wanting to drag out every second, take her to the peak, bring her back again and experience the euphoria over and over until neither of us could physically take it anymore. I just wish that when she fell asleep in my bed, with a content and angelic look on her face, I could have joined her in that tranquil bliss.

John's words came flooding back into my head refusing to silence in the dead of night. I sat down at the desk in my bedroom mulling over my options.

I opened up my laptop and began to scroll through my work emails. Over the course of my lunches with the designers, I had set them all the challenge to bring me a trendsetting, industry-leading design that would keep us in the top spot for jewellery innovation.

I had been inundated with amazing designs from my creative team and after many rounds of deliberation with Maxine, my Creative Director, we had agreed on our winning piece. Sitting here as the sun began to rise, I was conflicted between appeasing John and no doubt other members of the board by submitting it without the assurance that our firewall was solid or preserving the safety of the intellectual property until I received the confirmation that nothing could be hacked or leaked any more.

I minimised the email window to find a photo of my mother, father and me from when I was a child. Those were happy days, days when the biggest decision I had to make was what flavour ice cream I was going to eat on the beach or what game I was going to destroy Theo at! Sometimes I longed to be back on that beach in Cornwall with my scrappy best friend and his stroppy sister.

The dim light of the computer screen illuminated the contours of Delilah's face, sleeping restfully. I reminisced over how our relationship had changed over the past few months and how I could have never imagined that this would be my reality.

Taking a deep breath, I turned back to close my laptop, deciding I needed to at least try and get some sleep. My attention was caught by my rotating computer background as it switched from my family to the crystal-clear blue water, from a beach in my town in Colombia, that I took whilst I was living there.

I forgot how free I had felt in Cartagena. How I could breathe deeply and not feel my chest tighten or stress build. I felt the metaphorical light switch click in my brain. I needed some time to relax, I had been so stressed with all of this nonsense going on. I needed some headspace away from all the noise. Away from Graham, away from John, away from all of the white men who didn't believe I could do my job properly.

Colombia provided that and with the added treat of Delilah joining me for the journey, I might be able to switch off for a few days after all!

As soon as the thought entered my head, I couldn't stop imagining myself and Delilah enjoying the views of Colombia. Although I was proud of my home town, I'd never felt the urge to show it to anyone but as our relationship grew, I realised I wanted to share every part of myself with her, including the place that shaped me into the man I am today.

After some deliberation, I decided to rely on my Board's opinion and roll the dice. As different as these men were to me, I had always been able to trust them. I narrowed the recipients of the email to a smaller pool of Board members and Maxine. With the email sent and the fate of the work out of my hands, all I could do was focus on the trip I was about to take and pray that nothing went awry.

"I can't wait to lounge on a sunbed with a cocktail in hand!" Delilah sighed happily, snapping me out of my daydream. She really was gorgeous; all traces of last night's anxiety had dissipated. I'd never seen her look so at peace in my presence.

"I'm sure that can be arranged *mi Joya,*" I smirked, leaning forward to rub soothing circles on her bare knee. "We have a lot of sightseeing to do too, sweetheart." Her excited eyes met my own as she leaned forward to squeeze my hand on her leg.

"When was the last time you were in Colombia?"

"Over a year ago now, it must have been last spring." I sighed, running my free hand through my hair. "It's always nice to have a reason to go back and there's no better reason than to show you where I was born." The truth behind my own words caused my heart to pound.

"You do give me whiplash, Zane Moreno!" She laughed, shaking her head.

"You know, I am sorry about last night, Delilah." I looked at her, praying she could read the sincerity in my eyes. Her words from yesterday were still rattling through my brain. I didn't realise that my own stupid cowardice in the office was leading her to question our relationship. "It's never been my intention to make you think I don't care about you, *mi Joya.* All I want is to make you happy." I assured, lifting her hand to my mouth and placing a tender kiss on it. She smiled and nodded in understanding.

"I know Zane, I think this trip is exactly what we need."

For the remainder of the flight, Delilah cuddled into my side as we watched a cheesy romantic comedy, laughing at the obvious plot twists and predictable tropes. Eventually, the film became background noise as we chatted about Delilah's hopes for Colombia and what I was most excited to show her. The familiar tension between us became too much to ignore and we found ourselves once again lost in the intimacy of each other. There was something exhilarating about her screaming my name forty thousand feet above the ground with only the hum of the aeroplane surrounding us.

With the colourful port town coming into view, I already felt ten times lighter.

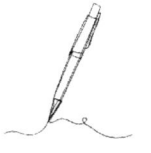

30

LILAH

After the four orgasms from Zane Moreno, it was safe to say I was well and truly over my fear of flying!

Stepping off the plane, the wall of heat surrounded me, despite it being 9pm. Zane already had a car waiting on the tarmac ready to take us on the short journey to his villa on the outskirts of the city. Even in the dark, Cartagena was one of the most beautiful places I had ever seen. Lights adorned every building illuminating the brightly coloured walls and irregular architecture, tropical plants grew along the windowsills and snaked up the brickwork. Zane placed his hand on my upper thigh as we drove down the streets. I felt his eyes glued to me for the entire journey.

"We're only a minute away now." He informed me as I rested my head on his shoulder, the exhaustion from the ten-hour flight and five-hour time difference beginning to affect me.

"I can't wait to explore tomorrow." I sighed dreamily.

"We have plenty of time for that, sweetheart." He moved his hand to play with my hair.

The car turned onto a thin winding road, edged with palm trees decorated with festoon lights guiding our way. As we turned the corner, a breathtaking building of wood and glass came into view.

"Fuck me!" I exclaimed, gobsmacked by the grandeur in front of me. Zane stifled a laugh.

"All in good time, Delilah." He smirked, causing a blush to taint my cheeks.

"This is incredible!" I replied, ignoring his innuendo. "I can't wait for the tour." We parked up and the driver helped us unload our luggage. Zane tipped the man before he drove away from the house, leaving the two of us alone in paradise.

As I reached for my case I squealed as Zane hauled me over his shoulder and spanked my arse. I couldn't help but giggle as he unlocked the door and carried me through to the kitchen, finally placing me down on an elaborate marble island. The coldness of the surface was a delicious contrast to the heat radiating from Zane's body. I wrapped my legs around him, pulling him closer as he claimed my lips in a passionate kiss. He stroked the curve of my hips when a very unladylike rumble disrupted us. He laughed as he broke the kiss and I whined in protest.

"Let's get you some food, missus." He pointed at my stomach, which I internally cursed for cock blocking me as he untangled himself from my grip.

"What's on the menu then?" I asked as he opened the fridge to reveal a plethora of food. Zane pondered for a second before reaching for the ingredients.

"*Bistec a caballo*, essentially steak and eggs?" He asked, peering at me to gauge my reaction.

"Sounds great!"

I sat cross-legged on the kitchen island watching Zane toil away, the smell of the garlic and other herbs filling the room. There was something heart-warmingly domestic about watching him cook for us. It felt, for the first time, like we were a real couple.

"Try this," he said, blowing on a spoon of steaming tomato sauce before offering it to me. The sweet, tangy flavour filled my mouth and I groaned in appreciation.

"Mmm, that's delicious," I complimented. "I never knew you were such a chef."

"I grew up cooking with my mother, I know you learnt some things from her too. I try to make time for it even in my busy schedule but it is nice to have someone to cook for." He smiled, turning back to the frying pan.

We ate our dinners on the dimly lit terrace by the pool, with a view of the cityscape and the sea in the background, making comfortable conversation.

"*Mi Joya,* this is the longest you've gone without back-chatting me." Zane teased as he put down his knife and fork.

"This is the longest you've gone without pissing me off," I replied, sipping my wine.

"Touché!" He laughed in response, picking up my empty plate and cutlery before stacking them on top of his own. He made his way with the crockery towards the kitchen, stopping to place a soft kiss on the top of my head as he passed.

Alone in the garden, I had a moment to reflect. I thought about the girl who was made redundant and hated a billionaire who stole her career. She was so unhappy and couldn't catch a break no matter how hard she tried. Sitting here now in this tropical utopia, I was thankful, in a weird way, for the events of the past few months as I'd never been happier. And that's not just because of the mind-blowing sex with the fit Colombian bachelor currently doing the dishes.

Opening my eyes in the morning, I was relieved to find that Colombia hadn't been a dream. I could hear the song of exotic birds and the running water from the infinity pool as the soft breeze blew through the open balcony doors. I turned to face Zane; the early morning light danced across his peaceful face. There was no sign of the overworked CEO, he looked younger, more reminiscent of the carefree boy from my childhood. I traced the contours of his cheekbones causing him to stir, his arm wrapped around my waist, and he pulled me closer to him.

"*Buen día, mi Joya.*" He rasped sleepily, snuggling me into his chest.

"Good morning." I smiled; I couldn't remember the last time I felt this content.

"What time is it?" Zane asked.

I leaned over him to reach for his watch on the bedside table. "9:30," I replied, Zane's eyes shot open finally.

"9:30? Whoa, I haven't slept in this late in months!" He sighed looking relaxed.

"Well, get up sleepyhead, I've got exploring to do and I need a tour guide!" I sat up, snapping my fingers at him. Zane's eyes trailed down my body, covered only by the white, delicate lace nightie. His gaze lingered on my breasts. I followed his eyeline to find my nipples giving my arousal away.

"Okay, okay, the first point on the itinerary: get to know a Colombian native." He smirked, pulling me back towards him as he lifted my dress over my head in one quick motion and began to explore my body. If this is what Zane is like in holiday mode, looks like we'll be booking a lot more annual leave!

As incredible as this morning's activity had been, I was excited to explore outside of the bedroom. Zane led me hand in hand, along the white sandy beach of Cartagena to two sun loungers which were shaded by grassy umbrellas.

"This is one of my favourite views in all of the city," Zane told me. The sun beat down reflecting light on the endless crystal-clear blue water. It looked like something out of a postcard. I took off my cover-up to reveal a black string bikini. I saw Zane's jaw tense, causing me to raise an eyebrow.

"Can you keep it in your pants for two minutes so we can enjoy the sights please?" I joked, picking up a piece of mango from the fruit plate that had just arrived at the small table between our seats.

"I *am* enjoying the sights." He smiled devilishly; I rolled my eyes.

"So, did you come here a lot as a kid?" I asked, changing the topic but genuinely interested in his history here.

"Yes, before we moved to Cornwall, this is where I would spend all of my summers with my friends."

"Oh wow, a bit of a difference to the Cornish coast then!"

"Well, luckily for me the beaches in Newquay are pretty beautiful too." He smiled kindly, "although the temperature left a lot to be desired!"

"That's true. Did you find it difficult moving to England?" I asked.

"It was a big change. I had started to learn English before we moved, but it was a difficult shift starting at a tiny local school and being the foreign kid who barely spoke the language. That's why meeting you and Theo was so great as you treated me as an equal. I looked forward to Summer every year where I didn't feel like an outcast."

"That's great but to be honest, that's the complete opposite of my summer experience over those years." I chuckled sadly, avoiding Zane's eye contact whilst popping another piece of fruit into my mouth. He rubbed his neck awkwardly. "But hey, we can make new summer memories, right?"

"Of course, *mi Joya*!" He leaned across the small

gap between us and kissed me tenderly. It's hard to believe I ever hated this man!

"Race ya!" I pulled back from him abruptly, running towards the inviting sea. I heard Zane behind me scrambling to take his shirt off as he jogged to catch up. I knew if he wanted to he could beat me easily but I sensed he was letting me claim the victory.

As the edge of the water was steps away, Zane whisked me up into his arms and ran full pelt into the crashing waves. I screamed as he threw me into the water, my head dunking, before resurfacing to a laughing Zane.

"You dick!" I shouted jovially, splashing him. We continued to play fight in the waves for a while before he pulled me towards his bare chest.

"I'm glad you agreed to come with me, Delilah," Zane said sincerely, brushing a wet tendril of hair out of my face as he stared at me intensely. "Your eyes are so extraordinary, not even the rarest emerald compares."

A warm feeling I'd never felt before, welled inside of my chest as his words washed over me, leaving me speechless. I looked back at the man before me, stunned by the adoration in his eyes. With nothing coherent to say, I wrapped my arms around his neck and kissed him hard. "Thank you for inviting me."

I spent the rest of the afternoon, drying off on the lounger, sketching aimlessly in my notepad whilst Zane swam in the sea. Eventually, I lost interest in my drawings and focussed my attention on the hunk of a man in the water. He caught my eye and began to wade out of the waves. The sunlight reflected off his wet, sculpted torso as he shook his head slightly to rid his curls of the seawater. I swear he moved in slow motion!

I sat, open-mouthed, mesmerised as he walked towards me like a Colombian James Bond. This view was doing more for me than any porno ever could!

"Can you keep it in your pants for two minutes so we can enjoy the sights please?" Zane joked, mimicking my earlier comment. I snapped my mouth shut, shaking my head.

"I'm sorry, I'm not the one walking around like a sculpted God." I could have sworn I saw the pride on his face at my statement.

"I think that's the first time you've complimented me outside of me fucking you senseless, Delilah!" I felt the crimson heat flush my cheeks at the mental image conjured up by his words. "Time to go home and get ready for tonight's plan, *mi Joya!*"

Zane took us to a beachside bar after a delicious seafood dinner at a nearby restaurant. The vibe of this place was unlike anywhere I'd been before. A roaring fire on the beach emanated a warm, orange glow onto the faces of the revellers on the sand. The music from the band filled my body and I let it consume me.

"Dance with me," I whispered into his ear as I pulled his arm towards the dance floor.

"I told you in Paris, I don't dance." He insisted, "But I love watching you." He let go of my hand as I twirled towards the group, his words causing butterflies to swarm in my stomach. I closed my eyes and ran my fingers through my hair as I twisted my body to the beat of the music. The tight black dress I was wearing accentuated my curves as I circled my hips and the iridescent material reflected the fairy lights hung between the palm trees.

I gazed seductively in Zane's direction. He was leaning on his knees with his hands clasped, his white linen shirt gaped open exposing his tanned chest, as he watched me hungrily.

"Hi, are you here alone? Would you like to dance with me?" An averagely good-looking man asked me with desire in his eyes as he offered me a hand.

"I'm not alone, no thanks," I stated, turning my body away from him as he disappeared back into the crowd. I felt a hand slide around my waist and pull me in tight towards them. Instinctively, I froze for a moment before the familiar woody scent enveloped me, causing me to melt into his touch. I felt his strong frame against mine, as he moved in time with me. "So, you can dance?"

"I said I don't, not that I can't." He spoke quietly as he stroked over my stomach. He rocked his hips against my backside, igniting the heat between my thighs as I felt the bulge of his cock. "Every man here wants you. But you're mine, *mi amor.*" He whispered into my ear causing a shiver to run down my spine. I tried not to dwell on the new nickname as I leaned my head back. He trailed wet, open-mouth kisses along my neck as I ground back into him. I felt his dick harden against my arse.

"Let's go home." I panted. "I need you, Zane."

31

ZANE

The door of my villa had barely closed behind us before we became a blur of entangled limbs.

"*Dios mi Joya,* you have been driving me crazy all night," I growled, breaking contact for only a moment as I guided us towards the open-plan living room.

"I can tell." She purred, reaching down to run her hand over the bulge in my trousers. My patience had run out. Bending down, I swept her up into my arms and continued to kiss her passionately as I carried her to the large corner sofa. I sat down with Delilah straddling my hips, her dress riding up her thighs. Instinctively, she began to rock against me, her breath coming in soft pants. The heat radiating off her clothed pussy made me insane.

"I can already tell you're soaking, Delilah!" I groaned as she sucked a sensitive spot on my neck. I began to pull the hem of her black dress over her hips before her hands stopped me. My eyes snapped to her at her hesitation but it was evident on her face that she wanted me as badly as I wanted her.

"Is everything okay?" I asked tentatively.

"Wait here," Delilah instructed a mischievous expression crossing her features as she removed herself from my grip and disappeared upstairs.

The seconds ticked by agonisingly slowly whilst I awaited her return, my mind wandering to whatever she had in store. Kicking off my shoes and unbuckling my belt, I turned the music system on to play quietly. I laid my head back against the cushions as I tried to distract myself from the growing anticipation. Images of Delilah writhing around on the beach, playing on repeat in my brain. The way the other men at the bar watched her made me simultaneously feel pride that she was coming home with me and fury that they were laying their eyes on what was *mine*.

After what felt like an eternity, I heard the sound of soft footsteps padding across the wooden floor.

"No peeking." The sweet voice of Delilah instructed again, as her delicate hands glided around my head to cover my eyes. My erection throbbed painfully. "Keep them shut." She said, as she removed her hands from my face and trailed one along my back as she moved around to the front of me.

I felt her stand between my parted knees, her supple thighs brushing against my own. She guided my hands over her shapely curves, starting at her full breasts, covered in a lacy material; over the indent of her bare waist and flair of her hips; past the mystery material hiding her most private area and along her smooth legs until my fingers felt the ruched fabric of her stocking. My eyes flew open - *I can't take this anymore.*

I stared at the Goddess before me, I'd never seen anything so beautiful. She was a breathtaking mix of elegance and sexuality; natural yet otherworldly.

My mouth dried as I traced every angle of her luscious frame, the black fabric accentuating the swell of her breasts and the lines of her legs. I followed her body up to her face and my breath hitched; it was like seeing her for the first time. Her red hair cascaded around her shoulders in fiery tendrils, begging for me to wrap my hand around it. The dim lighting highlighted her stunning features, the delicate slope of her nose, her cheeks flushed with arousal and her full lips, a perfect pink contrast to her pale skin, curved into a coy yet confident smile. Finally, I looked into her eyes, sparkling emeralds locked onto mine, shining with both adoration and mischief as she watched me take her in. I was truly mesmerised by her.

"Delilah" I breathed her name like a prayer. "*Eres la mujer más hermosa que he visto en mi vida.*" I whispered mostly to myself as I wrapped my hand around the top of her suspenders and pulled her towards me. She fell forward and kissed me tenderly before pulling away again and dropping to her knees, reaching up to tie her hair in a messy ponytail. I gulped, the pulsing in my cock intensifying until it was almost unbearable.

"I'm so fucking lucky!" I released a breath as Delilah reached for my trousers and pulled them down to reveal my iron-hard cock already glistening with pre-cum.

"Let me show you how lucky you truly are!" she teased before wrapping her hand around the girth of my arousal. I hissed at the contact as she began to draw her hand up and down my length with deliberate slowness, gliding her fingers over my helmet torturously. I leaned my head against the sofa cushions, revelling in the feeling.

"Your cock is so big, Zane." Delilah purred, "I'm not sure I'm going to be able to fit it all down my throat!" She looked up at me, batting her thick eyelashes with fake innocence.

"I'm sure you will try your best, *mi amor*," I smirked down at her, the term of endearment rolling off my tongue. She licked the tip of my dick before wrapping her lips around and sucking me into her mouth. All other thoughts vanished from my brain, the only thing that remained was the velvet warmth of Delilah's mouth as she took almost every inch of me.

"That's my girl," I growled as my cock hit the back of her throat. She gagged around me, her eyes watering as she adjusted to my size. She paused for a moment whilst acclimating to the full length of me before beginning to bob her head. I resisted the urge to close my eyes as I wanted to watch every moment.

"You look like such a pretty slut, with your mouth full of my cock." I praised, reaching down to caress her cheek, she moaned at my filthy words and delicate touch, looking up at me. I found myself lost in her eyes - big, round, pleading, doe eyes that darkened with desire.

"*Mierda* Delilah!" I wrapped my hand around the back of her head as she began to pick up pace, spit-soaked my length as she worked me towards my orgasm, her hand stroking my cock in time with her movements. "God, you're a vision on your knees!" As the pressure built into my lower abdomen, I began to thrust upwards to chase my climax. Her moans sent vibrations along my cock getting me even closer, just as the pleasure was about to reach its peak Delilah stilled before sliding her mouth off me. She smiled sweetly, taunting me, holding me prisoner on the edge. All I could do was stare dumbfounded at the vixen before me.

"Is there something you want, sir?" She asked innocently. Frustration and arousal burned through my veins in equal measure.

"You know what I want, Delilah," I growled in response, as she stroked the tip of my cock with her fingertips, causing a shiver to run down my spine.

"Come and get it then!" She sat back on her feet and opened her mouth wide for me, a clear invitation. *Fucking hell, this woman will be the death of me.* I stood up, grabbed her ponytail and slammed my cock down her throat. I barely gave her time to readjust to me as I fucked her pretty little face.

"What do you want Delilah? My cum down your throat, or covering that gorgeous face of yours?" I asked, she moaned around me, causing more jolts of electricity to course through my dick.

"I can't hear you, sweetheart!" I taunted, picking up speed, the filthy slick sounds filling the room. Sweat beaded on my forehead and my heart thumped harder in my chest as the force of my orgasm raged through me. With one last pump into her, I pulled out and painted thick ropes of cum over her open mouth and face. As the aftershocks subsided, I leaned down to kiss Delilah on the top of her head before retrieving a towel to clean her up.

"You magnificent woman." She giggled proudly at the compliment and began to stand. "Where'd you think you're going, *mi Joya?* It's not over yet." I stated, pushing her gently down onto the sofa. "Take your underwear off before I rip it off you," I demanded, kneeling on the floor and parting her legs, craving the taste of her pussy. I was enjoying these nights alone with her. No pressure, no time constraints, and no chance of being discovered. Just the two of us: free to explore. I tried to forget that this week would come to an end and force us back to reality in London. I wasn't ready to face that just yet.

****

The next two days were full of nostalgia. I wanted to ensure whilst we were here that I showed Delilah some of the most important places in Colombia to me. We visited the excavation site that I was first brought to when I moved back several years ago and it sparked my passion and inspiration to build my company. Delilah and I met with Diego and Juan Carlos, the first two tradesmen I networked with and have had on my payroll ever since. Delilah's charm won over the usually grumpy old-timers. She appeared to have that effect on people!

The next day we continued our exploration of the city, heading to the mid-week market to sample and purchase the delicious local produce.

"Oh, this place is gorgeous!" She stated. She wasn't wrong. The temporary stalls which had been erected in the middle of one of the squares, offered a rainbow of perfectly ripe fruit and vegetables which mirrored the colourfully painted buildings surrounding the market. The hot sun beat down on us as we casually wandered the aisles hand in hand, stopping regularly to sample the exotic offerings and buy ingredients for our dinner. We came away with two bags, full to the brim of food and drink for our evening at the villa.

For that night's activity, I taught Delilah another one of my family's favourite meals, *Sudado de Pollo*. A traditional Colombian chicken stew.

"Try this." I offered her a mouthful of the flavourful sauce that was bubbling away on the hob. "This was one of the most frequently made meals in my home growing up here. I lived on this as a child!"

"That's one of the best things I've ever eaten!" Delilah exclaimed as she scrunched her face in delight. I poured two glasses of white wine, offering one to her. I picked up an olive from the grazing plate of local delicacies that I had put together for us to eat, whilst we waited for the stew to cook down.

"So, what's on the agenda today then, Mr Tour Guide?" Delilah asked sleepily the next day, still wrapped up in my arms in bed as the sun rose.

"I'm going to take you to the house I grew up in."

Standing across the road from the coral-painted bungalow from my childhood, I was reminded of how small the one-storey abode was. As a child, it felt like a kingdom, full of love and happiness, but now as an adult, without the rest of my family here, the normalcy of the building was apparent.

"This is it. I try to make the effort to visit whenever I'm back. It reminds me of where I started and the joy I felt here, even when we had very little money and no plans to change that."

"So, it keeps your head from getting any bigger then?" Delilah teased, nudging my side. "It's lovely, Zane." I wrapped my arm around her shoulder and placed a kiss on the side of her head.

Standing there, where I was born with the bratty little girl I grew up with on the other side of the world, an unfamiliar feeling pulled at my chest. I could never have imagined that these two opposite parts of me would ever combine but it felt so natural. Although times were testing with the business currently, one thing I was sure of was Delilah was meant to be in my life and I'd be damned if I'd ever let her go.

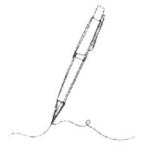

32

LILAH

After a whirlwind week of sightseeing and walking down memory lane, my step count was off the chart. So, I was looking forward to a day of sitting by the pool, drinking cocktails and not moving a muscle - well, maybe a bit of physical activity with Zane, but that was hardly a chore!

    The hot sun was beating down on the patio of the villa but I was hiding under the parasol to enjoy some shade and save my fair English skin from burning to a crisp. Zane, on the other hand, was far from relaxing, swimming laps in the pool.

    I took this quiet time to dig my sketchpad out and let my creative juices flow. It was incredible how being by the water, carefree and content had the ideas spilling out of me. I'd only been at this for an hour and already had half a dozen pages of various rough necklace, bracelet and ring designs drawn out. I was on a roll today! If my mum could see me now, she would be so proud.

Now and then I diverted my eyes from the page to the pool, distracted by Zane's tanned rippling back muscles which glistened deliciously as the sun reflected off of the water. It was like my own personal episode of Baywatch!

"Are you ever going to show me what you're scribbling in that book, *mi amor?*" Zane asked, flicking his dripping curls back as he stood, leaning over the edge of the pool.

"For my eyes only, Moreno!" I teased, snapping the book shut.

"I'll let you finish my portrait before I see it." He winked as he hoisted himself out of the pool, pushing up on the tiles with strong arms, causing every muscle of his upper body to bulge. *Jesus Christ!*

"Don't flatter yourself!" I mocked shuffling to the end of the sun lounger I was occupying. Zane walked towards me and bent down to kiss me. Or so I thought! Before I knew it, he wrapped his arms around my waist and hurled us towards the water, laughing as we hit the surface.

"Really? Again Zane?" I laughed, as I came up for air.

"I'm sorry Delilah, you just look so good when you're wet." He smirked suggestively, closing the distance between us and pressing his lips against mine. He ran a hand along the curve of my hip under the water. It landed on the tie of my bikini bottoms which he easily undid with one quick pull.

"How have you got any energy left?" I said coyly, as he trailed open-mouthed kisses across my neck, increasing my heart rate.

"I've always got energy for you." He breathed against my skin. I moaned as his hand reached between my legs and found my swollen clit. He began to move his fingers in a circular motion as I clung to his muscular body, pressure building as he guided us towards the side of the pool.

I felt my back touch the cold tiles before Zane's rough hands grasped my hips and lifted me effortlessly onto the edge. The chill from the porcelain shot through me as my bare pussy came into contact, causing the shiver of anticipation to intensify.

Naturally, my legs fell over his shoulders as Zane wrapped his arms under my thighs and pulled me closer to him, lining himself up with my core. I put my hands out to steady myself at the swift motion.

"*Dios*, I could eat your pussy all day, Delilah." He growled, centimetres from my begging sex, his breath ghosting over me. Before I had a chance to respond, he licked and sucked my bud with such precision, the pleasure already began to build to unbearable levels. I tangled my fingers into his wet hair, keeping him close.

I watched as Zane devoured me. He looked as though he got just as much enjoyment out of it as I did. The way he moved his head and moaned as if he couldn't get enough sent ripples of ecstasy directly to my clit.

"You taste so fucking sweet, *mi amor*." Zane groaned against me, my nipples hardening at his filthy words. He slipped a finger inside, making my breath hitch before I let out a moan. Zane continued to lick at my clit as he worked his finger deeper with each movement.

"*Zane!*" I whimpered as he drove a second finger in, stretching me wide open. Curling his fingers until he perfectly hit my G-spot. I swear with each thrust I saw stars! He began to pump slowly at first, then faster until I was writhing beneath him and screaming his name so loud, I was thankful there were no neighbours around to overhear.

The stars multiplied until the light they created was blinding as my orgasm crashed over me. My ears rang, my heart beat dangerously hard in my chest and my vision impaired as the intensity of my climax rolled through.

Zane's mouth continued to work me through the afterglow until I was an incoherent mess on the side of the pool. As the sounds of birds tweeting and wind through the trees became audible again, Zane slowly removed his fingers and began to trail hot kisses up my body until he reached my mouth. He tenderly pressed his lips against mine as I revelled in the taste of my arousal on his tongue.

"Come on *mi Joya,* let's go upstairs." Zane purred, hauling himself out of the water once again before leading me towards the villa. The giddy anticipation flooded back to the apex between my legs.

I can't wait for round two!

After what felt like hours Zane and I finally managed to tear ourselves off each other as he disappeared for the remainder of the afternoon. He didn't divulge any of the details and my heart was getting carried away that it might be a surprise for us. I tried to squash those feelings, reminding myself that he was likely just meeting with one of his business partners out here.

The last week had felt like a dream and the old Delilah finally felt like she'd returned. Laying back on the sun lounger I had occupied, I stared up at the cloudless sky reminiscing over the emotional rollercoaster I had been on over the past year. I was at last experiencing a constant level of happiness that I hadn't known for a long time. To be honest, I didn't know if I'd ever previously felt the way I did now. I wasn't even just talking about liking Zane more than I did as a child.

The way my heart swelled when I spent time with him; the butterflies that frantically fluttered when he smiled at me; and how my skin burned at his touch. I finally understood what this feeling was, but I still felt nervous to say it out loud.

Although, I would bet all of my money that Zane felt the same as me - his upgraded nickname hadn't gone unnoticed - I was all too aware that we were living in an unsustainable bubble in Colombia which made me realise I wasn't fully ready to give into those dangerous feelings. I needed proof that this effort and devotion would continue when we returned to London and then maybe I could call this what it was.

The sound of the front door clicking shook me out of my thoughts and I noticed the sun had already begun to set. How long had I been daydreaming?!

Through the bi-fold glass doors of the villa, Zane emerged looking fucking edible. He was wearing a linen blue shirt tucked into black trousers, which were rolled partially up his bronzed forearms, with enough buttons undone to expose his rugged torso. Silver rings decorated his thick fingers, matching the timepiece on his wrist. I finally diverted my gaze to his face. His dark black curls were coiled tighter and messier than usual, due to the humidity of the climate, but he still looked impeccable. I loved this version of Zane, slightly rough around the edges but still incredibly breathtaking. I wanted to march over to him and run my hands through his hair to mess it further and drag him upstairs for another sesh in our bedroom. However, my attention was caught by the large box he was carrying.

"A gift for you, *mi amor*," Zane announced, handing the parcel to me. "Go and put it on and be ready to leave within the hour."

I snatched it out of his hands, unable to hide my excitement and placed a soft kiss on his cheek as a way of thanks, racing upstairs to discover what was inside.

The next forty-five minutes blurred as I applied make-up, chucked my hair into a messy updo and slinked on the silky surprise. With a quick final check in the mirror, I was ready to return to my date.

The villa was silent as I clicked along the wooden floor in my strappy heels and began to walk down the stairs. Zane was stood at the bottom, flicking on his phone, whilst he waited for me. As the sound of my arrival reached him, I watched as his gaze started at my feet, along the silky pearlescent material of the satin dress which stopped just below my knees. He followed the slit of the dress up to my waist, then over my chest before landing on my face. It felt like it was our first date. I was overcome with nerves and self-consciousness for a moment whilst he examined me.

"*Mi Joya,* you look incredible." Zane declared, mouth agape in awe, as he held out his hand for me to take as I cleared the last few steps.

"Thank you, the dress is stunning!" I gushed. He took my chin in his hand, staring intensely into my eyes.

"I wasn't talking about the dress, Delilah, you truly are the most beautiful woman in the whole world." Heat spread across my cheeks at the compliment and I offered him a bashful smile in return. My previous insecurity melted at his words as he placed a loving kiss on my lips.

We rode in comfortable silence in the taxi, hand in hand, for the duration of the short journey. My mind raced across the various thoughts I had of what he could possibly have in store. However, nothing could have prepared me for what was waiting for us on the private rooftop.

If I thought that our first private dinner in London was amazing, this was out of this world. Beige woven blankets lay scattered on the floor with cushions and pillows for us to lounge on. More candles than I'd ever seen in one place were lit around the perimeter of the area creating a warm glow which was complemented by the abundance of fairy lights hanging above us. A small wooden table sat in the centre with a grazing platter on top with more kinds of meat, cheese, crackers and accompaniments than you could ever wish for!

"Woah Zane!" I gasped, taking in my surroundings. "Did *you* do all of this?" I asked as he led me towards the cushions and we settled ourselves down onto them.

"What did you think I was doing all afternoon, *mi vida*?" He reached for the bottle of Rioja on the short table between us and began to pour two glasses. Giddy excitement tingled through me at the thought of him going to all this work and the term of endearment falling from his lips so effortlessly.

"No one has ever done anything like this for me before." He handed me the glass before taking my hand in his. "Thank you."

"You deserve it, Delilah." He implored, lifting my hand to place a kiss on it.

"No thank you for everything, the dress, the holiday-"

"Even the job?" Zane smirked, cutting me off.

"The jury's still out on that one. My boss is a bit of a sex pest!" I laughed, winking at him.

"My sincerest apologies." He smiled coyly, as he fed me an olive. "Thank you too, I've never brought anyone to Colombia, and it's been wonderful to see it through your eyes." He took a swig of his wine.

"I've never felt so relaxed in my life." We began to pick at the food in front of us. A wave of confidence and eagerness to reveal more of my true self with Zane, as he had, washed over me. I took a nervous sip of wine before continuing. "You know you asked me what I was doodling today? It might sound silly, but I was drawing jewellery designs." I saw him raise an eyebrow in intrigue. "Not to pitch to you or anything. Don't worry, I'm not using you for your connections, Mr Moreno." He laughed. "It was something my mum and I used to do, she always dreamed of designing collections to be sold around the world but as you know, never succeeded at that, so the fantasy has passed down to me." A solemn look crossed his face. "When she died, I never thought I would pick up the pencil again but spending time with you over the past few months has helped to heal that wound and I've been feeling inspired lately." He retook my hand in his and squeezed it in a comforting gesture.

"Wow, that's amazing. Thank you for telling me." He smiled, leaning forward to kiss me. "And you should never be afraid of exploiting this connection, I'll always want to help you." My heart warmed at the declaration. A weight I wasn't previously aware of lifted off my shoulders, it felt therapeutic to share this part of myself with someone again, someone I truly cared about.

"Oh, I've never taken it that seriously, it's more of a pipe dream." I waved him off and took another sip of my wine.

"Well, if you ever want to pursue it, I will do everything I can to support you." He held up his glass. "We're a team now, Delilah, cheers to us!" I clinked my drink to his in agreement.

"Cheers to us." I echoed, smiling at the sentiment. "If you would have told me six months ago that I would be sitting on a rooftop in Colombia with Zane Moreno I'd have laughed in your face." I sighed in disbelief. Zane set his glass on the table and turned to me.

"I wanted to apologise again for how I made you feel growing up. I never realised how much of an impact it had on you until that night you got outrageously drunk and I took you home." I looked at him full of confusion. *What did I say that night?*

"You said we hated each other. I can't speak for you and I don't blame you if you did, but I've *never* hated you." His words washed over me as I let him continue. "As a child, I bonded with Theo over hobbies that didn't require us both to speak the same language. By the time I felt confident with my speech and in myself, you had long distanced yourself from me. I had become a stupid teenager, who didn't know how to speak to the pretty girl who I looked forward to seeing every year, without messing with her. It never occurred to me that my teasing was being received as bullying and I *do* hate that."

"I looked forward to those summers too, Zane, hoping that each year would be the one that we could build a friendship, but every time I was disappointed." He grimaced. "To be honest, it wasn't just the summers where I was let down. Theo's eighteenth birthday was awful. I still wake up in the night in a cold sweat from that Valentine's Day." I laughed awkwardly.

"This is no excuse, but I'd completely forgotten the extent to which I'd hurt you. I'm so sorry for how I treated you, Delilah. I was just a hormonal boy who didn't know how to process or express his feelings. I don't expect you to accept my apology but I promise to never hurt you again."

I stared back in disbelief at his confession, I couldn't fathom that all these years I'd been harbouring resentment towards Zane and it had never crossed my mind that he didn't feel the same way.

"I do accept your apology Zane and I appreciate it. Believe me." I smiled at him genuinely.

"That means more to me than you'll ever know, *mi amor*. For a long time now, I've operated on my own and never needed companionship. However, having you by my side, I realise I've never been happier and never want to be without you." He took a deep breath, a look on his face as though he was processing a thousand thoughts. "When we get home Delilah, I think it's time we tell the truth. I don't want to hide you away anymore. I want everyone to know you're mine." I couldn't believe the words he was saying to me, my heart felt like it was going to burst.

"I'm ready too, Zane." I beamed at him in agreement, trying to hide the child-like excitement and anticipation I felt at returning to London and starting our relationship out in the world, living normal lives together.

"I'm happy to hear that. And if I'm honest, I've never felt this way before but I know that I'm in…" Zane's phone pinged loudly, cutting off his sentence. He whipped it out of his pocket quickly to silence the notification but paused as the screen lit up. He took a deep breath with a concerned look on his face before turning to me. "I'm sorry, I'll be right back."

He got up and headed towards the door to the exit, leaving me alone to ponder the end of his sentence.

33

ZANE

It pained me to leave Delilah to read a text message after the incredible evening we had been having. However, I was all too aware that we were twenty-four hours from our deadline and Graham wouldn't be contacting me at 1am UK time if it wasn't important.

> Sorry to disturb your romantic getaway but I regret to inform you, the Valentine's submission has leaked. Graham

Fuck!

I read and re-read the message in the bathroom trying to process what I had been told. I apprehensively clicked the link that Graham had shared, and the blood in my veins turned to fire as I watched a video of Jason Sallow teasing his next product. I couldn't believe my eyes when he proudly displayed our Valentine's product as his own. I knew this could happen, I had been stupid to bow to peer pressure and share that email without the green light on our cyber security!

I threw my phone onto the sink and ran my hand through my hair in frustration. Where am I supposed to get a first-class design in eighteen hours?

I had been stupid to take my eye off the ball this close to the finish line. I should have expected something like this to happen again. I couldn't believe I'd allowed myself to become so distracted.

This was what I was afraid of when I first started getting involved with Delilah. Had my brain not been so preoccupied with dangerous thoughts about my Personal Assistant, maybe I could have prevented this or squashed it sooner. I ran my hands across my face as I tried to clear through a myriad of surging thoughts.

Fuck! Romantic getaway!

Why would he have said that? He must have found out about us. And if *he* did, what's to say that everyone else didn't know too? If my team thought I was off gallivanting with an employee instead of on a business trip this close to such an important date, what's to stop them thinking I don't give a shit about this company or respect them as valued members of my team?

I turned on the tap and splashed the cold water against my skin to bring myself back down to Earth as I had begun to spiral. I needed to get back to the Villa and on my laptop to see what I could do to fix this.

I paced quickly back to a waiting Delilah who smiled genuinely at my return.

"Wow, you were a long time! I thought you'd done a runner!" she laughed, drinking her wine. Seeing

Delilah so carefree would normally bring some calm to my brewing chaos however at this moment, I was envious of her tranquillity. I sat back down and poured myself another drink from a fresh bottle of wine, not caring to measure the amount as I tried to push the news to the back of my head and enjoy the last evening with her.

"Sorry, I had to go and deal with that. Where were we?" I asked, taking a large swig in an attempt to still my mind.

"You were in the middle of saying something." She reminded me with a certain glow about her. *Dios*, she looked stunning in the candlelight.

"Ah yeah, what was your favourite part about Colombia?" I bluffed the moment from before the interruption now firmly passed. I watched the glint in her eyes diminish slightly at my words.

"Oh right, erm, I loved seeing your childhood home. It felt really special to visit with you. What about you?" She sighed.

"Yeah, me too." I agreed, trying to fake my interest but all I could focus on were the damned designs. I checked my watch, before finishing my drink and pouring another.

"Are you okay, Zane?" She asked, concerned as I downed the Rioja.

"I'm fine, *mi Joya*. I'm just getting tired."

"Let's go home, I'm tired too." She agreed but the disappointed look on her face suggested she was bluffing too.

Back at the Villa, Delilah and I headed straight up to our bedroom however sex was the last thing on my mind tonight. We got ready for bed in silence and slipped under the covers, lying towards each other.

"Thank you for bringing me here, Zane. It really has been lovely." Delilah said sweetly.

"Thank you for being here with me, Delilah." I leaned over and cupped her face, placing a soft kiss on her lips. I felt her melt under my touch and before she could deepen it, I pulled back kissing her forehead. "*Buenas noches*, sweetheart."

She snuggled in under my chin as I wrapped my arms around her, tracing circles on her back until she fell asleep. I tried to join her in her peaceful slumber. However, after fifteen minutes of lying there hopelessly, I couldn't quiet my thoughts and needed to try and do something about the issue at hand.

Trying not to disturb her, I carefully shuffled out of the bed and headed towards the door.

"Where are you going?" she mumbled half awake.

"Shh go back to sleep, I'll be right back." She hummed in acceptance and rolled onto her other side. I retrieved my laptop and a glass of rum from downstairs and returned to set up on the balcony off of our room.

I opened my MacBook and sifted through the various designs that the team had been sharing with me over the past few weeks in the hopes that I'd missed something previously. It became all too apparent that these ideas were good, some were even pretty fantastic, but *none* were earth-shattering. I wasn't a quitter but even I had to admit the sense of dread that was settling into me. I had two choices: submit a subpar design just to have something to launch but risk the integrity and quality of my brand that our customers had come to expect from us or submit nothing and for the first year since running Moreno Jewellery, not put out an exquisite, limited edition Valentine's product.

    I leaned back in my chair, swirling the drink in my hand as I looked out towards the paradise below me.

    What I wouldn't give to be twelve hours earlier swimming in the pool, watching Delilah peacefully doodle away. My attention snapped towards the notepad still sitting on the lounger where she had left it, the conversation we'd had about Delilah's passion playing through my mind.

    Before I had realised it, I was outside picking up the sketchbook. My hands lingered on the leather exterior whilst I contemplated taking a look inside. I glanced towards the house before inhaling a deep breath and opening the cover. I took in the first drawing of a classic gold chain with a circle diamond hanging from it. I was surprised by the artistry in the sketch. I flicked through the next couple of pages carefully. It was like opening Pandora's box and before I knew it, I was frantically sifting through, amazed by the designs before me. I finally settled on a page with a ring. A large circular diamond at its centre in a gold setting. Intricate morganite stones shaped like leaves sat on either side along the band.

    This was it. This was our Valentine's piece. Taking another deep breath, I snapped a picture of the page and frantically fired it off in an email without thinking before placing the pad back down. I sat beside it breathing heavily as a wave of guilt flooded over me, far eclipsing any sense of relief I may have felt for saving the collection.

What the fuck have I done?

I had broken Delilah's trust. She told me she didn't want me to see this. She told me how personal it was. How would she ever forgive me for my actions?

But I had to deliver *something*. I had to prevent my company from a below standard release which would allow our competitors to get ahead. I would explain it all to her when the time was right and she would understand. I hoped.

I returned to the bedroom but paused at the sight of Delilah contently sleeping, not a care in the world. I couldn't bring myself to climb in next to her and take her into my arms.

I was going to tell her I was in love with her tonight. But how could I ever tell her now when I had betrayed her so badly?

Resigning myself to the fact that I was unlikely to get any sleep tonight, I walked quietly back to the living room and laid on the sofa, finishing the bottle of rum.

I had saved the launch, but at what cost?

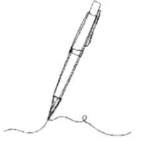

34

LILAH

Three days on and Colombia already felt like a distant dream. After what had been a romantic and insightful getaway, it was cut short slightly when Zane got that well-timed text on Thursday evening.

He had been opening up to me in a way that I never thought he would. I knew how that sentence ended and I would have said it back. But when he returned from the bathroom, it was like a different Zane. He seemed to have closed himself off to me again, just like when we started working together. I was hoping that it was some temporary bad news that would pass after a sleep, however, I woke to find him missing from the bed on Friday morning and that distance between us continued across the Atlantic Ocean and back into the office.

We'd still spoken daily via text however, he had made no attempt to see me over the weekend and I'd not felt like suggesting a date for fear of rejection. I had heard about another design leaking so maybe he had bigger priorities this weekend. Now back in the office, it was business as usual as he had been straight into meetings from 9am. Other than a fleeting hello, I had been working alone on the top level, dwelling on my thoughts. I was looking forward to seeing him properly when his string of commitments ended today so I could check that everything was okay.

I heard Zane's office phone ring in the other room and decided I should probably answer it in his absence. Walking quickly through, I picked up the receiver before it stopped.

"Hello Zane's phone, Lilah speaking," I answered.

"Lilah darling, it's so lovely to speak to you. You're sounding well." Instantly I recognised the female voice with the thick Colombian accent. Sofia Moreno, Zane's mum. The sound of her transported me right back to my childhood. Everything about Sofia was warm and loving and her disposition was a large part of what got me through my mum's funeral. I hadn't spoken to her since then.

"Oh, Sofia! What a lovely surprise!" I gushed, taking a seat in Zane's leather swivel chair and relaxing into it, ready for a catch-up. "How have you been?"

"Oh, you know, I can't complain!" She replied, "How about you *Cariño*? I'm very happy to hear that you and Zane have been spending more time together. I hope you've been having fewer arguments than when you two were children!" She laughed down the line. I was surprised to hear that Zane had been speaking to his mum about us but the news caused a cheesy grin to spread across my face and giddiness to travel through my body.

"Ha, no arguments anymore! No one is as surprised as I am that we've been hanging out." I replied, trying to conceal the emotions running through me.

"Oh, that's good, did you enjoy Colombia? Isn't the villa beautiful?"

"Absolutely!" I twirled the wire of the phone around my finger absentmindedly. "He showed me your old house, what an amazing location!"

"It is stunning, I haven't been back for quite a few years now. I've tried to convince Carlos to make time for a visit but you know what these Moreno men are like when it comes to work!" She chuckled.

"Well, I hope you get to go back soon!"

"Here's hoping! I know that it would have taken a lot for my boy to reveal such personal places, I'm glad he has you to open up to and share that part of himself with." A lump formed in my throat at her meaningful words as I thought about how much Zane had disclosed to me on the holiday.

"It was really special."

"Ah, sorry, I'm rambling on again! I'm sure you're busy, I'm judging by this conversation that my boy isn't available?"

"Yeah, he's in a meeting I'm afraid but I can pass on a message!" I scrambled for a Post-it note and pen but was unsuccessful. Damn you Zane and your lack of clutter!

"Oh no don't worry about it *Cariño*, just ask him to call me back when he's free."

"Yes, of course, I'll put a reminder in his calendar so there's no excuses!" I giggled, beginning to open up his laptop.

"Thank you so much, Lilah, we really must catch up properly soon!" We said our goodbyes before hanging up. I felt reassured after the conversation, the earlier stress regarding Zane forgotten about. Once his laptop had come to life I typed in the password and opened up his emails. Before I had the chance to set the reminder I noticed a priority email subject: 'Design For Urgent Approval' and curiosity got the better of me. I knew the Valentine's limited edition had been in the works for a while and wasn't free from its dramas so I was intrigued to see what the final submission was!

I double-clicked on the email, making it open as a separate full-screen window and read the text from the Creative Director:

> zane.moreno@morenojewellery.co.uk
>
> Design For Urgent Approval
>
> Zane,
> This is absolutely outstanding - you've knocked it out the park with this one. Which designer produced this?
>
> Please find attached a quick CAD that Jacob knocked up this morning based on the photo you shared on Friday, let's chat today to see if this has the green light and we'll get moving!
>
> Many thanks,

I clicked the attachment to have a nosy at this incredible design, full of fascination at what this year's centrepiece would be. My mouth dried and my heart stopped as the PDF loaded on the screen.

This is my design!

My pulse raced as a million thoughts rushed around my head. How did my sketch end up with the CD? I hadn't shown anyone!

A cold wave of realisation hit me.

I had opened up to Zane about my designs that evening at dinner and the significance of them.

Surely not!

He had been standoffish that night when we got home not to mention I'd woken up alone the next morning. The spineless bastard couldn't even face me. Did I mean that little to him that he would steal my work for his gain? My stomach twisted and nausea travelled through my body from the bitter taste of his deceit.

I glanced at the time through teary eyes as I realised Zane's meeting would be wrapping up any minute. I couldn't see him. I needed to process what had happened before I could think about talking to that fucking liar.

Racing back to my desk, I quickly gathered my personal belongings with trembling hands, purposely leaving my laptop and anything related to Moreno Jewellery. I held it together long enough to make it to the lift hoping I wouldn't bump into him en route to the exit.

The tears finally fell in droves as I scurried out of the office building and contemplated returning home. However, I knew that Zane would find me there and I needed the space right now. I texted Jacob, who was working from home, to see if I could stay with him for a while and he instantly replied to say it would be no trouble at all.

I hopped on the tube in my usual direction home to grab some essentials before I headed to the solace of Jake's place. My breathing quickened and my heart shattered completely as I replayed the past few months over and over, trying to find any sign of his impending betrayal.

Had this time together meant nothing to him? How could I have been so blind to believe that he had changed?

One thing I knew for certain was that letting Zane Moreno back into my life had been the most foolish, reckless mistake I'd ever made.

35

ZANE

"Honestly Zane, this design is one of the best we've ever had! Great work!" Maxine praised. I wished I could celebrate this success like the rest of the team but all I could think about was how I'd betrayed the woman I loved.

The wheels were moving so quickly due to the urgency of this project that I knew I had to speak to Delilah about this as soon as possible before she found out from someone else. In a few weeks, these offices would be littered with marketing material emblazoned with her design so I needed to explain myself before it got out of hand.

I spent the next two hours nodding along in the right places and signing off material that I had no right to approve. I felt guiltier with every i dotted, and t crossed.

"I look forward to catching up next week to see the progress. Thanks, everyone." I wrapped up the meeting heading for the elevator, feeling torn about returning upstairs. On one hand, seeing Delilah brought happiness into my life that I'd never known before and a smile from her seemed to make everything better, however looking at her now, simultaneously felt like a punch to the gut as I continued to lie to her.

I'd been unable to sleep stressing over the best way and time to reveal all to Delilah. Now that I knew the launch was progressing and the team had what they needed, I would give it the rest of this week to ensure this design didn't leak like the others and confess all to her this weekend. I'd invite her over and replicate one of the meals we ate in Colombia. I wouldn't leave out any of the details and she'd understand.

Delilah was forgiving, hell she forgave me for the shit I'd put her through in her childhood, this would be a minor blip in our relationship, I was sure.

As the doors opened, the want to see Delilah overruled the anxiety I had been feeling in her presence lately. Approaching her desk, anticipating her turning to me with a stunning smile, I noticed she was absent. Her laptop and notepad were still on the desk but she was missing. I checked my watch and realised the meeting had overrun into lunch. She must have been getting something to eat.

I tried to deny the disappointment I felt at not getting to see her for another hour and decided I would eat lunch at my desk to catch up on the week I'd missed while we were away. I'd never taken more than a day or two off at one time since founding the company, so after a week of absence my inbox was bursting at the seams.

I entered my office and immediately felt something was off. The air felt different, and items were out of place. My chair was pushed back, not tucked under as it usually would be. The drawers of my desk were half-open, their contents scrambled as if someone had rummaged through them. My laptop was open and skewed to the side—not in the middle, closed as I would have left it.

I sat on the chair and rolled back under the desk, closing the drawers as my mind raced with thoughts of who could have been searching through my office at a time when I clearly had someone who couldn't be trusted in the team.

I thanked my stars that only Delilah and I knew my laptop password as whoever had been hoping to find something they could sell on to that weasel, Jason, would have left here empty-handed after not being able to access my documents.

Breathing a sigh of relief, I typed in the code and unlocked the computer.

My heart dropped as everything around me blurred and a sharp high-pitched noise rang through my ears. The only thing in focus was Delilah's design full-screen on my laptop.

I slammed the screen shut not being able to bear seeing it any longer and let out a string of curse words, it felt like a vice was tightening around my chest. I held onto the edge of the wooden desk as if trying to keep my balance. My hands were clammy and a heat enveloped my body as I tried to make sense of my tangled thoughts.

Maybe I left it open?

Maybe it wasn't her?
Maybe she didn't see it?

I raced out to Delilah's desk, a terrible feeling crashing over me as I realised her personal belongings were missing. Opening her laptop for any kind of clue to her whereabouts, I felt a sharp, sudden pain in my chest as my heart ripped apart and my breathing stopped at the square of yellow paper stuck to the screen.

FUCK YOU ZANE

36

LILAH

I slammed the apartment door shut and fell against the heavy wood, my emotions spilling out of me now that I didn't have to conceal them. My legs became weak as I slid down into a pathetic heap on the floor. I let out loud, guttural sobs as the pain of Zane's betrayal flowed through me in uncontrollable waves.

"What the fuck's happened Lilah?" Theo came rushing into the hallway to find me useless on the laminate. He sank to his knees. "Sis, speak to me." He implored as he held me whilst I cried harder, shaking in his arms.

After what felt like forever my howls finally turned to whimpers. At last, I looked up into my brother's concerned eyes.

"Lilah, please tell me what's happened. You're scaring me!" Theo said, wiping away a stray tear.

"Zane." I managed to splutter before the tears came again.

"Okay, let's go sit on the sofa and chat this through." Theo guided me to our living room. As I settled down, he returned from the kitchen to sit with me, holding two cups of tea and a plate of biscuits.

"Right, start at the beginning. I'm all ears." Theo smiled at me encouragingly. I felt my battered chest ease a little at his kindness as I took a mug. The heat radiated through my shaking hands.

"All right but promise you won't be angry with me." I started. He looked back reassuringly and continued to listen intently as I spilt the topline information about our relationship and how it had ended, unable to bring myself to go into the full details of Zane's deceit. Every word I muttered felt like another splinter off my heart. Whilst I rattled on, I could tell Theo was trying to hide his shock at what I was divulging. I took a deep breath after word vomiting, feeling ever so slightly lighter by having him know the truth.

"Wow, that's a lot to process Lilah." He responded, sipping his tea before sitting back against the sofa cushions and running a hand through his dark hair. "For once, I'm at a loss for words." I released an exasperated laugh and managed a sip from my cup. "Firstly, I thought you hated each other and I'm impressed, if not also slightly concerned, at your ability to hide such a secret from me, Lils." He looked bewildered at me. "Secondly, I'm sorry this has happened, I'm here when you're ready to tell me everything but sounds like he's been an arsehole for how he's treated you and I can't promise I won't kill him when I next see him."

"Theo, he's not worth it. Just let me handle it." My phone buzzing in my pocket caught both of our attention. I took it out and declined Zane's call for the tenth time in the past hour.

"I'll swear off the physical violence but it's my right as your big brother to give him a piece of my mind." He ruffled my hair at the sentiment. "What are you going to do then? He seems to want to talk to you…" He nodded towards my phone, ringing again.

"I'm going to stay with Jake for a bit, he'll think I'm here and I know he'll come looking for me and I don't want to talk to him until I'm ready. I'm here to pick up some essentials and I'll let you know when I'll be back. Please if you see him, don't tell him where I am." I begged my voice cracking on the last word.

"Your secret's safe with me, sis. At least I know about this one." He winked, pulling me in for a one-armed hug before I packed my belongings and headed over to Jake's in an Uber to avoid scaring the general public and London tourists by my resemblance to one of the members of Kiss. I turned my phone off to avoid the endless stream of unwanted calls I was inevitably going to receive, and finally breathed a sigh of relief that he couldn't contact me again despite the unbearable emptiness settled within me.

Jake opened the door and did well to hide how taken aback he was at my dishevelled appearance.

"Oh babe, come in." He held out his arms and surrounded me with the most heartfelt hug which reduced me to tears again. He took my bags off me and placed them next to the sofa in his living room. My new bedroom for the foreseeable. If my career in the jewellery industry was now over, at least I had 'professional squatter' on my CV!

"I've completed my work for the day, so time to pop the wine and forget about stupid boys." I looked at him alarmed; *how does he know this was about a boy?* "Lils, you're in hysterics, at my flat, at 4pm on a Monday, what else would it be Hun? Who's the prick and what did they do?" He poured two large glasses of white wine before handing one to me.

"So…" I took a deep shaky breath. "It's Zane. We've been together for the past few months secretly and he fucked me over. So, it's done." The verbal confirmation that our relationship was no more, twisted like a knife in my heart. I looked towards Jacob to gauge his reaction to the bomb I'd just dropped.

"Pfft, that dickhead." he responded with less shock than I was expecting. He must have read the confusion on my face at his blasé response. "Hun, you both just disappeared off for a week and a blind man could see the way he looks at you!" The pain in my chest intensified as I recalled the adoration in his eyes that I'd never see again.

"How did you know?"

"Well, I never one hundred percent knew, but I had a hunch. He came swooping in like Superman and saved you from Simmons for God's sake. He's never done that for me and I've been legless plenty of times around him." I laughed at the mental image, trust Jake to make light of anything.

"Ha, for God's sake. If you know, do you think anyone else in the office knows? Zane was always afraid of that." Even now I was still worried about his feelings for fucks sake.

"Potentially but I never heard anything, I wouldn't worry babe." Jake smiled comfortingly. "So how did he fuck it up then?"

"Long story short, you know various designs kept getting leaked?" He nodded. "I had been sketching designs secretly as a hobby and had told him the sentiment behind it whilst we were away. I guess that same night he found out about the latest leak and he submitted my design for approval without asking me. I told him how personal they were and how I didn't want him or anyone else to see them and he completely disregarded that for his gain."

"That slimy bastard!" He announced, before suddenly putting his wine glass down on the table abruptly and covering his mouth with his hand. "Oh my God, I am so sorry but I was asked to CAD a sketch this morning from a photo of a notepad and I had no idea. Otherwise, I would have of course refused."

"Jake it's fine, how were you ever to know? You were just doing your job."

"It really was beautiful though, Lilah." I smiled weakly in response.

"I really thought I meant something to him but turns out I was just another person he could exploit, I'm so stupid Jake." I put my head in my hands trying to forget the events of the day as I gave in to the pain.

"Don't worry hun, we've all done stupid things for boys. I once dressed up as Dobby as this guy I was dating had a Harry Potter fetish." I snapped my head up to look at him through snotty tears. "And before you ask, yes, I recited all the quotes. Your boy was going through a dry spell." He shrugged as the two of us erupted into genuine laughter. I was so glad I came here. "Stay as long as you need by the way hun, I know it's just a sofa bed but it's yours with no expiry date."

How times had changed! Seventy-two hours ago, I was wrapped in Zane's strong arms in paradise, excited for our future and now I was going to be sleeping on a makeshift bed for the foreseeable, trying desperately to keep all the pieces of my broken heart together.

37

ZANE

I raced home to process my thoughts, unable to stare at Delilah's vacant desk any longer. I had been trying and failing to contact her for the past five hours. After the third hour, the phone started going straight to voicemail so I had resigned myself to the thought that she had turned it off - or blocked me - either way I had been shut out, unable to voice my side and the pain was becoming unbearable. I needed to see her. I needed to apologise and make her understand.

As the hurt spread from my chest to consume my whole body, the knowledge that Delilah was gone for good became crystal clear. A suffocating wave of dread washed over me as I imagined the look on her face when she opened my laptop, stealing her design hadn't just been a stupid mistake, it was a deliberate, selfish, desperate action to take. Not only was she gone but it was because of my own foolish actions. My phone fell from my grasp, landing next to my feet as I dropped my head into my hands and began to break down. I'd never been much of a crier. To be honest, I couldn't think of the last time I'd shed a tear. But now, with all hope of Delilah returning to me gone, I couldn't keep the emotion at bay. As the panic set in, my chest heaved and I gasped for air. With each inhale, I tried to catch my breath to no avail, tears fell from my eyes freely amid the anxiety attack.

I closed my eyes, giving in to the agony of my heartbreak. I had caused this. It was my fault and I deserved this. I could only imagine how Delilah felt right now and that thought alone crushed me.

The sound of my phone ringing brought me back to reality. Without looking at the screen, I answered. "*Mi Joya!*" I blurted hopefully, praying that Delilah had finally decided to give me a chance to explain myself.

"Wrong sibling." The sound of a male voice startled me. "Not who you were hoping for?"

"Theo, I-" I started, my heart stuttering, Delilah wasn't the only person I'd betrayed.

"No, it's my time to talk. Firstly, this is how I find out you've been sneaking around with my little sister for the past few months. I had to hear it from her in between sobs after you completely broke her heart." A fresh crack of pain ripped through me; I knew she'd be upset but hearing Theo confirm it made it one hundred times worse. "You're my best friend, you should have told me. She's my only family dude. I could have gotten used to the idea of you two in minutes if you'd been man enough to be straight with me but instead, you lied to my face so many times and now, you've completely screwed her over."

"I've really fucked this up, man." I managed to verbalise, trying but failing to keep my emotions under wraps.

"I don't know what you've done and nor do I care for the details but you clearly owe her a huge apology. Whether she'll forgive you or not is up to her as I've not seen her this upset in months."

"She won't answer my calls. Can I come and see her?" I begged. Fresh silent tears began to run down my cheeks as I attempted to hold it together.

"She's not here." He replied matter of factly, not revealing any details about her current location.

"I can't lose her, T." My voice finally broke, giving away my anguish.

Theo sighed sadly. "Well, I suggest you try to fix it then." He hung up leaving me broken and alone, with no idea of how I was going to get the woman I loved back.

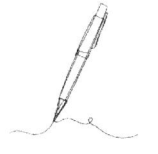

38

LILAH

Four days later and I was still holed up in the comfort of Jake's tiny apartment, nursing my broken heart with only Dairy Milk Buttons and Below Deck to keep me company whilst Jake was working from the office.

Bang on schedule, Jake walked through the door at 5.30pm with a bottle of wine and a fresh pack of chocolate treats - *it's such a shame he's gay, he always knows exactly what a girl wants!*

"I know what you're thinking, I'd make the best boyfriend in the world." He giggled, throwing me the unopened bag.

"I swear you can read my mind." I laughed back catching them as they fell.

"I sure can babe. Hence why I've invited some new crewmates on board this evening. I know how much you've been loving the yacht life whilst being here." He gestured towards the TV, the doorbell rang as if on cue.

For a moment, panic shot through me as I contemplated Zane being behind the door. However, the stress transformed into overwhelming joy at the sight of Amelia and Verity standing in the doorway with care packages.

I stood up from the sofa and burst into tears as Verity ran towards me with open arms. Although we didn't live that far away from each other in miles, our combined busy schedules meant this was the first time we'd seen each other in several months. To be honest it was the longest we'd ever gone without a physical catch-up! Her hug felt like home and I melted into her soft touch.

"What the hell are you doing here?!" I whispered in shock, pulling away from her.

"Jacob messaged me, he said you needed your girls." I turned to him perplexed at how he had contacted her.

"What? I DM'd her on Insta. You've literally got a hundred photos with her tagged and you're always going on about your bestie, V, it wasn't rocket science to piece it together!" He sassed.

"You're the best Jake. Thanks for coming you, guys." I looked at my three friends through teary eyes.

"Don't mention it," Amelia said kindly, squeezing my arm which was the most physical contact I'd ever seen her give anyone. We gathered around Jake's coffee table with cushions and blankets on the floor and popped on Don't Worry Darling to ogle at Harry Styles. I could tell my friends were trying to keep my mind off things and I was more than grateful for the distraction.

"God you can just tell he knows what he's doing." Verity sighed longingly at the table scene playing on the TV.

"Verity!" I laughed.

"I'd give anything to be Florence Pugh in that scene!" she continued as I threw a cushion at her.

"Well play your cards right hun and that'll be you one day soon!" Jake encouraged playfully regarding Verity's budding acting career. He raised a toast towards her.

"I promise you an invite to the wedding!" Verity joked as she returned the gesture.

"Don't forget about me! You know I love a musician and you'll be inviting lots on the guest list!" Amelia joined jovially. It warmed my heart to see my friends from both sides of my life getting on so well.

As the credits rolled, Amelia connected to the speaker and played one of her perfectly curated playlists.

"So, are we gonna address the elephant in the room then?" Verity broached the subject tentatively.

"Yeah, who are we killing?" Amelia announced deadpan, sending a chill up my spine. I had no proof but if anyone in this room could get away with murder, it was her! Jake and Verity cast a knowing look at each other. "What have I missed?" She continued, not understanding the implication of the glance.

"You're gonna love this, Mils!" Jake giggled, opening the third bottle of the night. She looked at me expectantly.

"I'd been in a secret relationship with Zane." I sighed bracing myself for the ridicule. Amelia's deep brown eyes widened.

"It's *inzane* right?" Jake joked emphasising the second half of his pun, gaining a nudge from Verity as Amelia processed my words.

"Wait, you were fucking Moreno?" she spluttered through her sip of wine. I nodded sheepishly as an awkward silence blanketed the room. "Good for you girl but what the fuck?" They all erupted into hysterical laughter. I filled my friends in on the past few months and specifically the latest events to a variety of shocked and empathetic faces.

"I know I've said it but I'm really sorry Lilah, you're going to move on to bigger and better things from this. If anything, hopefully, this will give you a bit of a confidence boost over the quality of your sketches. Shit way to find out though!" Verity consoled me.

"I know now might not be the best time but you've got to speak to him, he's profiting off of your work!" Amelia muttered. I nodded in agreement; I knew she was right but how could I face him again? "What a dick. You can never trust a man."

"Speaking of dicks." Amelia looked at Jake in surprise. "You've gotta tell us, hun, what's he packing?" Jacob asked tipsily. Horror spread across Amelia and Verity's faces as they looked at me to gauge my reaction to his inappropriate comment. An unladylike snort escaped me, sending us all back into fits of giggles. "I'm a stickler for the details." He joked.

"Ugh, I wish I could insult him. Unfortunately, he never disappointed me in that aspect." A faint pang of sadness twisted in my gut as memories of happier times crossed my mind.

"Well anyway, there's plenty of guys with big dicks who would be lucky to have you, and won't fuck you over." Verity pulled me out of my misery with her unusual vulgar language. Despite my heartache, I'd laughed more tonight than I would have thought possible considering the black cloud that was above me.

Thank God for wine, besties and Harry Styles!

39

ZANE

I survived here before Delilah worked for me but the hole that was left by her absence now seemed too much to bear. Not only was my working week affected but my lonely evenings at home were exacerbated by the silence on the other end of the phone. I'd stopped the cold calling but had resorted to shouting into the void, sending her pathetic text messages that didn't even deliver. I guess she'd now officially blocked me. But I continued on the off chance that the line of communication would open again and she would realise how remorseful I was.

I had become reacquainted with the coffee machine on the ground floor, in need of a lot more caffeine than usual due to the lack of sleep. As I waited for the machine to finish filling my cup, I made idle conversation with Dean from the Social Media department.

"Have you noticed this is the longest time we've gone without a leak? Hopefully, the snitch has been beaten!" Dean said positively. It hadn't occurred to me that this design had made it further than the others. All my thoughts had been consumed by Delilah of late. I wondered what was different with this submission.

"That's a good point raised Dean, I'll look into that," I said, as he nodded and returned to the main office.

The sound of another person entering the break room caught my attention. It was Jacob. He met my gaze startled and immediately turned to leave again. I left my coffee in the kitchen and walked hurriedly behind him.

"Jacob? Have you got a minute?" I called after him, sounding more desperate than I'd have liked. Seeing him reminded me how close the pair of them were and he would no doubt have information about her whereabouts. As I caught up to him, it was clear he was ignoring me. "Please Jacob, I need to know she's okay."

"She's fine." He replied curtly, stopping to face me. The tiniest hint of relief sparked in my chest at the statement.

"Do you know where she is? I need to talk to her." I questioned heavily.

"I know what you did Zane and I'm not surprised she's not talking to you." I reared back at his words, surprised that Delilah had told him everything. "If you don't mind Mr Moreno, I have designs to get back to, legitimate ones this time." He turned and walked away to his cubicle, leaving me winded.

Like a wounded soldier, I started to head back to the kitchen when my ears pricked up at the sound of Charlotte and Isabelle, from my design team, gossiping at their desks. Brittany from reception was leaning over the cubicle to join in.

"Has anyone seen Lilah?" Charlotte queried, digging for information.

"Not since she was whisked off to Colombia. I saw the stories all over Insta. With the amount of beach pics I saw, she was clearly never in the office." Isabelle bitched.

"Yeah, work trip my arse. Plus, Zane said he would be online through those few days but he was conveniently uncontactable every time I did message!" Charlotte added.

"I guess she's so exhausted from lounging around in her bikini all week she's had to take some annual leave off to recover." Brittany rolled her eyes.

"Wow, I wish I'd known about the PA position. It has amazing perks. Swanky holidays, an invite to all the senior work parties…" Charlotte listed.

"And don't forget fucking the boss!" Brittany interjected her voice soaked with jealousy. Anger bubbled through me at how they reduced our relationship to something purely physical.

The pair of them cackled like witches whilst Isabelle resembled a deer in headlights as she spotted me, listening to their conversation, just metres away. I watched as she tried to subtly change the topic but the two women were too deep in their malicious whispers to notice.

I approached, clearing my throat to draw their full attention to me. Charlotte and Brittany were startled at my arrival.

"Don't you have any work to do, ladies? Or do I need to find something to occupy your overactive minds?" I watched the three women fluster in front of me.

"Oh, we were just concerned about Lilah and wanted to make sure she was okay!" Isabelle bluffed, red tainting her cheeks.

"Don't lie to me. I heard everything you said and I won't tolerate this vicious gossip in my office." I replied, crossing my arms over my chest, appearing calm despite the fury bubbling below the surface.

"Well, where is she then?" Brittany brazenly asked, seeming to forget her place.

"Not that it's any of your business, but Delilah is not on annual leave. Although, as her boss, I could have granted her as much time off as she wanted. Same as I could remove you three from my company for this insolence." The women stilled in frozen shock. "But I won't. Not today anyway." I watched as Brittany gulped. I turned to the sea of onlookers, gawping at my uncharacteristic outburst. "That design you've all been fawning over was Delilah's and I had no right to share it with you all. She didn't submit it for consideration, I stole it and broke her trust in the process because I was selfish and blinded by trying to stay at the top of the game and in doing so, I forfeited the best person I've ever had in my life." I took a deep breath returning my attention to the witches. "She's unlikely to return, so I'd appreciate it if you'll refrain from discussing this matter any further."

After my unexpected and incredibly public declaration, I quickly headed upstairs to my desolate office for some privacy. I switched my brain to the conversation I had with Dean earlier this morning. He was right, it was strange that Delilah's design hadn't leaked. Based on the others, it should be firmly in Jason's thieving hands and plastered all over his TikTok by now.

I opened up the emails I'd shared all of the previous designs on and the one difference between the email I sent in Colombia was that I had sent it directly to Maxine. In the previous email, I had included two other members of the Board in copy. A cold sheen spread across my brow at the realisation that one of these two men, whom I had trusted fiercely, had been feeding information to my biggest competitor. We hadn't held a full Board meeting since I had submitted Delilah's work, so I doubt either of them knew the design yet. Thinking quickly, I dug out two of the previously rejected concepts from earlier rounds and shared one with each of my potential betrayers as a late entry for consideration. Now all I had to do was sit and wait to see which one Jason claimed as his own and I would have found the rat.

A quiet knock sounded at the door. The last thing I wanted right now was to discuss work whilst I didn't know who I could fully trust.

"Come in!" I called half-heartedly. I was surprised to see Jacob as the door opened. He entered my office awkwardly, surveying the surroundings as if he were taking note of every detail. "How can I help you, Jacob?"

"Look, like I said, I don't agree with your actions and Lilah's my girl, so I want to protect her. But I heard your soppy speech downstairs and I'm not saying she will forgive you but she deserves to hear how you feel about her firsthand." He approached my desk and handed me a scrawled Post-it note. "If it's not obvious, that's my address where she's hiding out." My heart rate increased as the anticipation of finally seeing Delilah again rose.

"Thank you, Jacob." I checked my calendar and cancelled the remainder of my meetings for the day. I couldn't wait a minute longer than necessary to see her.

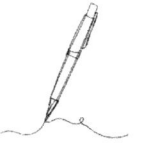

40

LILAH

After a full week of moping, I had decided to pull myself together and get my arse to the gym, it was certainly needed after the copious amounts of wine and chocolate buttons I'd been living off whilst slothing on Jacob's sofa.

An hour later, after sweating it out in an intense spin class, I paid my dues and headed to the changing room to gather my belongings. It was incredible how therapeutic it was to ride a stationary bike in a neon-lit room to Taylor Swift whilst some shiny bodybuilder shouted instructions at you! I checked my phone to see several missed calls from Jacob. I tried to return it but he didn't answer, however, I noticed a text from him:

> Please forgive me but trust me on this. xo

I pondered on the meaning of Jake's words as I left the gym and discovered that the heavens had opened and I wonderfully hadn't brought my umbrella as the sun had been shining when I left. Classic British weather! Talk about pathetic fallacy…

I walked quickly back to Jake's apartment, holding my hoody over my head and swung the metal gate open whilst I fumbled for the keys.

"Delilah." The raspy male voice caught me off guard causing me to drop the set of keys I had just fished out of my bag onto the floor. We both instinctively bent down to retrieve them, our hands meeting for a brief second before I pulled it back abruptly, finally taking in the man before me. The penny dropped at what Jacob's text had meant.

Zane stood up from the step in front of the door, his dark curls soaked through as if he had been waiting here for a long time. His suit was dishevelled and sodden from the downpour. As much as I couldn't bear to look at him, I couldn't deny how devastatingly handsome he looked like this. The pain of his beauty hit me like it was the first time I laid eyes on him, causing the air to be knocked out of my lungs and the fragments of my shattered heart to throb excruciatingly as it clenched tightly.

"Please can we talk?" He pleaded as I pushed past to unlock the door in an attempt to escape, avoiding eye contact.

"I have nothing to say to you, Zane," I stated as I walked into the building preparing to close the door behind me. As I began to shut it, Zane's strong hand stopped the motion. I finally looked into his eyes, taking in the devastation and desperation within them.

"Delilah, please, hear me out and once I've said my piece, I'll leave I promise." His vision appeared glazed over, seemingly holding back tears. I took in his features, deeper and more unkempt than usual. His stubble was longer than before and his eyes darker as if he hadn't been sleeping. I thought back to Jake's message and decided to give him one chance to explain himself as I pushed the door fully open to allow him access. A faint look of relief appeared on his face as he hurriedly walked in, as if worried I would change my mind at any second.

We stayed in silence as we walked up the stairs and into Jake's empty apartment.

"Thank you for letting me in and not allowing me to freeze in the rain, *mi amor*." The nickname made me feel sick. Nausea rose within me, burning my throat.

"Don't you dare call me that, Zane!" I snapped. "I've only let you in on Jake's request, so say what you've got to say and then you can go." Anger and upset coursed through me in equal parts. Having him here was breaking me further.

"I don't know how I can ever prove how sorry I am for betraying you, Delilah. I let my ambitions and desire for commercial success cloud my judgement and I'll forever pay the price for that. I prioritised my business over you and that is completely unacceptable. Just say the word Delilah and I'll halt the production and throw the entire launch away. You mean more to me than some silly limited edition."

"How can I ever believe a word you say again, Zane? You violated my trust. The first time I opened up to you so vulnerably, you threw it in my face for your own selfish gain. I should have known you could never have changed. Once an arsehole, always an arsehole."

"I know, I'm sorry. It was a split decision made out of desperation; I didn't have time to think about it. You're right, I never wanted to be an arsehole but I am and I made an idiotic decision but believe me, it was never my intention to hurt you." His eyes glistened with unshed tears as the weight of my assessment hammered home.

"That's a pathetic excuse, Zane, you could have spoken to me, I would have wanted to help you. You said we were a team!" My voice wobbled as a sob escaped from my throat, I flinched as he reached out to comfort me before pulling back. He was wounded by my reaction, but I knew if he touched me, I'd have shattered completely.

"I know, I know." He repeated desperately, his tears affecting his speech as he stood metres away, his eyes pleading with me.

"You could have asked me. I would have said yes!" I finally fell apart, sobbing hard as my emotions came flooding out.

"It's the biggest regret of my life. I can't live without you. I love you, Delilah." The three words I'd waited for him to say in Colombia which would have made me the happiest I'd ever been, now caused me gut-wrenching pain.

The air between us felt thick with unspoken words and destroyed trust as I thought over my response. Zane stared exhausted after baring his soul to me.

"I appreciate you coming here Zane, but I need to be alone right now. Please can you go?" I finally requested though it killed me to see him like this, there was nothing I wanted more than for him to pull me into his arms and soothe my anguish but I knew I couldn't fall into that trap again. He opened his mouth to speak but seemed to resign himself to the hopelessness of the situation before turning and leaving me alone once more.

Watching him go in so much pain made my heart break all over again and I was unsure of how I would survive it a second time.

41

ZANE

As expected, one of the designs I planted got leaked to the world by Mr Sallow, in record time. I'd been monitoring his social media activity and it only took three days for the *ladrón de mierda* to claim it as his own. Previously, when one of my designs appeared on Jason's feed my heart would drop. However, this time I was disappointed at the discovery of my betrayer but jubilant that I had been the one to catch him.

Sitting here now, a week on from determining who the rat in my company was, despite the general gloom surrounding my days, this one triumph sparked my confidence, even if only for the next thirty-minute meeting, the old Zane was back in the desk chair.

"Please come in and take a seat." I gestured to the vacant space in front of me.

"Good morning, Zane, what can I do for you? This dropped into my calendar at the last minute so I assume it is an urgent matter." The snake asked with fake concern.

"Awful to see yet another one of our designs has made its way into Jason's grubby hands," I stated matter-of-factly as I turned my laptop around to display a screengrab from the latest live stream.

"I wasn't aware of the latest design leaking, I assumed when you missed the deadline they were no longer interested." The way the weasel lied to me so naturally made me grit my teeth.

"I have to admit, I expected to hear from you after the deadline passed. It was the first time this company has failed to launch a limited-edition line and with your stake in the company, I'd have expected some concern around the matter." I saw him shift awkwardly in his seat at my fake friendly tone.

"Oh well Zane, I didn't want to add to the noise I'm sure you were hearing and I know how you beat yourself up. But hey, at least you submitted something, even if it was a week later and you know, is unviable now given the subsequent leak."

"Yes, it's very unfortunate." I agreed, shutting the laptop between us and looking at him intensely.

"Although I must say, Zane, I would have thought given your position, you would have been pulling this place apart to find your rat, however, I guess you had other distractions." He said brazenly, a smirk formed across his mouth. That smug prick. I understood the implication of his words. That I had allowed my relationship with Delilah to take priority over a business, admittedly, I had been intoxicated by her during those months but I'd never taken my eye off of the ball. I lost her by putting my company first for fuck's sake.

"The thing is, I *have* been looking into this leak further." A flicker of panic crossed the traitor's face. "We didn't miss the deadline or at least *I* didn't," I opened my top drawer and produced a piece of paper featuring Delilah's design from within. Seeing it twisted my gut at the reminder of my *own* betrayal. I mentally pulled myself back together, I needed to be focused right now. I dropped it in front of him.

The backstabber picked up the design with shaky hands. "You see, I was in so much of a panic the night before the submission date, I forgot to copy you into the email." As the realisation began to settle in, I continued reciting my exposé. "It turns out that was the best decision I could have made." I couldn't prevent the sly, smug smile from forming on my lips.

"So, I thought it over, why had this one not leaked when all the others had?" I tapped my chin mockingly with my finger, pondering the rhetorical question as I stood up and began to walk around the desk. "Surely, a member of my own Board wouldn't backstab me!" The viper gulped anxiously as he waited for the killing blow. "I had to find out for sure. So, I shared one different fake design each with a select number of people and low-and-behold, yours ended up on the live stream being paraded around by Jason Sallow himself." I could've sworn he had stopped breathing. "What did he offer you for my designs, Graham?"

I leaned against the desk to the side of him in an act of intimidation. He resembled a cowering mouse who had fallen right into my trap.

"Do you know what it's like to have the company you headed up for years acquired and completely cease to exist? Not to mention, that the man you now had to answer to and work below was barely out of nappies, with no business experience in this country." His pathetic whinging poured out of him as he rose from his chair to face me. "I've been in this industry long before you were barely even an itch in your daddy's pants. I should have been an equal to you, not one of your lackeys."

"You had a choice to stay here, don't make snivelling excuses for your petulance Graham. You didn't answer the question, what did he offer you?"

"What I deserve." Graham snapped at me. "Jason's a busy man with lots of different ventures to focus on. He values my experience and knowledge. In all but name, that company would be mine." He was almost vibrating with anger but his attempts to rile me up were futile.

"You're right on one point there. Jason is a *very* busy man! That is why when I offered to buy him out at a generous price, he gladly agreed. That's the thing with influencers Graham, they're full of ideas and his other businesses were a much higher priority to him."

I watched amused as the colour drained from his face. "So unfortunately, I don't think there's a job waiting over at Crystal Cascades for you." The door opened to reveal two members of my security team waiting to escort

Graham off the premises. "And there's certainly not one here. Get the fuck out, Graham!"

"You jumped up little cunt!" He spat as he began to throw a punch in my direction. I stepped instinctively to the side, avoiding the contact with ease. I couldn't contain my laughter at the idiocy as security grabbed him and dragged him out of my office.

"*Adios* Graham." I waved sarcastically as he left.

I should be happy that I'd caught the snake and, in many ways, I was but I couldn't shift the sadness that the only person I wanted to tell all about this, was the one person not returning my calls.

After the adrenaline of this morning subsided, the hollow ache in my chest quickly returned and I was certain it was there to stay.

I stared out of the open office door, my eyes fixed on what was Delilah's desk, bare and unoccupied.

Pull yourself together Moreno!

I was done with moping around and feeling sorry for myself. Yes, I had caused this. But I was also going to be the one to fix it and get my girl back.

42

LILAH

"Have you given any more thought to whether you're going to pull the plug on the launch?" Jake asked over a steaming cup of coffee. It had been a couple of weeks since Zane's surprise arrival at Jake's flat and after that had occurred, I felt it was time to return home to Theo's as my hiding place had been found. I could no longer, in good conscience, occupy Jake's sofa any more. However, since I wasn't going into the office, I missed my daily gossip with him, which brought some sunshine to my dull days. So, we tried to meet every morning at an overpriced coffee shop halfway between our addresses to shoot the shit.

"I'm conflicted. It was always mine and my mum's dream to design jewellery so letting it go through, albeit in a way we wouldn't have hoped for, feels like I'm ticking that off. However, he stole it and he'll profit from it. Come February, I won't be able to go more than a few feet without it being plastered all over the place and I'm unsure of how that'll make me feel. If I'm honest, I worry it'll take me right back to that day in Zane's office, when I saw the email and I've worked hard to get myself out of this hole." I confessed.

"It's a mindfuck, that's for sure!" Jake agreed as I sipped my latte.

"And if I stopped them progressing now, think of the money they'll lose. That could affect the company and in turn, could affect you!"

"I get ya hun, but you've gotta do what's best for you!" Jacob encouraged kindly. "What's your plan for today then?"

"Hmm I know, thanks, Jake. I'm going to go and see an old family friend, hopefully, he'll help me to decide what's right!"

"Aww lovely, well can't wait to hear how it goes. Same time tomorrow hun?" Jake asked as he stood up from our table and I nodded in agreement, already looking forward to tomorrow's catch-up as he headed out. I would have to start drinking tap water or applying for new jobs soon as I was rapidly rinsing through my savings again!

The door shut behind Jacob, changing the air around me. It now felt heavy from the emptiness of my heart. The past few weeks I had barely held it together, all of my thoughts circled back to *him*. I knew that I should hate him for what he had done, and on some levels I did, but ultimately, I missed him. The way he'd grab me my favourite lunch on Fridays in the office; the way his hands felt on my skin; his Good Morning texts; even the way he said my name for Christ's sake! I knew the easy thing to do would be to give in and run back to the comfort of his arms, but I had to stay strong. He'd betrayed me and there was no coming back from that.

I finished my coffee shortly after Jacob had left and headed to jump on the tube, hoping I had now avoided the rush hour madness. A pang of guilt hit me as I passed each stop. Brian was like a father figure to me but amongst the chaos of starting at Moreno Jewellery and the whirlwind of my time with Zane, I had neglected to visit him since the day I left Timeless Treasures.

I rang his doorbell, hoping he wouldn't turn me away at my ignorance for not checking in on him sooner. The door opened and there was Brian. All five foot two inches of him!

"Lilah my dear, what a lovely surprise, come in, I've just popped the kettle on!" Brian said, a wide smile appearing that travelled up to his eyes which accentuated his laughter lines. Immediately, my nervousness melted away as the warmth radiated from him.

I settled into the tartan-printed sofa and slouched into the cushions, taking a biscuit from a plate of treats that Brian had produced.

"How are you, Brian? I'm sorry it's taken me so long to come and see you!" I idly dunked the custard cream into my tea.

"Never better dear, it's been a lovely summer so lots of time out in the garden! Don't you apologise, you've been busy at your exciting new job!" Not a hint of bitterness behind his words.

"I'm glad. That's actually why I'm here. I need

your fatherly advice." I pleaded.

"Of course, what's wrong Lilah?" he questioned, concern twisting his aged features.

I breezed over the past few months, leaving out my and Zane's relationship. "...and I know that Mum always wanted our designs out in the world; however, this just feels wrong," I concluded.

"That's awful, pet! Yours and Esmeralda's designs were always so beautiful. Honestly, I think that people would be lucky to have the chance to buy them and your mum would be so proud to see your designs out there but I can understand why it wouldn't feel great, all things considered." He emphasised, squeezing my knee reassuringly.

"I wish I could enjoy this moment, but he neglected me, Brian. He put his livelihood before my own. Much like how he treated you!"

"What do you mean, dear?" He asked with a puzzled look on his face.

"He bought out your company without a second thought of how it might affect you!" I explained.

"I'm absolutely fine, Lilah" Brian laughed. "I had been contemplating retirement for a few years, I'm not getting any younger, so when Zane approached me, I was happy to entertain the offer." I was shocked to hear that Brian had been thinking about stepping back after so many years at the helm.

"That still doesn't excuse him leaving you high and dry after all the love and care you poured into that shop!" I argued.

"He didn't at all! He offered me a seat on his

Board due to my lengthy experience," my mouth dropped open. "However, it felt like the right time to hand it over so I declined. Any normal CEO would have left it at that, but he was gracious enough to put several stocks within the company in my name to keep me set. I can never thank him enough for protecting me and my family for the remainder of my life." I listened gobsmacked as Brian explained a side of the story I'd never considered before. "Although I'm sure he's not without his faults, from what I got to know about Zane Moreno, he seems like a very good man indeed." He gave me a look which conveyed he understood there had been something more going on between us. "I'm sure if you gave him a chance to explain himself, you'd find his heart was in the right place."

43

LILAH

I couldn't be arsed to get dressed up for a Thursday night Simmons visit, so decided to invite Jake and Amelia over to my flat and managed to coerce Theo into mixing up some drinks for us on his evening off. I was sure the broken heart card would run out soon!

The three of us huddled around our tiny kitchen table as Jake and Amelia filled me in on the office gossip.

"Honestly Lilah, you should have seen the look on Brittany's face when Moreno took her to task. It was hilarious!" Amelia chortled, sipping on her Spicy Margarita.

"I haven't heard a bitchy word out of her since - even with Zed man being out!" Jake added, swirling a Cosmo.

"What do you mean with Zane out?" I queried more concerned with his whereabouts, although I did love the idea of Brittany being taken down a peg or two!

"Oh yeah, did I not mention it? He's been MIA for weeks!" Jake said.

"And when he is in, he's certainly not the same Moreno," Amelia added.

"How so?" I queried, more interested than I cared to admit.

"Don't get me wrong, he's still in a three-piece suit and polite enough to everyone, but there's something less put together about him and he clearly doesn't want to be there when he does show his face!" Amelia explained, finishing her drink.

Theo's bedroom opened as he sauntered into the kitchen. He paused for a moment when he looked in Amelia's direction before stopping at his bar cart to the side of us.

"Same again, ladies?" Theo offered, beginning to fill the cocktail shaker with ice. "Thanks for the review, by the way, cutie." He winked at Amelia with a cheesy grin, flashing his dimples.

"Don't mention it," she replied flatly, clearly unimpressed by his playful pet name.

"Although I missed the part where you mentioned the drop-dead gorgeous guitarist." He joked, shaking the drink.

"Theo, get out!" I ordered.

"Okay, okay, I'm going!" He laughed, putting down the ready-to-drink cocktail mix on the table before heading back to the hallway. "Second door on the right, by the way!" He smirked towards Amelia jovially, shooting a finger gun before disappearing.

I watched Amelia shiver in blatant disgust at his cheesy lines. If there was anyone less likely to be bowled over by Theo's cringey words, it was her.

"Was that an open invitation?" Jake piped up, causing Amelia and I to burst into fits of laughter. "What? Your brother's fit!"

I rolled my eyes. "To each their own I suppose." I laughed. "Sorry about Theo, Amelia, he prides himself on being a bit of a lady's man, but I know you've got a boyfriend so please ignore him!"

"Yeah well, not anymore." Jake flashed a look in my direction as she sighed. I silently cursed myself for sticking my foot in it. "But yes, I think I'll be staying out here with you two nutcases regardless rather than following your brother into his room if that's okay?" She smirked, taking a sip of her newly made cocktail.

"Of course, never follow that man in there, you'll never escape!" I joked as I patted her hand caringly and Jake giggled away between us.

The three of us continued to laugh and drink until the early hours of the morning keeping any negative feelings I may have had at bay.

The next day, I awoke later than usual, I think the copious amounts of cocktails were to thank for that! After Jake and Amelia left, I couldn't get the thought of Zane out of my head. The way they described how he stood up for me, the modesty he had shown regarding the kindness he showed Brian, and the description of him in the office made me feel a conflicted mixture of gratitude and concern. Despite the overarching feeling of betrayal that reared its head whenever thoughts of him crossed my mind, I felt it was time I saw him again to bring me closure.

Although it was a Friday, I was banking on what Jake had mentioned about Zane barely going into the office and decided to take a punt that he would be at home.

My palms were sweaty and my stomach was in knots when I approached the front door, a million thoughts raced through my head as I tried to decide if this was the right decision. *Why do I even care if he's okay?* I pondered for a moment until I decided that I owed myself this closure. I tentatively knocked on the heavy wood and immediately regretted my decision. I wasn't ready for this. Before I had a chance to scurry away the door opened.

My heart flew to my throat when I saw him. Although it was Zane he wasn't the Zane that I recognised. Gone was the perfectly curated businessman and here stood, a softer, more casual figure. But he was equally as breathtaking! Who would have known grey sweatpants and a black slouchy hoodie could look so good? My eyes travelled up to his face, his hair, usually not a curl out of place, was ruffled in all directions as if he had been running stressed fingers through it, it was also longer now much like his overgrown stubble.

I was frozen there speechless as he stood bewildered in the doorway, shock and surprise clear in his tired-looking eyes.

"Delilah?" He breathed as if he couldn't believe I was standing in front of him.

"Hi." Was all I could muster. I wasn't prepared for how much seeing him would affect me, it almost hurt. The irony wasn't lost on me that the only person who could soothe this pain was the one who had caused it.

"Do you want to come in?" He asked sheepishly as if expecting me to decline. I nodded silently as he widened the door and I shuffled inside, the warmth from his body as I passed made me shudder. Entering the hallway, I felt a wave of sadness wash over me as I remembered back to the last time I was here. I was so happy that evening when he finally opened up to me and invited me into his sanctuary. I made my way through to the living room remembering the layout of the modern townhouse, Zane trailing behind me. I was too nervous to sit so I stood in the arch of the bay window and turned to face him but kept my eyes glued to the floor.

"Can I get you anything?" He asked uncomfortably with his hands in his pockets.

"No, I'm fine," I said, suddenly unsure of why I had decided to come. Shifting my weight awkwardly. "Jacob and Amelia said you hadn't been at work recently, and not that it is any of my business, but I wanted to check you were okay." My voice sounded strained. I finally met Zane's gaze, he looked broken.

"I can't believe you're here," he rubbed his eyes as if I was an illusion.

"I'm glad you're all right," I responded, immediately losing all ability to think of anything else to talk about.

"I'll leave you be now." I didn't want to go but it was dangerous to stay. Standing metres away from Zane, my brain told me I should run away but my heart wanted to pull him in closer. I finally moved and began to head back to the door. As I passed Zane, his hand wrapped around my wrist stopping me in my tracks. Heat flared at his touch. I was scared to look at him in case I crumbled.

"Delilah, please don't go," he pleaded. I looked up at him, my heart breaking at the desperate way he stared at me. "Please sit down, I want to show you something." My body defied my mind and before I knew it, I was sitting on the sofa waiting for Zane to reveal what he had to show me.

He returned and perched beside me. I was all too aware of the small distance between our legs, electricity surging between us. I wondered if he felt it too.

"Excuse the amateur level of what I'm about to show you, it's not finished yet." He said anxiously, stumbling over his words. My pulse spiked as I waited for him to turn over the piece of paper he was holding. "I wanted to prove to you how sorry I was and how much I care about you. I know I went about this all in the wrong way, but you truly do have amazing talent, Delilah." He turned the paper. "So, if you want to come back, I present to you our next capsule collection." I began to scan the paper. It revealed a list of ten jewellery pieces, a marketing plan and a timeline. At the top of the page, it was titled 'THE EMERALD HART COLLECTION'. My heart stopped at the block letters before me. "You would have full creative control; nothing passes without your express approval and sign-off. I've not shown anyone this so if you want me to rip it up and burn the scraps of paper, it will never see the light of day." I felt the familiar sting of tears at the back of my eyes.

"Zane I..." I started.

"I can never apologise enough for breaking your trust Delilah, but you are so talented and I know you don't believe in yourself, so I want to give you a platform to live out your and Esmeralda's dream." The tears began to stream down my face as I stared in awe at the paper before me.

"I don't know what to say…This is too much" I choked on my words, the emotion in my chest almost unbearable. "This is incredible but I need time to think about this." I looked up at his teary eyes. I didn't think the pain in my chest could get any deeper but looking at him now was agony. "How could I ever trust you again Zane." My words cut like a knife; I saw the pain crack through him. "I'm sorry, I have to go." I stuttered, needing to get back to the safety of my apartment. As I stood to leave Zane sunk off the sofa onto his knees in front of me. His strong hands found my hips and he looked up at me with pleading eyes. The combination of the collection and the look on his face was breaking down the barriers I had built.

"I will forever hate myself for what I did to you..."

A strangled cry escaped my body. "Please Zane…let me go." I cut him off.

"I can't. I will spend every day of the rest of my life proving how sorry I am. I never wanted to hurt you. I was stupid and selfish and I will do anything to make it up to you." He took hold of my hands. "You mean everything to me, Delilah. I've been lost without you, and since having you in my life again I'm a better man. Please please, I know I don't deserve it but give me one last chance." He begged up at me like I was the only thing in the world that mattered. I felt my guard dissolve completely.

"Promise me."

He looked up at me with a glint of hope in his eyes. "I promise." He kissed my hands. "*Te lo prometo.*" He kissed them again before wrapping his arms around my body and kissing me repeatedly over my stomach, muttering promises between each peck. "I vow to you with everything I am and have. *Tú eres mi Joya, mi vida, mi amor.* I love you Delilah and I promise to never let you down again." Full-body sobs wracked my body at his confession. The weight of his words caused me to fall to my knees in front of him bringing us face to face.

"I love you too." I declared, the happy tears coming in full force. An overjoyed smile began to spread across his features. He grasped my jaw with both hands before crashing his lips to mine. It was like being able to breathe again after drowning.

"*Te amo,*" he whispered against my lips, "*te amo,*" his hands snaked around the back of my head holding me to him as mine did the same. Tangling in his overgrown hair as he whispered confessions of his love again and again, each word felt like a stitch mending my broken heart. I was putty beneath his touch. His fingers glided over my ribs, grabbing my waist and pulling me tighter against him as I granted his tongue access to my mouth. God I'd missed this, God, I'd missed him.

"Zane, I need you." I breathed desperately as pressure built between my thighs. That was all he needed to hear. In one movement he had shifted us and lifted me onto the sofa, he looked up at me from his position between my legs, kissing my bare thighs and pushing my skirt up.

"I've missed you, *mi Joya.*" He kissed upwards, goosebumps rising on my skin as he pulled my underwear down.

"I've missed you too." I choked out, looking at the beautiful man before me with a mixture of love and desire coursing through every part of my body.

I gasped breathlessly as his mouth made contact with my centre, his tongue licking between my folds. He groaned in appreciation.

"*Dios mio, mi amor,* you taste delectable." He purred against me. My hips rolled beneath his touch as he continued to devour me like I was his last meal. I swear. I was a mess beneath him, thrashing under his grip, just as the pressure began to build at the bottom of my spine he stopped for a moment, and I whined in protest. A sly smile pulled at his lips before he pushed two fingers inside me with ease.

"Zane!" I moaned as he began to pump his ring-adorned fingers in and out of me in time swirling his tongue around my swollen clit. His free hand found its way beneath my white t-shirt, snaking up over the lace of my bra and pulling it down to free my full breast and squeeze my nipple. My breath hitched at the sting of pain mixed with pleasure.

"God I'm gonna come!" I cried out. Zane's eager licks quickened as the pressure built to its peak and a tsunami of euphoria crashed over me. Before I had a chance to come down from my orgasm, Zane crawled up my body and trailed kisses along my torso, removing my clothes as he made his way up to my face. I moaned at the taste of myself on his tongue as he pushed it into my mouth.

He pulled back to stare deeply into my eyes, making me blush at the intensity of his gaze.

"Si estoy soñando, no quiero despertar." Zane breathed, inches away from my face. *"Soy completamente tuyo."* His words felt like a confession but one that I couldn't understand, he must have seen the confusion cross my face. He leant down to whisper in my ear, "I am completely yours." The warmth of his breath against my neck paired with the weight of his words caused my blood to surge. "And you are mine." He finished; his fingers found my clit again.

"Fuck me like I'm yours then." I challenged, reaching down to stroke the bulge in his tracksuit bottoms. The thin material leaving nothing to the imagination. Zane moved away from the side of my head to face me, a surprised look across his face which quickly formed into a decidedly more wicked smirk.

"As you wish." I wrapped my legs around his strong abdomen as he lifted and carried me up to his bed, throwing me onto the cloud-like duvet. I lay there, sprawled out naked, waiting for him to join me. I watched as he removed his hoodie, pulling it up from the back of his neck and over his head in that sexy man way!

I instinctively reached between my thighs to alleviate the growing arousal. It's incredible how turned on he made me, just from sight alone!

"Uh huh, Delilah." Zane's gruff voice stilled my motions as I looked at him mouth agape. "That cunt belongs to me tonight." He finally removed his tracksuit bottoms to free his rock-hard length. Just the sight of his dick made my pussy clench and drip in expectation.
"I love seeing you like this…so ready for me." He stared hungrily, his eyes travelling across my body and landing on my bare centre. He took a step towards me before lifting my legs onto his shoulders, my heartbeat accelerated at the angle. My body filled with anticipation, knowing how much deeper he could fill me in this position.

"How badly do you want it?" He asked, teasing my opening with the wet end of his cock.

"More than anything." I implored breathing heavily, moving my hips to try and make better contact with him. He stopped still as I looked up at him, begging with my eyes.

"I'm going to fuck you until you can't take it anymore." With that declaration, he slammed into me with full force. I cried out his name at the impact. His movements didn't falter as he fell into a punishing rhythm, I grabbed the duvet beneath me tightly as my back arched off the bed.

"Good girl, you take my cock so well." I moaned at the praise though his words were hardly registering as my thoughts scrambled in my head. He hugged my legs towards his chest with one arm and leaned on the bed over my head with the other, folding my body in half. I was merciless to him as he thrust deeper into me. Each vigorous motion was pure ecstasy as he focused purely on my pleasure. I stared in disbelief at the dominant Colombian God, sweat glazing his rippled muscles, his breathing ragged, each exhale mingling with my own heavy breaths. I clenched around him, he hissed in response, looking away momentarily to regain his composure.

I was utterly and unequivocally intoxicated by him.

"Fuck, you look so good!" I whimpered pathetically as I tried to catch my breath amidst relentless thrusts. He released a deep rumble from his chest at my words before he spun me over onto all fours, quickly grabbing my hips and pulling me back to him.

My vision blurred as he pounded into me, with one rough hand placed on my upper back for support, pushing me harder into the mattress as the other spanked me hard. The spark of pain bloomed into pleasure, as I forced myself back onto him. "You look incredible with my handprint painted on your arse, Delilah." I moaned at the filthy image, his hand sliding further up my back and twisting around my dishevelled hair.

He pulled my head back, his muscular body leaning over mine to whisper into my ear. "It's like your cunt was tailor-made for me, *mi Joya*." The combination of his filthy words and unyielding rhythm pushed me over the edge. My orgasm ripped through me with such force that I collapsed onto the sheet. All-consuming, relentless waves of ecstasy washed over me again and again in a blinding haze of pleasure. Zane continued to grind into me until I was a useless, limp heap on the bed. I felt his body tense and his warm load spill inside me with one last thrust as he released a guttural moan.

We lay breathless together, in a state of blissful exhaustion, my legs still tingling and my heart pounding from the aftermath of my orgasm. Zane pulled out of me, rolling onto his back and cuddled me into his chest. He stroked my hair out of my face and placed a kiss on my forehead. I sighed happily, snuggling into his embrace feeling both drained and deeply satisfied.

"You are my everything, Delilah Hart." He confessed still stroking my hair. "I'm never letting you go."

I stared up at the beautiful man beside me, whose eyes were full of adoration, as he traced lazy circles along my back. Listening to his heart thud, I felt my own fill with more love than I could ever imagine.

"I'm not going anywhere, Zane Moreno."

EPILOGUE

TWO YEARS LATER

ZANE
"I will have to run this past Delilah. Thanks for your time."

It had been a year since Delilah joined me as co-owner of the newly named Moreno Hart Jewellery company. After the success of the Valentine's launch and the Emerald Hart Collection, nearly two years ago now, I couldn't think of anyone better to be fifty/fifty owners with. She took a lot of convincing, honestly, she would have happily settled for a Senior Designer role however after the betrayal from Graham and the loyalty I had always felt from Delilah, there was no one I trusted more. And no one else I would want to have to cosign every decision with!

I closed the Zoom application on my laptop and set my out of office for the week. As well as her ambition, Delilah also showed me the importance of taking a break and letting go of the reins now and again. We tried to get away at least three times a year on a beach vacation, or an adventure holiday and always returned to Colombia.

This year I planned the location of the beach excursion and so far, Delilah was none the wiser to our destination. This time we wouldn't need to use my private jet!

I pulled onto the driveway of the red brick, Edwardian house covered by climbing honeysuckle that was flowering in the summer sun. I parked my black matte Tesla beside the light blue Mini Cooper. I couldn't hide the smile at the juxtaposition between my sleek expensive sports car and Delilah's classic vehicle.

Clicking the lock on my key over my shoulder as I approached the forest green panelled front door, which complemented the foliage on the brickwork, a warm feeling of contentment filled me.

"*Hola mi Joya!* I'm home!" I called cheesily into the spacious abode.

"I'm in the kitchen!" she said in response. I made my way towards the open plan room, following the delicious smell of something cooking on the stove. I found Delilah with an apron tied around her waist, stirring a pot of sauce. Wrapping my arms around her, I buried my face into her neck and took in the sweet and spicy scent of her.

"I've missed you, gorgeous." I purred into her ear as I placed a kiss on her cheek. She giggled and turned towards me.

"I've missed you too, but you know I work better at home" She leant up to peck me on the lips. "My co-worker can get a bit handsy!" She laughed as my touch snaked over her arse.

"Who can blame him!" I teased, spanking her playfully. She squealed before turning back to the food, still with my arms around her. "This smells amazing, *mi amor.*"

"I'm just about to dish up if you want to sit down." She explained. I placed another kiss on the top of her head before grabbing two sets of cutleries, two glasses and a bottle of cold Sauvignon out of the fridge. I laid the table and poured the wine as Delilah joined me with the bowls of pasta.

"So, when are you going to reveal all about this mysterious holiday then? We leave in twenty hours and I need to pack accordingly!" Delilah asked, sprinkling parmesan over her meal.

"I was going to tell you tonight anyway *mi Joya,* don't think you've succeeded in breaking my willpower," I smirked, causing her to laugh and shake her head at me, waiting for me to elaborate. "I'm taking you back to Newquay." Delilah's eyes lit up.

"I haven't been back in years! I can't wait." She clapped her hands together, beaming at me. My chest tightened at her excitement.

"I thought we could remake some of those summer memories." I winked.

"Wow, I can't wait to keep myself busy while you game all week!" She joked, "When will Theo be arriving?"

"Like I said *mi amor*, remake them, not relive them!" I rolled my eyes as I watched Delilah twirling a forkful of spaghetti. She moved into my house shortly after we reconciled - much to Theo's enjoyment! He was thrilled to have his bachelor pad back. After a few months of blissful co-existing, we decided to set up a home together for our future and fell in love with this property in Hampstead Heath. Between my minimalist style and Delilah's eclectic taste, it was a mixture of us both: a home not just a house.

There was a time in my life when I could never have imagined living so domestically. I was a man who always prioritised work and business but losing Delilah due to this, made me rethink everything. I couldn't imagine walking through the door of my office or my home and not being greeted by her stunning face and sunny disposition. She was truly my better half, my best friend and the love of my life.

LILAH

Being back in Cornwall felt like a dream, so many of the places we visited I recognised but my memories were hazy after not returning for over a decade. However, it hadn't seemed to change much over the years. The local shops' quaint decor remained in the windows and the houses were still painted in various pastel shades. Zane and I had just finished a delicious romantic meal of mussels at a restaurant a short distance from the beach and were walking hand in hand towards the sea to watch the sunset. I had forgotten how beautiful they were by the coast!

As we walked down the stone stairs to reach the sand below I spotted a set-up of blankets surrounded by three dozen candles and an assortment of my favourite flowers - multiple colours of peonies. Cushions lay scattered in the centre next to a bottle of Dom Perignon and two glasses, mirroring our final date in Colombia. My pulse quickened, thinking a million thoughts as I tried not to get ahead of myself. Zane surprised me with romantic dates all the time, why would this be any different to the norm?

"This is beautiful Zane, you've outdone yourself." I commended looking up at him. He squeezed my hand tighter as we approached the glow of candles.

The two of us turned to face the water as the orange glow of the sun crept below the horizon. Zane took me into his arms from behind, kissing the back of my head.

"I wanted to recreate our last night in Colombia. I know I've said it to you a thousand times since and I'll never stop reminding you for the rest of our lives. But I should have told you then. I love you with every part of me, Delilah Hart." He said quietly into my ear. My heart beat sporadically in my chest at his meaningful confession. I felt his grip release and heard the sand crunch beneath him as he stepped back away from me. Instinctively, I turned back to see where he was going. Nothing could have prepared me for what I saw.

Lit by the final golden rays of the August evening sun, Zane was a vision down on one knee, the sunlight highlighting his coffee eyes and glinting off his sea-enhanced curls. A black velvet box was perched on his palm. My chest squeezed and my eyes watered as I waited for him to finish his speech.

"You are it for me Delilah. You are the one that I want to go to sleep with and wake up next to every day. I want to share all my laughter, tears, highs and lows with you. I can't wait to grow old and grey with you surrounded by our children and their children, reminiscing over all of the memories we have created together." I couldn't stop the tears from running down my cheeks looking into his vulnerable eyes as he took my left hand in his.

"You are the love of my life; will you marry me?" I released a sob at the question as he opened the box to reveal the most exquisite ring I'd ever seen. A thin gold band adorned with various shaped diamonds surrounded a large, stunning oval cut emerald. Sinking to my knees, I grabbed his face and kissed him hard. "Well, *mi Joya?*" He questioned; his voice shaky with apparent nerves.

"Yes, yes, yes!" I squealed, kissing him over and over as he slid the ring onto *that* finger. A dazzling smile formed on his perfect face at my acceptance as he led me onto the cushions and popped the bottle of champagne to celebrate. I clinked my glass to his in a toast to our future. The giddiness was overwhelming as I tried to sit still and listen to Zane as he explained the secret planning, he had been doing up until now.

"Do you like it, *mi amor?*" Zane asked, his eyes glinting with excitement.

"It's the most beautiful thing I have ever seen. Where did you get it? It's not one of ours!" I questioned eagerly, admiring the glittering jewel.

"One of the perks of being the CEO of a jewellery business is that some skills start to rub off on you after a while." I looked at him intently as the cogs were turning in my head. "I wanted to give you a ring that was worthy of your beauty. One of a kind. So, I've been designing this item with a Colombian gemmologist for a year."

"*You* designed this?" I stared back at him in amazement as the penny dropped.

"Don't act so surprised!" He winked. "No prizes for why I chose an emerald, hey *Joya*!"

I looked down at the stone which emulated my eye colour. Thinking back to my childhood memories on this very beach, I could never have imagined I would be sitting here now with Zane's ring on my finger excited for the life we'd build together. He caressed my jaw, turning me to face him before capturing my lips in an all-encompassing kiss. The two of us sat in comfortable silence, his arm wrapped protectively around my shoulders as we stared out at the twilight sky. I watched the sun finally dip below the horizon taking all of the light with it and took a moment to reflect on our journey, illuminated by the candles around us, listening to the waves crash.

From childhood enemies to complicated lovers, to blissfully happy fiancés. The story of us was anything but linear, it had been passionate and messy, however, it was ours and it was perfect.

ABOUT THE AUTHORS

Ria Alice and Jessica May are two friends from the UK with a shared love of steamy romance novels. Their book contains pop culture references galore, fun, supportive friendships, and a spicy relationship to top it all off!

When they're not writing, you can find them at a 2000s emo night, a karaoke bar, or marathoning cheesy rom-coms over a charcuterie board.

ACKNOWLEDGEMENTS

Zane and Lilah will always hold a special place in our hearts as the focus couple of our first book baby. We have loved writing their story and bringing them to life.

Thank you to our beta readers who have given up their own time to support us and provide valuable feedback to help us create the best version of this book.

Thanks to Pat and Harry, who have had to put up with a new man consuming our lives for months and for us abandoning you multiple times for all-day writing sessions and late-night editing. Also, you were forced to film videos for content on our TikTok.

Thank you to the boot sale we went to at the end of June 2024. Some people may have been discouraged when the sales of our clothes and household tat were non-existent, however, we made lemonade out of lemons and Zane Moreno was born.

Lastly, thank you to you for reading this story. We hope you love it as much as we do and look forward to more adventures in the Hidden Universe.

Ria and Jess

x

Printed in Great Britain
by Amazon